A BEGINNING

TO AN END

C. A. BLAKE

First published in Australia by Aurora House
www.aurorahouse.com.au

This edition published 2024
Copyright © C. A. Blake 2024

Typesetting and e-book design: Amit Dey (amitdey2528@gmail.com)
Cover design: Donika Mishineva (www.artofdonika.com)

ISBN number: 978-1-7635727-2-0 (paperback)

 A catalogue record for this book is available from the National Library of Australia

Distributed by: Ingram Content: www.ingramcontent.com
Australia: phone +613 9765 4800 | email lsiaustralia@ingramcontent.com
Milton Keynes UK: phone +44 (0)845 121 4567 | email enquiries@ingramcontent.com
La Vergne, TN USA: phone +1 800 509 4156 | email inquiry@lightningsource.com

DEDICATION

To all the women who struggled with
their body because society said your weight mattered.
This is for you.

ACKNOWLEDGEMENTS

To sixteen year old me, who wrote this book wishing for someone to love her the way Ruel loves Valarie.

TABLE OF CONTENTS

AUTHOR'S NOTE + DISCLAIMER

Thank you for reading *A Beginning to an End*.
Out of all the books you could have chosen, you've decided on this one and I'm super grateful for that—so I want to give you a huge thank you.

This book, though it is under the category 'romance', isn't something that is light-hearted. Please note, that going into this book there is huge talk and discussion on bullying, body image, domestic violence, fatphobia and mental health issues related to the same, and more.

I wrote Valarie Dale, the protagonist, as the inner thoughts of myself. As a plus-sized woman, who has always struggled with her body image due to the way I was treated purely because of my size. I wrote Valarie from a lot of my past and present experiences and at the time I was experiencing them.

Originally, when I began writing *A Beginning to an End*, I was sixteen/seventeen. I was still in high school, and I was handling a lot of personal shit, which is very much projected into this book and Valarie.

It was a tough year, 2022. But without the hardships I faced, I never would be here, writing this author note two years later. Alive, healthy and happy.

So, if there is one thing to ask from you, as the reader, it is to understand Valarie Dale.

And if you can understand her, you can understand me, and your friends who may be going through a similar experience—maybe even yourself.

But no matter who it is, or what it is, believe me when I say everything happens for a reason.

It will get better.

Happy reading,

C. A. Blake

If you'd like to know more about C. A. Blake, you can find her on Instagram at https://www.instagram.com/cablakee/

The Before

"Just because she knew it wasn't right,
didn't mean she knew how to stop it."

1. SOULMATE BELIEVER

"**D**o you believe in soulmates?"

Simple answer, difficult question. Before she could answer the 'do you believe' part, she first had to ask herself what the actual *definition* of a soulmate is. Because according to Google, a soulmate was 'a person ideally suited to another as a close friend or romantic partner'—basically insinuating that a soulmate was someone Valarie Dale should find herself connected to on a level different from her friends and other relationships.

But for that to happen, for Valarie to answer the big fat "yes" that Harmony Davis was waiting (and hoping) for Valarie to respond with; she'd first have to *believe*. And Valarie didn't believe in a lot of things—especially things that came out of Harmony's mouth.

"Me and Daniel are getting married one day," Harmony used to say. "I just know it!"

"Addison's a really good person, Valarie. Don't you trust me?"

"You're my best friend Valarie Dale."

Okay—whatever, you get the point. And maybe Valarie should start believing in things—like dogs are better than cats, or Vegemite is actually tasty. But she doesn't. And probably never would.

Valarie's eyes flashed over to the ice cream counter on her left. "Nah," she said, answering Harmony's question.

Harmony frowned. "What about platonic soulmates? Y'know, like friendships or sibling love?"

"If you say your sibling is your soulmate, I'm instantly calling the fucking police." Valarie coughed. "That's just weird."

Harmony Davis giggled loudly, her hand brushing through her blonde shoulder-length hair. "Not like that, dumbass. A soulmate doesn't have to be romantic in the sense of like sex and shit. It can be someone similar to a best friend or a pet."

Valarie raised an eyebrow. "What if you're having sex with your best friend?"

"Then you're having sex with your best friend?" Harmony repeated with a shrug of her shoulders. "You're not—*ugh*—Valarie just answer the bloody question!"

"I already said no!" Valarie huffed. "I don't believe in that shit, you know this."

"Why not?" Harmony whined.

Valarie rolled her eyes. "Because I just *don't*. I swear, every single wedding where the word soulmate is thrown around in the vows, those so-called *soulmates* are now divorced with three kids."

"That's depressing," Harmony frowned, looking at Valarie oddly, "and really specific."

Valarie shrugged, spooning at her melted ice cream, refusing eye contact.

"I can't believe we start Year 11 tomorrow," Harmony exclaimed suddenly. "I'm super excited, with Addison now sitting with me it's gonna be sick."

Addison—*fucking Addison.*

Valarie gulped down the ball of frustration in her throat. "Well, not *just* Addison. Me and Tessa too. *Remember?*"

"Oh. Yeah, right. You two, us *four*." Harmony smiled, "We'll be like the Kardashians or something."

"What the hell are you talking about?"

Harmony giggled. "Like we're one big family. All supporting each other and stuff."

"That's..." Valarie just shook her head with a small smile painted on her lips. "Okay, yeah sure. Weird analogy, but I get what you're trying to say." The two laughed noisily.

"What's this about the Kardashians I hear?"

Valarie peered to her left, catching sight of the old, rugged man in his work uniform, which consisted of a black shirt and jeans with his name tag on the top of his right pec. A missing tooth was difficult to ignore when his lips pushed away from one another and curled into his famous and friendly smile.

A smile Valarie had been familiar with since Year 7.

"Don't you worry about that Mr Diego," Valarie chortled, taking a sip of her melted ice cream.

"I worry about you girls twenty-four seven. Can't have my best customers sad or worried now." Mr Diego took a few steps towards the girls' table.

Harmony giggled again, her right leg crossing over her left as she moved her body, so she could lean against the white-bricked wall, her eyes now able to flick between the two a lot easier. "The only worry you should have is the lack of faith Valarie has towards things like true love."

Valarie groaned, causing Mr Diego to raise an eyebrow and cross his hairy arms over his chest.

"I thought we were over this," Valarie mumbled. "Listen, Harmony has made good points, I won't lie, like the shit she said earlier about true love and stuff. But I just don't believe in all the soulmate and teenage love stuff everyone goes on about."

"You just don't believe in love at all!" Harmony exclaimed.

"Not true," Valarie said. "Love is real—you'd be stupid not to believe that. But what I *don't* believe is that you can fall in love at the age of fifteen and decide then and there you're going to marry them. The chance of your relationship surviving out of school is lower than five per cent! And don't get me started on your soulmate shenanigans."

Harmony rolled her eyes, waving a hand towards Valarie as her eyes stuck on the amused yet intrigued older man. "See what I mean?"

"No, I get what she means," Mr Diego nodded along, humming slightly. "Valarie's right Harmony. Sorry."

Harmony threw her head back, banging a hand on the table. "You were supposed to be on my side!"

He just shrugged his shoulders.

"See, he even agrees!" Valarie grinned. "I'm not saying you can't date in high school and stuff, but I just think it's stupid that kids get into relationships at such a young age and expect to be with them for the rest of their lives. Just be realistic y'know."

"You've never even dated anyone. What would *you* know about love?"

"Hey!" Valarie recoiled from Harmony's sharp tone of voice. "Don't get pissed at me. You asked for my opinion, and I gave it to you. If you don't like it, don't ask for it."

Harmony looked away.

Mr Diego smiled awkwardly. "Okay girls. Well, do you want any more ice cream?"

"No." Harmony and Valarie both mumbled.

"O-kay," he said, and walked off.

Valarie turned her body to face Harmony front on. "I know that face, what are you thinking?"

"Doesn't the idea of finding a prince charming... *excite you*?"

Valarie said nothing, shocked at Harmony's sudden condescending tone of voice. "Just imagine someone caring and treating you like a princess, holding your hand through all your troubles and fears, through the ups and downs. It would be an *amazing feeling.*"

Valarie didn't believe it. She *couldn't.* Things like that only happened to girls like Harmony. Maybe in her dreams or the fake scenarios created in her head while listening to a Taylor Swift song. But not to Valarie—not in real life.

Not to someone who looked like her.

"That shit only happens in fairy tales Harmony," Valarie breathed, flicking a hair behind her ear.

"It happened with me and Daniel."

"And look how that ended up."

Harmony stayed quiet, a flicker of shock passing over her.

Valarie's face instantly dropped, guilt tugging on her heartstrings at the sight of tears filling up Harmony's eyes.

"Sorry," Valarie began, "I shouldn't have said that..."

Harmony rolled her tongue through the inside of her cheek just as Valarie sighed. "Let's just change the subject alright. Like... have you talked to Addison recently?"

Harmony's lips twitched into a smile as if just saying the name automatically brought her great joy.

"I talked to her yesterday," Harmony smiled. "She and Arthur broke up a few days ago."

"That's that Year 12 from Hale, right?" Valarie confirmed.

Harmony hummed, leaning forward in her seat. "He was rich *and* hot. A bit of a shame they broke up."

"He goes to Hale, Harmony. I think that's the biggest red flag there is. Who cares if he's rich and hot?"

Harmony shrugged. "Only live once."

Valarie rolled her eyes. "Well, he was a dickhead. We should be happy they broke up."

"He's Oliver's best mate—wouldn't want to call him that."

"And what's Oliver going to do?" Valarie spat. "Call me a *whale* again?"

Harmony shuddered slightly. "You know he only says shit like that as a joke. It's his way of treating his friends."

"I don't see him going around calling you names," Valarie mumbled, leaning back in her seat and running her hand angrily through her wavy hair.

"They're dickheads, Harmony. Oliver *and* Arthur."

"It's Oliver's way of joking with his mates Val," she repeated with a frown, eyes blinking slowly. "He's mean to people he likes—it's his way of being sarcastic."

"Whatever." Valarie pushed her chair backwards, picking up both her and Harmony's empty ice cream cups and throwing them in the bin. "Let's just go. I've got to get a good night's sleep before school tomorrow."

Harmony bit her lip, but complied anyway, standing up and following Valarie towards the store door. "Bye-bye, Mr Diego!"

"Bye-bye girls!"

The bell on the door echoed around the empty room, a surprise for both the girls as usually around that time the store was packed. But it was completely empty.

"You excited for school?" Harmony bumped her shoulder into Valarie's side, a teasing and excited grin on her lips.

Valarie forced a smile, trying to hide the tightness that was threatening to harden her lips. "Sure."

Harmony just grinned more, pushing herself down into the driver's side of her car and flicking on the ignition, the engine revving and, in an instant, Valarie shoved herself into the passenger's side.

"To your house, we go!" cried Harmony.

Valarie forced out a laugh.

Valarie Dale didn't particularly like this part of the day. The part where the sun began to set lower and lower and the realisation of what time it was came to light. Where she blinked once and suddenly found herself slowly dragging her feet over the driveway outside her house. And it wasn't like she wanted to go in, but what choice did she have? It was her place of living. A roof over her head that also provided food.

But it wasn't a home. Valarie would argue that with anyone who'd listen.

And yet, there she was. Standing outside her front door, her heart feeling so heavy it ached. There was nothing stronger at that moment than her subconscious forcing her shaky hands to pull at the handle of her front door.

And she was met with silence.

She'd never complain when the sound of nothing filled her ears, but she wished it would fill her mind too. Her brain was running at a million miles per hour, thoughts pouring into her ears, ringing loudly and blocking out any silence that could potentially give her some peace of mind.

Her eyes flicked to the white clock hung on the wall a few metres from the ceiling, the longer black hand clicking to the side indicating the time was now officially six-thirty p.m. Her father, Matthew Dale, would be home any minute now and her mother would be at least another hour and a half. Valarie could only wish her father would be late, that maybe he would decide that today was the day he wasn't coming home and he would run far, far away and never return. Like an ending to a fairy tale.

Fairy tales don't exist, Valarie.

And of course, her wishes were not granted as about twenty minutes later, after she had finished her shower and skincare routine, and changed into some comfortable clothing for the night, the dangling sound of a key being shoved into the keyhole of the front door echoed throughout the house. Instantly, the moment the door opened, the house turned ice cold.

When Valarie peered around the corner of the wall she was hiding behind and got one look at her father's face, she knew the rest of her night would be her hiding out in her room and finding herself asleep before her mother even got home, just to ignore her father. Even if that meant she missed dinner.

"Valarie?" An hour later, the voice of her mother, Cindy, echoed from behind Valarie's bedroom door, where she had been cooped up.

"Come in."

Valarie first noticed the blank emotion on her mother's face before anything else. Not even the dark, crumpled blue nurse uniform her mother wore, or the tired look in her eyes from the long day at work. One glance at her mother's face and it told Valarie everything she needed to know.

"How was school?"

"I didn't have school today." Valarie held back the urge to laugh like her mother just said a joke.

Valarie wished her mother was joking.

"Oh," Cindy Dale muttered, shoulders slumped (like always) and leaning against the wall of Valarie's bedroom door. "I thought it started today? Did it not?"

Maybe, Valarie thought, *if you listened to what I was saying last night you'd know.* "No Mum," she sighed. "It starts tomorrow remember?"

Cindy's eyebrows raised slightly, as if it finally hit her, "That's right, I forgot school starts on Tuesday this year. Sorry 'bout that, my mind's been all over the place." She tried laughing it off, but the laughter only got cut off by the awkwardness in the room. Valarie's eyes dropped from her mother's gaze.

Silence filled the air for a minute, with Valarie tugging down on her oversized hoodie to let the sleeves hang over her hands while the older Dale in the room just kept her eyes on her daughter.

"How was work?"

Valarie didn't hate her mother. She would do anything for her mother and thought the world of her. But she wasn't the brightest of souls. She was forgetful and often acted and looked a lot older than her age. But Valarie, as much as she wished her mother would change or start actually acting like a parent—she didn't blame her.

She blamed Matthew Dale.

"Long." Cindy's shoulders untensed. "And tiring, very tiring." Cindy curled her thin lips together in a tight smile. "How was your day? If you didn't go to school, what did you do?"

Hung out with Harmony. Listened to Harmony's rant about this boy she likes, listened to Harmony talk about Daniel, listened to Harmony talk about whatever came to her mind... "Just hung out with Harmony," Valarie shrugged. "Nothing much else, to be honest."

"Oh. That's it?"

"Yeah..." Valarie furrowed her eyebrows, "What else did you expect?"

"Don't know, to be honest."

And without a goodbye, or a hug, or a loving motherly smile, Cindy walked away. Forgetting to close the door behind her too.

2. TIMETABLE THIEF

The sunshine soaked itself over Valarie's sleeping body, shining through the cracks of her cheap and flimsy curtains that covered her bedroom windows, inviting itself to awaken the girl from her once peaceful sleep, to her now squinting eyes and annoyed mood.

She laid there, no real urge to move or get ready for the day; and only when the clock struck seven-fifteen and her body hadn't moved for twenty minutes did she then force herself up and out of the comfort of her bed to begin getting ready for school. The birds were still chirping outside, though to Valarie it was like white noise.

But something she did notice was the complete silence in her house.

A small grin landed on her lips, her mind processing that she was once again, alone, and a sense of relief washed over her body as she began rummaging through her messy closet and finally found her school summer uniform; the white polo shirt with the school's logo on the top right and a pair of navy-blue shorts to finish it off.

Valarie grimaced at the sight of the shorts. She quickly threw them back into the pile of clothes and began searching once more for the school trousers instead.

Though the temperature would be in the high thirties, Valarie refused to wear the school shorts, finding them uncomfortable against her pale and fat thighs. She preferred the pants where her thighs wouldn't be shown to the public eye, as well as being able to walk without having to pull down the ends of her shorts every five steps.

Wearing trousers was not part of the school uniform, but Valarie got an exception after a humiliating incident in Year 8. Her shorts had torn from being too tight, so she had a lengthy discussion with her head of house, Mrs Baker. She left the office with a yellow note and a signature to justify her clothes to anyone who asked.

With a quick slip of her school pants over her thighs which began settling comfortably around her waist, just above where her hip dips were prominent, she began pulling at her shirt subconsciously. She hated how it seemingly clung to her stomach.

Valarie found herself stuck in front of her bathroom mirror moments later; quickly blending in a few strips of concealer on a couple of small pimples on her chin, brushing her eyelashes with some mascara and pulling her hair into a quick ponytail.

Her hands swiped at her phone that sat on her bedside table, the electronic light shining into her still slightly sensitive morning eyes.

She found herself travelling into her kitchen with her school backpack on her right shoulder and her phone in her left hand. Quickly stuffing three bags of original Smith's chips, two packets of Oreos and a half-eaten pizza into her bag before filling up her water bottle and walking out her front door, shutting it locked behind her.

Since Valarie wasn't seventeen (not for a few more months anyways) she couldn't get her driver's license just yet, but lucky for her—Harmony Davis had turned seventeen over the Christmas break and had offered to pick Valarie up for school and drop her home too.

Eight o'clock hit and right on time, Harmony arrived. A sense of relief washed over Valarie as the summer heat was already becoming too unbearable to stand.

"Why are you wearing pants?" Was the first thing Valarie Dale heard when she pulled the car's side door open and plopped herself down into the passenger seat.

Valarie raised an eyebrow, clicking in her seatbelt and turned to Harmony who was already looking at her with a disbelieving look.

"Because I fucking can," Valarie shrugged, moving in her seat to get comfortable. "It's comfortable, and I've been wearing them for the past three years."

Harmony gaped, "It's like forty degrees outside!" Ignoring the rest of Valarie's comments.

"So?" Valarie shrugged again. "Never too hot for pants."

Harmony just shook her head, before moving the gears out of reverse and beginning the journey to school.

"Harmony!"

Light blonde hair swept in front of Valarie's face so quickly that if the hair in question hadn't stopped in front of Valarie, she probably would have missed it. Small arms wrapped themselves around Harmony's body, squeezing tightly around the brown-eyed girl who laughed happily back. "I missed you!"

Valarie gazed at the pair, arching an eyebrow as the bitterness towards Addison Archer subsided. Addison and Harmony were like two peas in a pod; similar types in boys, a similar type of personality, a similar type of smartness and looks. Valarie could only roll her eyes at the pair.

"You're acting as if you guys didn't see each other only a couple of days ago."

A light laugh came from beside Valarie; one that she knew all too well. Tessa Reed. Short, soft, light brown hair covered her head, dimples on each cheek, and a slit between her eyebrows from when she was in her rebel phase (though, you could argue she was still in that rebel phase).

"How's your girlfriend?" Valarie asked.

"Never was my girlfriend," Tessa shrugged off, eyes peering to where Addison and Harmony were now happily talking as if Tessa and Valarie didn't even exist. "Though, I wouldn't be opposed to the idea. But what about you Val? Any boys I need to know of?" She wiggled her eyebrows suggestively, grinning heavily as she bumped shoulders with Valarie. "Or girls—I wouldn't judge."

Valarie sighed joylessly. "Nope." She popped out the 'p' while her eyes quickly glided over to Addison and Harmony who were *still* talking. "None at all, except if you count the old guy on the bus."

"Was he hot?" Valarie cracked out into laughter, teeth showing. Tessa only grinned more if that was even possible. "The question was needed, Valarie."

"It really wasn't." Valarie shook her head in amusement. "And for the record, *no* he wasn't hot. He was old and had really bad breath." Valarie scrunched her freckly nose up in disgust as the memory replayed in her head.

"Oh, hey Valarie." Addison Archer finally looked at the two girls. "How were your holidays?"

Shit, boring, lonely. "Great yeah, yours?" Valarie answered.

"Amazing," she sighed gently, a soft smile covering her red lips. "I went to Fiji for two weeks and saw *so* many cool things. It was *super cool.*"

"*Super cool!*" Valarie repeated jokily.

Tessa snorted like a pig.

Addison's smile twitched—as well as her eye. Like her real personality was trying to jump out. But it's not like anyone would notice—especially Harmony. To her, Addison could do no wrong.

"You ready for classes this year Harmony?" Tessa looked over at Harmony.

Harmony's face instantly dropped. "Are any of us ready?" She muttered, "I have *six* ATAR subjects this year."

"I have three," Addison shrugged, rolling her arms over her chest.

"None," Tessa smirked.

"I have four," sighed Valarie, breathing out a puff of air, "think I'll regret it though after the first week."

"Then why'd you choose ATAR?" Harmony's eyebrows creased.

Valarie shrugged. "Because I want to just try it."

"Yeah, nah *fuck* that," Tessa snorted. "You see, I'm smart, unlike you three." She pointed and waved her finger at the three girls.

"For what, choosing all general classes?" said Harmony.

Tessa nodded with a grin. "Yeah, basically. 'Cause, you see, when exam period comes around, and you all are stressing your tits off about it; I'll be chilling at home re-watching all the *Vampire Diaries* seasons."

Valarie rolled her eyes, just about to chip in when the bell rang indicating that homeroom was about to begin.

Tessa groaned. "How is it, that after being at this school for five years I never get use to the sound. Anyways, I'm off," she continued. "To the *best* house colour by the way, just thought I'd remind you all."

"Shut up Tess," Harmony shook her head, shoving Tessa's shoulder in a joking way. Tessa only winked back and skipped away.

Harmony, Valarie and Addison began walking off in the other direction. Towards the area where the Yellow house was located for their homeroom.

"Gooood morning girls!" A bright and bubbly voice was heard nearly instantly the moment Valarie, Addison and Harmony walked into the classroom already filled with students. Miss Candlewood, better known as Miss C for short. All the way from India, Miss C held herself with a smile at all times. There wasn't a day she was unhappy, and being Valarie's homeroom and human biology teacher, she never failed to lift up Valarie's mood. Even if just for a second.

She stood there, her hands sitting comfortably on her side as her silky black hair sat up in a high ponytail. "How are we today?"

"Amazing, Miss!"

"Happy to be here."

"Eh, she'll be right."

"Well, that's good to hear." Miss C exclaimed, skimming over Valarie's comment. "Are we excited for the year to come?"

Harmony grinned happily. "Very." Her arm was linked in with Addison's.

"Well, I must give you three your timetables for the year before you head off." Miss C took a few steps to the side, her hands plucking out three sheets of paper from the lone table and quickly handing them over to the girls.

Valarie smiled, her eyes skimming over the paper in her hands as her feet began following after Harmony and Addison. The three sat down around a group of familiar faces, both men and women combined. A small smile grew on Valarie's lips when her eyes locked onto Layla Graham—a black woman Valarie was casual friends with.

Harmony and Addison grabbed two empty seats from near tables, pulling them together and settling down across from Layla's spot. Valarie took it upon herself to take a seat beside Layla.

Her eyes locked onto a smaller figure sitting on the opposite side of Layla, one Valarie didn't actually notice was there until she perked up.

"Oh, hey, Jenny." The girl in question smiled softly, tucking a soft piece of her thin, black hair behind her olive-skinned ear. "How were your holidays?"

"Good, yeah good, thank you for asking. How was yours?"

Valarie shrugged her shoulder with a fake smile. "The same old, nothing really interesting to talk about."

The timetable that was settled on her lap suddenly disappeared, causing Valarie's head to spin over to the source of the thief.

"Only Human Bio together," Harmony Davis muttered, her forehead creased, and her head tilted to the side as she read between both hers and Valarie's stolen timetable. "You're doing Drama? *Why?*"

Valarie held herself back from rolling her eyes. She leaned forward on her chair towards the blonde woman and snatched back the paper that was taken from her. "Yes. I am taking Drama as a subject. And yeah, no worries, Harmony, you can take my timetable, thanks for asking." This time Harmony rolled her eyes, not bothering even trying to hide it from Valarie's view.

"Don't be a bitch, Valarie."

Valarie's eyes snapped over to Addison, who was already glaring at Valarie. "Shut the fuck up…" Valarie began to retort.

"Hey! I'm doing Drama too!" Layla suddenly spoke up, cutting in. "What a coincidence!" A small, awkward laugh escaped through Layla's lips. Valarie smiled tightly.

From the corner of her eye, Valarie noticed Addison tugging at Harmony's shoulder, forcing her body to look at her, not Valarie. And this time, Valarie didn't bother hiding her scoff.

"So, what class are you in? Can I take a look?"

Valarie nodded her head, her bottom lip curling under her top as she leaned back into her seat, offering the sheet of paper over to Layla who happily took it from her.

"There's only one Drama class this year by the way," a voice suddenly cut in. Sitting on a table across from Valarie and right next to Harmony, Justin Bradson spoke with a small grin. His body pressed between two other boys who looked literally identical to each other—Caleb and Brady Solomen. "So yeah, you would be in the same class."

Layla beamed widely at the information. "And what about you Jenny? What classes have you got?"

The girl in question perked up, seemingly surprised someone had called her name. "Er... Business General."

"You're doing Business?" Beside Valarie, Layla gasped with joy. "I am too! And Valarie—it's on her timetable."

Jennifer smiled softly. "Fun."

"Oh, isn't this great news! I won't be alone for that class," smiled Layla. "What other classes are you doing? Hmm, English, Math, History... hey, I think Jenny's doing History ATAR."

At the sound of Jennifer's name being mentioned, she popped her head up. "Huh?"

Valarie threw her head back in laughter.

3. TESSA'S FUTURE HUSBAND

Homeroom
History ATAR
English ATAR
Recess
Human Biology ATAR
Business General
Lunch
Drama ATAR
Math General

Valarie peered down at her timetable once again.

"You've got History, right?" Jennifer smiled from beside Valarie, curiously staring down at the sheet in her hand. "If so, we're in the same class."

"Brilliant," Valarie fake-moaned.

Jennifer Graham was an interesting soul. Valarie would consider her a friend, a mate, but she wasn't that close to her. More like that person she would say 'hi' to if she walked past her within the hallways, but definitely not the type of friend she'd spill her deepest darkest secrets to.

Jennifer was kind, soft and sweet. She reminded Valarie of the really expensive flowery perfume you could get from Myer. When you first met her, she was shy, and it took a few minutes, sometimes longer, for her to really get out of her shell. But once she did, she was a ball of fun and happiness. With a gorgeous smile and stunning southeast Asian features, the girl was the definition of beautiful.

The two girls walked through the main hall of the school, students of all different shapes, sizes and year groups brushing and pushing past Valarie while trying to get to their first class of the day. Year 7s ran through the halls, not stopping for anyone or anything, while Year 12s took their sweet time, laughing happily with their friends with no urgency to get to class.

"So… are you excited for this year?" Jennifer asked. Her brown eyes peered up at her, which made Valarie grin at the height difference.

Valarie was taller than nearly everyone in her year. At nearly six feet, (five foot eleven, to be exact) she was one of the tallest among the girls. The boys, not so much, but there were still a few that were below her. And with Jennifer's height of around five foot five, the height difference was laughable.

"Of course," Valarie smiled widely, her hands pulling on the straps of her heavy school bag that hung low on her shoulders. "The French Revolution seems super interesting. But also, there's a lot of content to cover which I don't think will do me any good for these exams we've gotta face in May and June."

Jennifer drew in a breath of air sharply. "Don't remind me." She rubbed her forehead just as the two turned a corner, the classroom coming into sight. Valarie could already see a few familiar faces standing outside waiting with their books, pens and laptop in hand. "I'm *totally* going to fail this class. My parents are up my ass about this year. Saying all this shit like…" She stopped just in front of the classroom and turned to Valarie, pointing a stern finger at her, creasing her eyebrows, drawing her lips together to become thinner and using her other hand to lay on her hip. Kind of like how an old mother would look.

"This is one of the most important years of your life Jennifer!" Her voice was stern and high-pitched, and her finger waved threateningly in front of Valarie's face. "If you do not do well this year, you will not graduate school and you'll be grounded for the rest of your life. Your ass will be as red as a tomato!'"

Valarie stifled a laugh. "Let me guess, your mother?"

Jennifer groaned, puffing out her lips as she took a seat on the wooden bench outside their classroom. "Both actually. My mum said that, but my dad didn't deny nor disagree with her." A soft and bitter sigh left her lips. "They're acting as if this year will determine if I survive and live to the fullest extent of my life. Like it'll be the end of the world if I don't get an A for each subject." Her glassy eyes peered up at Valarie.

"God, I'm already wanting to cry and it's only the first hour back at school." Jenny let out a harsh muted moan, leaning back so her shoulders hit the cold concrete wall behind her as she rubbed her forehead again.

Valarie frowned, sitting beside her and letting her bag fall off her shoulders onto the floor. She didn't know what to say, truthfully. Valarie had never had to deal with expectations from her parents as… well, they didn't really care. They had no interest in what she was doing or how her grades were at school.

"It'll be okay, you'll get through this. You always do," Valarie said, awkwardly.

Jennifer shrugged, "Hopefully."

"Come on," Valarie nudged her towards their classroom door. "Let's go."

History was fantastic as always. As she had guessed, it looked like the French Revolution *would* be exciting to learn, but Valarie Dale was also correct when she said that there would be a lot of content. The class would cover the period from 1771 to 1793, and judging by the content and handouts she received, it would require a lot of effort to remember it.

She was excited though. Shaken with nerves, maybe even a little petrified, but nevertheless, excited.

Valarie couldn't say the same for any of her other subjects; *especially* English.

It was laughable really, that Valarie hated English and yet chose it willingly. She knew she was going to be sacrificing her mental health to do English and History as ATAR courses. Essays weren't something she picked up on easily, and neither were short stories or exams—anything involving writing really.

So not only did she have to write essays for English, but also for History. She knew the consequences of choosing two subjects that were as difficult as each other, but if she wished to attend History class, she'd have to suck it up and do the exams and essays.

And English—well, she needed the course to get into uni. Gaining an ATAR score in high school was the easiest and quickest way to get into uni. Without one you'd have to go to TAFE and do another six whole months of schooling to obtain an ATAR score. And the last thing she wanted to do was an extra six months of school *after* graduating.

Valarie had no clue what she wanted to be when she was older, so she thought the best way to leave her options open was to choose English ATAR as one of her subjects.

But by twenty minutes into her first English class of the year, Valarie was already regretting her choice.

Blah blah *blah*. That's all Valarie could remember once she'd made her way out of the classroom of hell. Something about reading 'Jasper Jones' in the first semester of the year with essays and more essays about the book expected.

She had only sat down for a moment before her three friends who completed their friendship group of four came striding towards her, taking their spots on the cold bricked floor right out front of the Music office. Valarie hadn't even taken out the food she'd packed for recess before Tessa began jumping out of her skin about whatever was on her mind.

So clearly nothing had changed since last year.

"I think I just fell in love!"

Valarie's eyes flickered to where Addison and Harmony sat. Both held a similar teasing grin, obviously amused by Tessa's dramatics. "His voice. Oh. My. Fuckin' God, Valarie!" Tessa stood up swiftly, a dreamy expression stuck to her face. "You don't understand how perfect this man is… he's literally made by the Gods above, I'm tellin' you, Val!"

Valarie's blank face gave no indication to Tessa that what she was saying made zero sense to the Dale girl.

Addison exhaled. "Tessa babes. You've had *one* conversation with him over a period of an hour, and for fifty-five minutes of that hour, you sat there in your chair staring dreamily at the back of his head." Valarie detected a slightly agitated tone to Addison's voice. "It was fucking *creepy*."

It seemed Valarie was the only one who noticed, too.

"The back of his head is *hot* okay Addison," Tessa's tone was sharp, yet playful at the same time. "And it's *not* creepy. You just don't understand Addie, when we made eye contact it was like the world stopped."

"He only made eye contact with you because you decided it would be a *brilliant* idea to knock yourself against his desk, so…"

"It's beside the point *why* we made eye contact Addison," Tessa huffed, crossing her arms over her chest while Valarie stifled a laugh behind her hand. Tessa took a deep breath before continuing. "We're *soulmates* Addie, believe me when I say this is the start of our beautiful love story. Where from one moment we're making eye contact—with those gorgeous eyes of his—to the next smiling and the next marriage."

"Marriage?" Valarie cut in, curling her lips, struggling to keep her amusement and laughter at bay. Tessa was dramatic, always had been, and Valarie thoroughly enjoyed it. She was always overreacting about something that had happened to her. But sometimes, during her theatrics, Valarie found herself struggling to figure out if Tessa was just being dramatic or was using her dramatic nature to hide her true feelings.

"You're already planning the wedding after knowing this guy for what, an hour maybe?"

Tessa only huffed playfully at Addison's comment, pouting like a child whose toy had been taken from them. From the corner of her eye, Valarie could see Harmony watching with amusement painted on her face, while Addison seemed to be growing more annoyed by the minute.

"Of course, I have. I've already made my Pinterest board and looked at venues in Margaret River. No fucking way am I getting married in *Perth*." Tessa scoffed. "I swear he's straight out of a Disney movie." She stopped for a split second before her face lit up like Christmas lights. "Oh, *oh*! He kinda looks like that guy from Rapunzel. You know the love interest, er, what's his name?"

"Ryder?" Harmony answered with a laugh, causing Tessa to let out a big grin as if she'd just won the lottery.

"Yes! *Him.*"

Valarie didn't believe it.

As much as she wanted to, she just ... didn't. Her school was full of rude, immature boys who found it funny to make cruel 'jokes' about women and still got amusement from making fun of each other's mothers. Valarie refused to say these kinds of jokes out loud, but she sometimes made them too.

So, for Tessa to come out and say that a man with such beauty and grace—who happened to be Valarie's first movie character crush—was walking the halls of this very school ... well, it was near *impossible.*

"Obviously this man is not Ryder from Rapunzel. What is his real name?" Valarie asked, raising a curious eyebrow.

"*Ruel.*"

The rest of recess, Valarie Dale spent her time eating and listening to Tessa harp on and on about Ruel, and her plan to live happily ever after with him. It was entertaining, to say the least, and a good distraction from the nervous feeling Valarie had in the pit of her stomach. She was worried the rest of her classes would be shit and from the looks of things, they would be.

"Kill me now," she muttered to herself, literally having to drag her feet into the Human Biology classroom behind Addison and Harmony who were already halfway inside, searching for an empty table.

The three girls were the last ones to walk inside, and limited tables were available. It became clear that the only spots left were in sets of two.

Valarie's lips curled and her hands clutched the books against her chest. "Hey Harmony..." She stopped in her tracks.

Harmony hadn't even looked back to see where Valarie was. She was too busy giggling with Addison as they took it upon themselves to sit beside one another.

Valarie let out a breath of air, shaking her head as she swiftly took the last empty two-seater table at the front of the class.

Why, Valarie wondered to herself, *is choosing where to sit on the first day of school so difficult and stressful?* She threw her books down onto her desk, and pulled at her shirt to unstick it from her stomach before wrapping her arms around herself. *This isn't too bad,* she thought, glancing at the empty seat beside her before looking up to the teacher's table which stood proudly in front of the whole class; Miss Candlewood's long flowy brown dress shifted in the breeze from the open windows.

"Good morning class!" Miss C exclaimed happily. "I'm Miss Candlewood, but you can just call me Miss C for short. Though most of you I know, there are an odd few in here I've never taught before so, welcome! Now, before we start with our lesson today, I would like to go through the assignments that you will be expected to complete and what we will be covering throughout this year—*Valarie*."

Valarie's heart dropped out of her chest. Her eyes widened in dread with thoughts already beginning to form about what she had done wrong. She could feel the whole class peer over at her, eyes boring into the side of her head, into her face, into her soul.

The teacher raised an eyebrow at her, seemingly noticing her shuddering state. "You're not in trouble Valarie, I just need you to move seats as this year will include group work involving whoever you share a desk with."

Group work? Chatter stirred up, and grunts and moans echoed throughout the classroom.

"Class, class, calm down," Miss C shushed slowly, one of her pointy fingers coming up to hover at her lips. "Everyone please quiet down!"

The teacher came out from behind her desk and walked towards Valarie, still smiling as always. She peered down at her. "Would you be a dear and move next to Ruel up the back for me."

Valarie's eyes nearly fell out of their sockets. *Ryder?* She twisted the upper half of her body and turned to look behind her. Her eyes landed on the possible future husband of Tessa Reed. Or more like, the husband of Rapunzel...

Jesus. She was right. Tessa was right.

Miss Candlewood went back to behind her desk, facing the now quiet class but Valarie paid no attention.

He was... *gorgeous.* Tessa wasn't being dramatic when she said he looked like a prince straight out of a Disney movie. He wasn't looking directly at her, but in her direction, which allowed Valarie to get a good view of him from where she sat. He was pretty. There was no denying that. He sat there peacefully, not doing anything special, his skin radiant against the glow of the summer sun through the window. His beautiful brown eyes gazed up at the teacher, and all Valarie wanted to do was to get lost in them.

His eyes made the colour brown appealing and elegant, and for the first time in Valarie's life, she was actually enjoying looking at the colour. He sat so gracefully on the table with his hands folded and shoulders straight. There was a beautiful neutral look on his face, with a hint of a smirk as if he knew she was staring bashfully. When Valarie looked closer, she could see—*green?*

His eyes are green? No. Brown. Valarie was certain now that they were brown. They gleamed against the sunlight, just a simple gaze lighting up the room.

"Miss Dale." A crisp voice came from behind her. She spun her whole body back to face the front, taking her eyes off Ruel. "Please move spots as I asked."

Embarrassment flooded through her veins, the metal poles of her chair scraping against the floor as she slowly pushed it backwards. Her hands scooped up her unopened books and pencil case, and with quick small steps, Valarie Dale found herself plopping her books down on her new desk and her body on a cold stool.

She hung her head low as the teacher finally began the lesson.

A small cough came from beside her.

"Hi."

His voice... Valarie gulped.

His hand stuck out in front of her face. With a soft grin, he peered into her eyes as she slowly peeled her own gaze from the table below her to his face.

"Why do you have two eye colours?"

It was more of a statement than anything else. But Valarie didn't even care what it sounded like. She cared more about *why the fuck* she had said it out loud. It was meant for her brain, no one else's. She turned her head away from him, curling her lips tightly from the embarrassment she could suddenly feel in her gut. But her body paused, and her eyes flickered back up to meet his when she heard him laugh, a small chuckle echoing from his gorgeous lips as he pulled them together. *Stop staring at his goddamn lips, Valarie.*

"Yes, I do. Thanks for noticing, Valarie."

He chuckled again. Valarie's mouth was slightly agape and at that exact moment, all she wanted to do was dig herself a hole; one that could guarantee her departure from this awkward and humiliating moment. He knew her name? *Of course, he knows your name, idiot,* she thought. *The teacher just said it out loud.*

"I... I didn't mean that," she breathed out an awkward laugh, a small and tight smile struggling to stay afloat on her lips. "I... I just noticed that you had brown eyes earlier on and then when I sat down, I saw you had green *and* brown eyes which I think is super cool by the way so don't think I'm trying to like, make fun of you or anything."

Die. She should die. The best possible ending to this conversation and the best possible outcome would be for Valarie Dale to die. Or maybe disappear, like what Thanos did in that one Avengers movie to half of the population.

"Want to know something *super cool?*" He was... taunting her?

She narrowed her eyes at him. But he paid no mind to the sudden protective shield she showed, he just leaned forward. Her breath stuck in her throat and suddenly no words or actions could be made as he licked his lips and looked into her eyes again.

"You have blue eyes."

A breath finally realised from her throat. Ruel leaned backwards on his chair, pushing his body down so his legs spread slightly, and his hands crossed over his chest. She gulped again. He shifted his gaze to the teacher once more. As if nothing had happened.

And though he was faced forwards, his side profile did nothing to hide the cheeky grin that was settled on his full nude-coloured lips. Valarie just kept staring at him, blinking at him, until a few moments of silence between them turned into a near minute.

And suddenly, her heart was fluttering, and a small blossom of red began spreading across her cheeks as she let out a soft laugh.

"Hi to you too, Ruel."

His grin widened.

4. IN HER DREAMS

Miss Candlewood spent the rest of the lesson running through what their curriculum would look like for the year, as well as what was expected of them regarding their behaviour and involvement.

And for the whole hour, Valarie found herself stuck in a predicament. Because as much as she knew she shouldn't, she did—she looked. She smiled. She made eye contact. She even went as far as 'accidentally' knocking her knee against his under the table, which caused Ruel to grin at her and raise his eyebrows.

Who knew an eyebrow could be so attractive?

He was attractive. She was *attracted to him.* And she knew she shouldn't be. Not when in the back of her mind all she could think of was the name *Tessa.* But Valarie had never felt like this before. Never in her life had she been so attracted to someone so quickly, or even at all.

She'd had crushes before, but never in real life with people she knew. More like celebrity crushes, like all the guys on *Bondi Rescue.* But there was no doubt she was intrigued by Ruel. He wasn't mean, he didn't seem to be disgusted by her and in fact, he seemed to actually *enjoy* sitting next to her.

Valarie had never experienced it before. A man as attractive as him, or a man at all, not ignoring her. Not disgusted by her.

This shit didn't happen to her. Not to *Valarie.*

She couldn't stop herself from romanticising the situation. She promised herself one hour—one hour of her crushing on this guy she'd barely even met, one hour of sneaking glances and smiles.

And then she'd go back to reality.

"I already *know* this class will be the death of me." Addison held her head high like she always did, her black school boots with a bit *too much* heel clicking against the brick floor. Students weaved past Harmony and Valarie who stood beside Addison after the end of Human Biology class. "Five assignments this term *alone,* and two of them are research tasks. Does Miss C not understand that there are only *ten weeks* in this term? Not bloody twenty!"

Addison stomped her right foot on the ground, angrily pushing past a small Year 7 who only looked up at the blonde with utter awe and admiration. As if the kid had just been pushed by an angel.

"It's not as bad as my Chemistry class though," Addison went on, the hallway slowly clearing as they turned a sharp corner.

Valarie quickly rushed to the other side of the two girls to make sure she didn't get cut off by the wall.

"So, thank *fuck* for that." Addison finished.

Harmony chuckled, peering over at Valarie who had stayed quiet during Addison's rant. "So, Valarie, you and Ruel…" Valarie knew that tone of voice. The clear teasing as if they were back in fifth grade and she'd just admitted her crush on the popular boy.

"There isn't a *me and Ruel,* Harmony," she rolled her eyes, "I just sat beside him in class."

"And? What was it like?" Addison added, giggling as she bit her lip suggestively with a teasing tone in her voice. "Is he as attractive up close as everyone else is saying?"

Valarie rolled her eyes. Again. "Wouldn't know, I didn't spend time looking at him," she lied. "And anyway, he's Tessa's, remember?

Or did you forget Tessa's life plan to live happily ever after with her Disney prince already?"

Harmony snorted while Addison rolled her eyes. "I don't think I could forget even if I *wanted to*," said Addison with a laugh. "And anyway, I'm allowed to call him attractive. It's not a crime."

"I know," Valarie muttered, curling her bottom lip in between her teeth. "I was just saying."

Addison didn't respond. Instead, she quickly waved Valarie goodbye before pulling Harmony the opposite direction, leaving her alone.

Pulling out her timetable, Valarie quickly confirmed to herself that Business was her next class. Turning around, a small gasp left her lips when her body bumped into something.

Or more like someone.

Her hands instantly came to clutch around her stomach as she took a step back. She found herself staring at Ruel, and an instant rush of warmth ran through her body. "Shit, sorry," she muttered, embarrassment flushing her skin. "Didn't see you there."

"Clearly," he dragged out, the words rolling over his tongue with a hint of amusement. *Why is he always so amused?* "Where you off to?"

"Er," she gulped. "Business."

"General, in room fifteen?" Valarie nodded, one of her arms dropping to her side while the other stayed covered around her body. He smiled. "Guess we're in the same class then."

"We are?" She instantly regretted her enthusiasm, and quickly managed to recover herself by coughing into her hand and saying, "I mean, cool. Okay."

"Cool." He nodded with that confident grin that he seemed to be always wearing and began to walk forwards, stopping and flipping his body around when he realised Valarie hadn't moved from her spot. "You comin'?"

Her feet pattered quickly against the floor, her cheeks red as she fell beside him.

What are you doing? Her mind blanked. All she could hear was her heart banging against her ribcage.

"Are you alright?"

Her eyes shot up to look at him, and her head tipped to the side. She hesitated for a moment before she finally got the words untangled from her tongue. *"Huh?"*

Ruel stopped, with Valarie following right behind him. "I said," he licked his lips, looking down at her as she began to feel the air leave her throat. "Are you okay?"

"Fine."

"So, you're not then."

"I just said I'm fine so… that means I am."

Ruel chuckled. "You sure?"

Valarie frowned. "Why are you questioning me, I just said I'm fine."

"I'm just asking a question."

"Well, don't," Valarie muttered, shaking her head before beginning to walk off.

"Do you want to be friends?"

She stopped in her tracks, turning her eyes to lock into his. "What are you, five?"

"I just thought we could be friends."

Valarie's jaw dropped in disbelief. "Are you high?"

"Why would I be high?"

"Because…" Valarie's lips parted. "I have no words."

"But you just said words."

She scowled. "Fuck off."

Valarie began to storm off until his hand caught hold of her wrist. Instinctively, she pulled away.

"I'm sorry," he said, his eyes not wavering from hers. She felt slightly intimidated. "I was being a smart-ass. That wasn't cool."

"Don't worry about it…" she shrugged. "I was being an asshole too. Just forget about it."

"No seriously, I'm sorry but… I just thought, well… I thought we got on in Science and well, I just want to get to know you better."

Valarie tried her best to not show how hard her heart was beating against her chest. "Listen, if this is some kind of joke," she looked around as if she was searching for secret cameras, "if someone put you up to this, I'll pretend for your sake the joke worked but *don't* sit here and pretend you want to get to know me." Her eyes began watering.

"No, *no!*" His voice turned stone cold, and he looked *hurt*. "No one is putting me up to this. I would never do something like that to you."

I don't even know you. "Just leave it alone Ruel. I understand you're new and you're probably just trying to be nice to everyone you meet but I'm not the type of person you want to befriend." Her breath came out shaky. "Just leave it alone. Leave *me* alone."

"Of course you're someone I'd want to befriend."

Her eyes moved back to his, her lungs feeling like they were collapsing inwards from the eye contact.

"Give me a chance."

She ignored his comment. "I've got to go. Class and all." She awkwardly muttered.

"I'll tag along if that's alright?"

She took a moment to respond. "It's a free country mate, you can do whatever the fuck you want."

Valarie started walking. She could hear his feet patter against the concrete floor as he caught up to her—staying by her side.

For the minute and thirty–five seconds it took for them to walk to their next classroom, it only took about ten seconds before Valarie was struggling to hold back her smile.

Because for a moment there, she liked to believe that it wasn't a joke, and he was interested, and that she could maybe be friends with him.

That she was the girl who caught his attention. Not anyone else.

In her fucking dreams.

5. PROMISED

Business class was a bore. Well, except for the fact that Ruel decided to sit directly across from Valarie and kept throwing over small crunched-up pieces of paper at her throughout the lesson. With small written notes inside them.

She did her best to ignore it, and act like she didn't enjoy it, but when Layla Graham raised an eyebrow in suspicion at the two, Valarie quickly threw a piece of paper back with her own note: 'Stop it'.

He, unfortunately, did.

When the bell went off, indicating that lunch had begun, Valarie was the first out the door. She shook her head at Layla, silently indicating not to mention the notes before running off. Lunch dragged out, and before she knew it Drama class had started.

Valarie arrived at Harmony's car after school before she did. Though, Harmony wasn't far behind her. And the car hadn't even pulled out of the carpark before Harmony suddenly began screeching in anger.

"That bitch!" Valarie stilled in shock. "The last thing I want to do is go home and do fucking homework, but noooo!" Harmony drawled out, the car taking a sharp turn and causing Valarie to clutch suddenly onto the edge of her seat. "Mr Kit has other plans!

I know he's divorced but just because your life is hell doesn't mean you need to make mine hell too."

Valarie struggled to hold back her laughter. "You knew what you were signing up for when you chose ATAR Physics."

"I signed up for exams and harder work, not five pages of homework due by the end of the week," she exclaimed, throwing her hands up in the air and making Valarie's eyes widen. She had the urge to lean over and steer the car herself. "How does he expect us to do this homework if we don't even know the content properly? We haven't even finished the introduction yet."

"Not sure," Valarie shrugged nonchalantly. Harmony just sighed in annoyance.

"So, fucking annoying. Actually," Harmony paused her rant. "I think Addison's free this arvo, you reckon you could message her to call me later?"

No. "Sure."

"Thanks." Harmony grinned. "Just use my phone."

Valarie nodded her head, not muttering another word as she pulled out Harmony's phone from the small pocket on top of her school bag that sat in between Valarie's legs. She quickly unlocked the phone with the passcode she knew by heart.

"Do you want to quickly stop by Mr Diego's for some ice cream before we go home?"

Valarie shook her head, shoving the phone back into the pocket where she found it. "I can't, sorry, I don't have a lot of money at the moment, and I'm trying to save up for a car."

"But you could spend money yesterday?"

Yeah, because I stole the five bucks from my parents' wallet. "It was just leftover change. I can't Harms, I'm sorry not this time."

"But you don't need a car, you don't even have a license!"

Valarie groaned internally. "So?" She said, running a hand through her messy hair. "Doesn't mean I can't start saving up. It's a lot of money and I don't have a job right now. Plus, I turn seventeen real soon so I'll be able to go for my driving test then."

"Okay." Harmony shrugged, the wheels of her car hitting the familiar spot of Valarie's concrete driveway.

She turned to Valarie, their eyes meeting. "So, no ice cream tonight?" Valarie just blinked. Harmony smiled tightly. "See you tomorrow then."

She didn't know why, but she felt guilty. Maybe she should have said yes to Harmony's offer of ice cream, but then she remembered all the times Harmony had said no to her and as quickly as it had arrived, the guilt disappeared. "Definitely," Valarie smiled, pushing open the car door and stepping out. "Thanks for the ride by the way. See you tomorrow, same time as always."

"Yes, see you then."

Harmony gave another tight smile, no teeth showing, before driving off into the sunset, leaving Valarie with the smell of the gasoline and a heavy heart.

Dinner consisted of vegetables, mashed potatoes and steak. Served along with an awkward and eerily chilly silence, it wasn't very delightful. Not even the scrape of a metal fork or knife hitting a plate could help with the unsettling tone.

Valarie's blue eyes refused to meet her mother's or father's; she kept them peering down at the food settled on her plate, her hand twisting her fork through the soft mashed potatoes to try and distract herself from the inevitable: her father.

"How was school?"

The question made Valarie's heart skip a beat, and she would be lying to herself if she didn't say she was nervous. But she did her best not to show it, and instead gulped down the lump in her throat, swallowing a forkful of food before replying. "Good," she nodded, licking her lips unintentionally. "How was work?"

"Shit," he spat, with no remorse. Valarie flinched.

"Why?" She was hesitant to ask, but maybe if she could get him to let out his anger now, he wouldn't need to let it out later. On her.

"Because I work with a bunch of idiotic cunts who don't know how to do their jobs properly!" He flared, his jaw tightening.

Valarie's tongue ran across the inside of her right cheek.

"How difficult is it to just listen to instructions?"

She heard a little hiccup of fear slip out of Cindy's mouth. Valarie's stomach began twisting when she noticed her father's eyes moving to his wife's. His sharp knife cut through his steak with one single movement, and he suddenly pulled the piece off his plate and into his mouth. With one chew, he gulped. A glimmer of disgust and anger suddenly flickered over his face and all Valarie wanted to do was run and hide.

He finally spoke again. His words, though, did not ease the tension in the air. "And do you know what I thought of while I was at work today?" His words hit hard, an invisible knife cutting into Valarie's mother's heart. But Cindy stayed quiet. *"Do you?"*

Cindy shook her head, her eyes beginning to squeeze tightly. "Coming home, to see my two favourite females, a nice warm cooked dinner, and peace and fucking quiet. But instead, I got a wife who cannot even bother to ask me how my day was—" Valarie caught her breath, "—loud music booming through Valarie's room—" Valarie gulped, "—and a fucking cold *steak!*"

In a split second, the steak that sat on Matthew's plate went flying across the room. The loud slap of the meat hitting the floor rang through Valarie's sensitive ears. Her mother flinched, and her body hunched over. Valarie froze.

"*Stupid fucking…* " He stood from his seat, muttering profanities under his breath.

Valarie's eyes didn't waver from the steak on the floor. But she knew her mother was crying. She could practically feel her fear. A lone tear ran down her wrinkled face, hands clenched together in her lap and her head hung low. And suddenly tears began streaming out of Valarie's own eyes, anger blossoming at the bottom of her stomach.

The chair scraped underneath her, the sound echoing through the air. Her mother's eyes snapped up to the girl who was now standing up tall, a look of determination and anger painted on her face.

Cindy shook her head violently. "Valarie, *don't*."

Valarie pushed past the words of warning, ignoring the feeling of her mother's worried eyes on her as she stomped into the kitchen. Her father was just standing there; fist clenched around the edge of the sink as he stared daggers into the air. "Father." Valarie's voice was crisp, Its shakiness was covered by confidence she found somewhere deep within her.

"Go away Valarie," he muttered, teeth clenched together.

Valarie took a step forward.

"You don't get to come in here and yell at either of us like that just because you've had a bad day, it's not fair." She spoke through her teeth.

Steam seemed to burn out of Matthew Dale's ears as he snapped around and took two angry steps towards Valarie, pointing a shaky finger straight at her red face. "Don't you come in here, girl, and try to start something you *won't* be able to finish," he stared her down, like a lion going for its prey.

She gulped, taking a step backwards. It was then she realised how close she was to the wall behind her. "I fucking *warned you* to go away, and now look at the situation. All because *you* wanted to come in here and fucking tell me how to act."

Another step forward, another one back.

"I have *every right* to be fucking mad at your mother, and same with you. Do you know how loud you are, how annoying your music is?" He took another step forward; she took another step back. Her gaze never wavered from his. Even though she wanted to look away, she just... couldn't. "Do you know how much I want to throw that goddamn fucking speaker out the window?"

Her back hit the wall. Her hands fell against her sides. Her bottom lip quivered as her eyes burned with hot and heavy tears. The anger that burned in his eyes was something Valarie had never seen before—because yes, he was angry, he was always *fucking* angry but this... *this* was something new, something different.

It was frightening.

Valarie *never* backed down from him. Since the ripe age of thirteen when she promised herself she would never let him talk to her or her mother like that, with that anger laced in his voice, and get away with it. Ever since, she'd never stopped *fighting* back, talking back. Except for today.

Except for the day she could only see red in his eyes.

"I just want peace and quiet. I just want *one thing* to go my fucking way and instead," he scoffed, "I end up with a *heartless cow* of a wife and a loud, annoying *excuse* of a *daughter.*"

He was inches away from her, glaring into her eyes. She could feel her knees begin to shake and wobble, feel herself begin to cry, the tears like lava burning against her cheeks. She never cried in front of him—she wouldn't allow him to see that side of her. But she couldn't help it. This was different.

Daughter and father, two generations of people; staring into each other's eyes. With two different emotions, two different stories, two different reactions.

"Fuck. *You.*"

Thousands of little strings were wrapped around Valarie's heart, keeping it upright, keeping it safe and secure. But when she stumbled out those two words, and his large hands wrapped around her neck, the largest string of them all snapped.

Gasping and crawling for an escape, Valarie's feet were lifted off the ground slightly, the tips of her toes clinging to the floor as hard as they could. But the pain of that heartstring splitting into two hurt more than the loss of breath. Her eyes were squeezed shut, until an extra bit of pressure pressed into her neck from her father's large hand and her eyes quickly opened wide. Her pupils dilated to their fullest as she looked into Matthew Dale's eyes.

Those eyes used to hold so much love, so much happiness. What happened? Why is there anger, why is there red, why didn't he stop?

It was pure anger, fury, hatred. It was like he didn't even know what he was doing, as if he didn't know *who* he was hurting.

"*Matthew!*"

The fast beating of her heart drowned out all outside noise, including her mother's screams. Valarie didn't register it when she tilted her head up as she silently begged for air, or when her hands began crawling and scratching at her father's. She didn't know when he finally released her, but when he did, a rush of painful air hit her lungs.

But he had walked away. And her knees had hit the wooden floor harshly, her hands cradling her neck. She was still gasping for air, and her heart was still crying and begging for help.

"*Valarie…*"

Her arms wrapped around her body as she turned into a curled-up ball. She shook her head from side to side, tears streaming down her face like a waterfall.

A hand touched her shoulder suddenly, causing her whole body to violently shiver, a painful, silent scream coming out of her chapped lips.

"Valarie, it's okay."

She kept shaking her head, her back pushing itself even more against the wall, trying to get away from the voice, trying to get away from whoever was trying to speak to her. Valarie blinked through her stinging tears, and that's when she saw a glimpse of her mother's hand. A hand of help.

Cindy was kneeling on the ground. Her arms wrapped around Valarie and all she could do in that very moment was lean into the chest of her mother; allowing the comfort and touch of another human being for the first time in a long time.

Breathing felt like a struggle, it was difficult and painful, but Valarie didn't know how to stop it, didn't know how to make it better.

"Breathe Valarie, breathe. It's okay, I'm here."

"H-h-he," her lips were shaky and cold. Her sobs weren't getting any slower and her breathing wasn't getting any deeper. "H-he..." she let in a big gasp of air. "Y-you promised Mum," Valarie hiccupped. "You promised h-he wouldn't touch me."

Another heartstring snapped.

6. HOODIE

"Valarie and I have created a plan."

The middle-aged woman sat in her wooden chair, one leg swung over the other. Her long brunette hair was clipped up, with two strands falling over her ear as she held a clipboard in her hands.

"It's called 'the safety plan', and it's something I have been working on with Valarie during our sessions together. She has expressed concerns about both her and your wellbeing and safety."

Thirteen year old Valarie Dale trembled in her seat. She could feel her mother watching her, but she refused to look back.

The school counsellor continued talking.

"The idea is simple. I have given Valarie my personal contact details so if anything *were* to happen, Valarie and yourself would have someone to contact—"

"What exactly are you insinuating here?" Cindy cut in. Valarie sucked in a breath of air.

"Nothing, Mrs Dale. I am merely informing you of what we've been talking about in our sessions. And I believe this is something you should be aware of as it involves you too."

"Well, we don't need it. I don't know what Valarie has told you in your sessions together, but should you know, Valarie loves to play up the dramatics when it comes to things like this." Valarie's mother said sternly, turning to Valarie. "When I agreed for you to see the school counsellor, you said it was to deal with your body issues and trauma from primary school—to talk about how sad you are or whatever. Not... *this.*"

Valarie whimpered. "Mum—"

"Isn't that, right?"

"Yes, but—"

"End of conversation." Her eyes snapped back to the other woman. "There is nothing to worry about. And I would appreciate it if you would keep out of our business. Starting today, I don't want you to talk to my daughter anymore, are we clear?"

Valarie teared up. "Please, *Mum.*"

"No more Valarie," Cindy said. "I'm not kidding. I've talked to you about this multiple times."

Valarie's bottom lip quivered. "I'm sorry. I just thought—"

"You thought nothing," she snapped. "I promise you, Valarie. Nothing bad is going to happen to you, to us. There is nothing to worry about."

Sixteen year old Valarie Dale winced in pain as the cold of her concealer touched the sensitive skin on her neck. She held the makeup sponge with both hands, shakily trying to spread the makeup across the large bruise that had grown overnight. Her head was titled upwards, but it was becoming more difficult by the second as her eyes were becoming blurry with tears.

Never, in a million years, did Valarie think she would be in this situation. Where she was too scared to leave her room, going to great lengths to stop the outside getting in, by for instance wedging a chair under the door handle.

She'd always been frightened, nervous at the thought of what was outside her bedroom door. But she had never been scared enough to forcefully shake at the mere thought of being anywhere but her bedroom.

Her skin burned every time she tried to move her head. Even *thinking* about the fact that she had bruises on her face made her skin tingle with pain. Her head hurt from how much she'd been crying the past twelve hours—and it didn't help that she was running on a maximum of two hours of sleep.

Valarie wasn't stupid when it came to her home life. She knew what her father was doing wasn't right; the yelling, anger and fear he created in their shared house wasn't normal or positive. But just because Valarie knew it wasn't right, didn't mean she knew *how* to stop it.

There had been multiple times in her sixteen years of living that she thought, *maybe this is the time he'll do it,* put his hands on her skin, her body; break the last bit of trust she held in her heart towards the deadbeat of a man she shared DNA with.

Hope. She had hope, and that hope was diminished the moment she watched the man who promised to protect her the day she was born be the one to hurt her in the end.

How *dumb* was that? That throughout the years of abuse, bullying and everything in between she *still* had hope.

Maybe he was right, Valarie thought. Maybe she was *fucking stupid.*

She felt utterly mortified at the situation she was living through— looking at herself in the mirror, she struggled to maintain eye contact with herself, wanting nothing less to look away but she just... couldn't.

And so, she didn't.

She kept looking. Seconds ticked by, then minutes, until half an hour went past. It got to the point where she didn't have any more tears left to cry and she ran out of concealer to rub over the bruise on her neck. Where the humiliation became too much, and all she could think about was wrapping her bedroom curtains around her neck and hanging herself with them.

She hadn't had a thought like that since primary school.

She slowly slipped the school hoodie over her head. The top of her shirt clung in between her teeth as she tried to stop any screams of agony and pain from leaving her mouth.

But now, as she began tying her shoelaces, Valarie had to worry about school and how the fuck she was supposed to pretend everything was okay. She was pretty good at hiding how she truly felt, but as they say—everyone has their breaking point.

And Valarie knew she was nearly at hers.

The sound of tires rolling into the driveway of her house made her heart skip a beat. With a quick breath in, Valarie closed the door behind her and slowly made her way to the laundry, opening the glass sliding door to rush down the side of her house and through the side gate, unlocking it with the four-digit code before rushing over to Harmony Davis's car.

"Why'd you come out the side gate?" Harmony asked, raising an eyebrow as she began reversing the car out of Valarie's driveway.

She just shrugged uncomfortably, tugging at the top of her hoodie to make sure her neck was covered. She tilted her head to the side, not caring about the pain, to stare out the window so she wouldn't have to look at her best friend.

"Front door wasn't working."

"Why are you wearing a hoodie?" Addison questioned at recess, with a distasteful tone. She peered up just in time to see Valarie sit directly in front of her with an unhappy look on her face.

"'Cause," Valarie shrugged, though if anyone were to look closer, they'd see the way her throat gulped in nervousness, and how her hands came crawling up to the top of her hoodie to pull up and over her neck as a response to Addison's curious question. "I can."

"Fair excuse," Tessa butted in, with a grin, pulling out a peanut butter sandwich from inside her school bag. And it was then Valarie realised she never actually stopped past her kitchen before school to get herself food for the day.

Valarie suddenly found the floor very exciting.

"Just curious that's all," Addison shrugged, slowly examining her nails. "You do know it's like forty degrees outside so it's just *kinda* weird how you're wearing a hoodie, you get me? And for someone who's always got something to say you've been pretty quiet this morning." Her voice was sweet, yet her face did no justice to the fake kindness of her tone.

"How about, Addison," Valarie spat, her clothes suddenly becoming too restricting against her body, "you just worry about keeping my name out your fat fucking mouth *okay?*" Her voice was disdainful, high-pitched—a tone that not only shocked Addison, but also Tessa and Harmony.

Addison's eyes snapped over to Valarie, a glimmer of *malice* behind her eyes. "What the *fuck* Valarie," she shook her head, scoffing in distemper, "who pissed in your cup of tea this morning?"

"You." Valarie blurted angrily. "You and your fucking opinions about me and what I'm wearing. Who gives a *shit* if I'm wearing a hoodie?" She threw her hands up in the air. "Or anything actually. Who gives a *shit* about *anything*? Life is so fucking pointless, and you get angry and stressed all over a shitty fucking job, Dad. And for what? Huh? Was it worth it? Being a bitch to the people you're supposed to love?"

Valarie shot daggers at Addison, her face flushing red in frustration. "Is it worth it Addison? Being a downright fucking two-faced little *cunt?*"

Silence fell between the group of four girls.

"Fuck you, Valarie," scoffed Addison under her breath, arms tightening around her chest as she moved herself closer to Harmony.

Valarie looked over at Tessa, whose mouth was slightly ajar, but Valarie didn't bother waiting around. After watching Harmony wrap an arm around Addison's shoulders, she made her way up onto her feet, grabbing her bag with a little more force than needed before storming off down the corridor. Not bothering to look back.

Staring at the floor, she moved swiftly through crowds of people before rushing inside the women's bathroom, her head hung low as she brushed past the few girls who were taking photos of themselves and re-applying their makeup in front of the mirror. She rushed to the toilet stall furthest away from everyone and quickly slammed the door behind her, flipping the toilet seat down and taking a seat with her face falling into the palms of her hands as her shoulders shook from sobbing.

A rush of guilt trailed through Valarie. The sudden realisation of what she'd just done, just said… she had let her emotions get the best of her. She had let the anger control her.

Just like her father did.

And *no one* deserved that.

Her hands were shaky when she wiped the tears streaming down her face. Her heart was pumping out of her chest when she unlocked the toilet door minutes later after calming herself, moving swiftly through the crowded bathroom, adjusting her hoodie before walking outside. And it was only when her name was called that she stopped dead in her tracks.

She found the source of the voice; the familiar face of her Human Biology partner came into view and instantly her whole body tightened up. He was standing directly in front of her, the boy's bathroom directly across from the girl's.

Valarie's eyes widened, and as quickly as she stopped, she began dabbing harshly at the red bags under her eyes, trying to control her flushed cheeks which she just *knew* were bright red.

But Ruel—well he was just staring.

No words were said, no judgemental stares or curious glances. Just a look. But for Valarie, she felt like she was being followed by a camera, the lens zooming in on all the insecurities and emotions she wore on her face; from the blackheads on the tip of her nose to the soft, nearly unnoticeable jawline. Not to mention the mark on her neck.

"You, okay?"

Valarie gulped, looking into his green-brown eyes. "Yeah. Are you?"

He blinked without an answer. The tips of his eyebrows creased together as his eyes circled her face. His gaze fell on her tear-stained cheeks, on her reddened eyes and then her neck. And the once-creased eyebrows were now separated, his jaw slacking as his eyes narrowed in on her neck.

Her heart dropped out of her chest.

"Valarie—"

The trill of the loud school bell stopped Ruel mid-sentence. And with the escape route whoever was living above gave her, she took the help and swiftly left. And in the blink of an eye, she was walking to her next class with her head hung low and her arms crossed over her chest.

Not bothering to look back at Ruel who she knew, was watching her with a hint of uneasiness and concern.

7. DRAMATIC

Valarie apologised.

She couldn't handle the guilt, the humiliation. She managed to catch up to Addison before period three started, and profusely apologised for lashing out at her.

All Addison did was mutter "okay," and walk off.

So, Valarie went about her day, ignoring everyone and everything as the time ticked by. And then Human Biology rocked up. She spent the entire hour with her head laid in her arms as she pretended to be asleep.

She knew he was watching her. His gaze spent more time on the side of her face and neck than on the teacher.

When the bell went off at the end of fourth period, Valarie didn't bother putting her things away properly before she rushed outside, grabbed her school bag from one of the lockers and ran off. Not waiting around for Addison or Harmony. Ignoring any curious glances caused by her quick getaway.

For the whole of lunch, Valarie didn't speak once. She just played with the string of her hoodie.

Math came next.

And Math was just... Math.

Drama ATAR was the last class of the day. Her first official lesson of the class, as the day before she was stuck in the library with a relief teacher. It was a nice change to find herself in a large open room, Layla standing beside her with a smile that made Valarie smile too.

"*Oh,* I'm *so excited.*" Layla squealed. "And look!" Her fingers tugged on Valarie's arm, forcing her to look to her left.

Valarie held back a snort of laughter at what she saw. Half the wall was *covered* in pictures, and most of the students that were staring at them were in them. They were all from last year's production.

Valarie cackled out loud when she saw a picture of herself during their *'High School Musical'* play, dressed in a wig and old grandma look to imitate the drama teacher in the musical.

"Terry, look at you!"

"You look like a fucking idiot Rachel!"

"What the hell are you wearing, Joel?"

Mumbles mixed with laughter and giddiness from the class quickly ended when the voice of Natasha Campbell let out a horrid dying pig squeal. "*Why* is there. A picture. Of *me*," she pointed to herself with one long finger, while holding a disgusted and sickened look over her picture-perfect face, "looking like *that.*"

The picture she was referring to was her standing in the middle of the stage, wearing a *god-awful brown* wig on her head with a smile that brought most of the boys to their knees.

"Why am I on here?" It was a demanding question. The tone she used was just like the leading commanders you see in military and war movies. "Why the *hell* am I on here?"

"Miss Campbell, what is the meaning of all this *yelling?*" A mystic and echoey voice spread throughout the class, silencing the heavens above and bugs below. All eyes turned to the older woman, whose flowy flowery dress dragged across the floor behind her as she glided her way towards the students. Her name was Miss Apple-Berry, better known as Miss Fruit, Miss AB, Miss Crazy or Valarie's favourite (which she also coined for the teacher) *Miss Trelawney.*

Miss Campbell had large eyes, red-rimmed like she'd been smoking weed just before class. She always glided around the classroom on tippy toes, like an angel.

She was weird, that was for sure. But her love of drama and the arts was very inspiring. Most people didn't have any issue with her weirdness—as a matter of fact, most students loved her.

Well, except for Natasha.

"I gave *no* consent for my picture to be taken and put on show for everyone to see!" Natasha stomped her foot on the ground and crossed her arms over her chest.

Valarie noticed Layla rolling her eyes. Miss AB only chuckled mystically, her hands crossing over one another behind her back as she came to stand right in front of the girl.

"Now Miss Campbell, your parents not only complied with written signatures approving your consent for your picture to be taken, but also shown for school use. You, my dear, are not the only person up on that wall—it's nothing to be ashamed of."

"I can see that, *obviously*," Natasha spat out, scrunching up her nose. "I'm not *stupid*."

"Never said you were dear," the teacher smiled sweetly, which clearly only made Natasha angrier. "I was just stating the truth."

"I don't *care* about the truth!" Her face went red with anger. "I look absolutely *horrible*," she took a step towards the teacher, "and I'm painted up on this wall looking my absolute worst! What if someone important sees this?"

Valarie rolled her eyes, holding back the urge to shout out "shut the fuck up."

"If you have any issues regarding the photos, please come and speak to me after class." Natasha's mouth opened wide once more, but she went quiet when the teacher spoke again. "Okay class, come and take a seat in front of me please."

The students mumbled to one another, moving towards the front of the class and finding empty spots on the carpeted floor. Valarie and Layla quickly found a spot near the edge of the room.

Valarie met Natasha's eyes for a split moment once she got comfortable, and she swore she saw her mouth shaping the venomous word *'pig'*. Valarie quickly moved her eyes away from her.

"I can't believe you used to be friends with her."

Layla's voice was soft from beside Valarie. Her eyes on Natasha.

"Don't remind me," Valarie muttered, her body shivering in disgust. Layla only smiled sympathetically. "It was only for a year though, in year seven. Before she became a bitch."

She looked back over to Natasha, a sense of disappointment and hurt crossing over her when she saw the way Natasha laughed with her friends. She'd started making gestures at her stomach, pretending to be a pregnant woman. Blowing her cheeks out so they were enlarged.

Valarie Dale swallowed down the lump growing in her throat.

"I don't know what to do with her anymore."

Both women in the house stayed deadly silent.

"She's a useless excuse for a human and the last thing I need is someone asking about it."

Valarie had never needed to hold her breath before. The number of times she had snuck out to overhear what her parents were arguing about—she didn't have enough fingers.

But to be literally holding her breath until her face turned the same colour as her neck…

"Fucking little cow. Where is she anyways?"

"I don't know. Probably at school." Valarie could hear the fear laced in her mother's voice.

"I need to talk to her."

Valarie's heart began to rattle in her chest. Her knees wobbled and she had to grab a hold of the wall she was leaning against to hold herself upright.

"Why?"

"Don't be fucking stupid Cindy. Why do you think?"

"She won't say anything, you know this. I—I promised you."

"She better not." Matthew grumbled.

"No one will believe her. Everyone knows how dramatic she can be." Valarie's lips parted in shock. "Dinner's nearly ready, come on. Just…" Cindy sighed, "forget about her."

Matthew hummed under his breath. Valarie could hear the two of them make their way up from the living room couch. The stacking of plates and cutlery echoed through the silent house.

Valarie cautiously made her way back into her bedroom, where she'd been for the past hour. She closed her door and shoved her chair back under the handle before breaking down into a fit of sobs.

It was midnight when Valarie realised she wasn't going to sleep—again.

She would have done anything to get some sleep or have a break from the long-lasting headache—even better, for the pain in her chest to stop.

And there it was, a distraction. A notification had popped up on her phone, one from Instagram to be exact.

She nearly dropped her phone out her hands when she saw what it was.

'Ruel_Diego1 has followed you'!

8. BORED

Thursday. What a fucking crazy thing to name a day.

Two days it had been since well… *everything*. It was all very ironic, Valarie laughed to herself, that the saying 'everything has changed' now had meaning in her life. Because as fucked up as the whole situation was—it *did* change everything for Valarie Dale.

In that one hour of her life, her trust was broken. She had cried more tears than ever, and had the realisation that no matter what that man does to her, Cindy Dale will *always* protect her husband.

Valarie looked at herself one last time, tilting her head to the side—back and forth, up and down—taking in every inch of her body until she was squinting from how much disgust her heart held for it.

The bruise on her neck wasn't fading. It was still obvious and frankly looked worse than it did two days ago. But Valarie had perfected the amount of red lipstick, foundation and powder to cover it up. Due to her skin being so pale, sticking on a bit of colour to cover it up worked like a charm.

And all it took was a few hours in front of the mirror late last night to make it work.

Her father was already gone and off to work. She knew this purely by the footsteps she overheard earlier that morning. No words had been spoken. With the little talent she had, being able to distinguish between her parent's footsteps came in handy.

She triple-checked that her neck was covered before making her way into the kitchen. She ignored any and all eye contact with her mother to stop any possible conversation she might want to have.

"Good morning, Valarie."

Fuck.

Her voice was soft, *and sad.* It made Valarie stand up tall for a second, her instincts kicking in and the questions beginning to pour throughout her mind quicker than she could mentally handle. *Why are you sad? What happened? Was it him, again?*

Valarie again tried her best to ignore her mother altogether.

But she couldn't help it. It was automatic for Valarie to want to protect her. Care for her. Make sure she was okay.

A tear fell down her cheek.

She was sick of crying.

She finally looked at her mother.

Did he hit her too? Does she feel remorseful that she's allowed the situation to get worse? Is she blaming herself?

There wasn't anything to indicate physical assault—her mother looked normal, actually. Her body was hunched over the dining room table, a coffee settled in between her always-shaky fingers and the permanent look of melancholy still painted on her wrinkled and tired face.

Does she even fucking care?

"Hi."

Valarie gulped.

"Are you off to school?"

Can you give a shit about anything else?

"Yes." Valarie turned around, struggling to continue looking at the older woman. She kept herself busy by filling up her reusable water bottle.

"Okay."

"Well, I'm off."

"Okay."

I'm okay, thanks for asking by the way.

Valarie huffed at Cindy's answer, looking at her mother who was staring down into her cup of coffee. Valarie's mouth opened, only to shut closed almost instantly. She shook her head and rolled her eyes before storming off towards the front door, giving a tight smile to Harmony Davis who had just rolled into her driveway.

"Perfect timing!" Harmony shouted, grinning as Valarie quickly moved herself to the passenger side door.

"Yes."

Harmony raised an eyebrow. "You okay?"

Valarie let out a shaky breath, deciding to curl her arms around herself and squeeze at her stomach.

"Yes."

Neither talked the rest of the drive.

Valarie ignored everyone.

Don't get her wrong, she didn't particularly like all the looks she got when she just muttered the quickest responses known to humankind—but she just couldn't muster the energy to pretend she cared.

Her first three classes were a bore, and for the fourth period, Valarie slowly made her way to Human Biology. Where of course, he was there.

Ruel fucking Diego.

Valarie had yet to confess her findings in regards to Ruel's last name to Harmony.

"Good afternoon, Valarie, how are we today?"

"Afternoon."

"Are you okay?"

Valarie let out a shaky breath. "Yes." Her voice was sharp, yet soft.

Ruel nodded in response. She could feel him looking at her, but she refused to acknowledge it. The last thing she needed was to be distracted by him.

Or maybe... she did.

A few minutes had passed. Miss C's words went through one ear and out the other. She could still feel him watching her. Her body twitched at the sudden human touch when his finger pressed on the side of her shoulder, clearly trying to get her attention.

It made her want to smile.

It also made her want to punch him in the face.

She let out an annoyed sigh and turned in her seat, looking straight into his eyes.

Valarie wanted to cry.

Ruel sat there with a smile, and a sticky note on the tip of his nose read 'everything will be okay'.

She did start to cry.

Wiping the tears from her cheek, she flicked her gaze back to the front.

But suddenly everyone's attention was on her. Or to be more precise, on the man next to her.

Ruel had his hand up in the air, a determined look in his eyes. "Valarie's not feeling too well, is it possible that I could take her to first aid?"

Her head snapped over to him, confusion in her eyes.

"What a nice thing to do Ruel. Thank you." Miss C answered. "Here, take this." Ruel stood up, taking the pink sheet of paper from the teacher before beckoning Valarie to follow.

He stood at the front door, and though Valarie knew it was only a few seconds that he was standing there, it felt like a lifetime as she stared into his eyes.

She was embarrassed, and pissed at the fact that he'd put her in a humiliating situation where if she didn't go with him, people would ask questions. But if she went along with it, they'd still ask questions.

Valarie saw his shoulders lift as he let in a deep breath of air, his lips curling into a supportive smile.

Her lips twitched.

Realising her staring problem, and the stillness in the room, she swiftly stood up and followed after Ruel.

Standing awkwardly with her arms tight around her stomach, she watched Ruel shove his stuff into his school bag, before grabbing a hold of Valarie's things and stuffing them in hers. He gave a small smile to her when he turned around to face her.

"Let's go."

"Where?" She didn't mean to sound so aggravated, but frankly, she was. She had no clue what was happening, where her head or heart were at. Without the words to explain how she felt, Valarie followed after Ruel who had led them down the stairs and out back of the science building.

If someone was to look, they'd see them both as clear as day. But on the huge oval where classes of different ages were holding their P.E. classes, no one was going to look their way.

Not when Ruel had settled down against the bricked wall, ample green leaves from the trees hiding their location reasonably well.

She stared at him, and as if she knew what he was thinking she muttered, "What the fuck do you want from me?"

"Sit."

Valarie's eyes narrowed. "Why?"

He shrugged, pushing down his shorts from where they were riding up his tan thighs.

Valarie gulped.

She wordlessly sat beside him, keeping a comfortable distance between them.

"Did you know roller coasters were created in America to try and distract people from sinning?"

Her head rolled forward. "I don't think you forced me out here to talk about that."

"No, I didn't," he responded. "I didn't force you out here either."

"Well, you didn't give me much of a fucking choice, yeah? It was either get questioned by the teacher and students or you."

"And you chose me?"

She turned to face him. Her mouth went dry. "Listen," she began, licking her lips as her hands began playing with the small weeds in between the cracks of the bricked floor to distract herself from… him.

"I—I'm really struggling at the moment and the last thing I need is you coming in and fucking everything up."

He thought for a moment. "Am I fucking everything up for you?"

Yes. I don't know how to think or be around you. It scares me. You scare me.

"No—yes." she rubbed her hands aggressively over her face. "Not like it's any of your business anyways but I've just got some personal things I'm handling at the moment, and I'd appreciate it if you could leave me alone."

"I don't think I've asked about your difficulties, have I?"

Her bottom lip curled into her teeth. "No, but I know you want to."

She swore his hands twitched towards her, as if he was going to reach out and take her hand.

"I've never been one to believe in mind-readers but I wouldn't be surprised if someone out there had superpowers—"

"Don't be a smartass."

He grinned.

Her heart fluttered. "Seriously, I'm not in the mood, Ruel."

"I like the way you say my name."

Valarie blinked. "You're an asshole."

His lips smirked sideways. "Sure."

She continued to stare at him, and for a few fleeting seconds everything was silent; her head, her heart, her thoughts. It was peaceful. Nice, like how it feels to hold a small kitten in the palm of your hands. The way your heart aches from the touch of its soft fur.

And then it all comes rushing back to you, like a train—all the loud noises, screams of people telling you to get out the way, the honk of the horn from the train driver.

"Hey kids! Can you kick the ball back?"

Valarie's old P.E. teacher shouted from across the oval, his hands pointing towards the yellow footy ball at the feet of a tree in front of them, snapping her out her daydream.

She went to stand and retrieve the ball, but the palm of Ruel's hand laying on her knee gently pushed it down, making her stop in her tracks.

She froze at the touch. Her mind went haywire, and she didn't know what to do with herself.

Valarie watched him grab a hold of the ball, throwing it back at the group of school kids who were waiting for it.

She swore she started drooling.

"Hopefully none of them snitch on us," Ruel sniggered as he took a seat back beside her. She noticed he was closer to her than they'd original been.

"Hmm," she hummed.

"Can I be real with you?" She blinked at him. He laughed. "Okay, stupid question. But the real reason I brought you out here with me was because I was bored."

She laughed unexpectedly—and that showed in the shocked expression on her face. "Seriously? You embarrassed me in front of the whole class just because you were bored?"

He grinned, his body relaxing at her openness to continue the conversation. "Yeah."

"Fuck you."

"I would."

Her jaw dropped. It took a moment to respond—she was too shocked at the confession that had seemed to slip off his tongue so easily. *He was only joking Valarie, don't get ahead of yourself.* So, she laughed it off, responding with a "dick," and, ignoring the bubbly feeling in her stomach, she punched his shoulder lightly.

Her neck became exposed at the sudden movement. She quickly realised it the moment the conversation stilled, because he was staring at her neck.

She tensed up.

Ruel's face became sharp with desperation. "No Valarie—don't block me out. It's okay."

She went to stand but his hands wrapped gently around her wrist to stop her. She turned her back towards him and with no hesitation Ruel let go and held his hands up in the air.

"I'm sorry, that wasn't right of me to do…"

His lips curled inwards. "Just, stay. It's okay."

Valarie hesitated.

"Please."

With a sigh she untensed her shoulders and sat back down, her hands instantly pulling up her hoodie to cover her neck.

"Do you know why I really brought you out here with me, though?"

She shook her head lightly, still a little hesitant.

"Because I knew you were just as bored, so I thought, why don't we be bored together, you know?"

"I wasn't bored," responded Valarie. "I was just tired."

He didn't question it.

In fact, for the remainder of the time they spent together, he didn't ask a single question.

9. DON'T MAKE HIM ANGRY

Valarie Dale knew she couldn't avoid him forever.

It was inevitable that Valarie and her father would eventually make eye contact, talk to one another, bump into each other. They did live in the same house after all, under the same roof and hidden behind the same walls. The only thing that had been keeping them apart was her.

She managed to make it to Friday evening before she saw him. Four days, a personal best. But now that it was the weekend, and her father only worked weekdays, unless she wanted to skip showering and eating for three nights, she had no choice but to walk out of her bedroom.

As she stepped towards the dining room table, where she knew her parents had begun dinner, questions raided her brain.

How would he react to seeing her? Valarie had taken the makeup off her neck in the hope that showcasing the aftermath of that night would hit a spot in his heartless chest.

Would he be apologetic? Would he feel guilty? She knew her father didn't know what the word *sorry* was, but she still hoped that maybe he would apologise this time. Maybe he would change after seeing the damage his anger had caused.

Her eyes locked in on her mother's first, but as she scanned the room, she discovered only Cindy was in it.

"Where is he?"

Cindy sighed. "Bathroom."

Valarie let out a puff of air as she took a seat across from her.

"Don't start today, Valarie." Cindy said. "Please, don't make him angry."

"I haven't even done anything."

Valarie watched her mother's eyes gaze down to her neck, a flash of something Valarie couldn't decipher ran across Cindy's face. But like the speed of light, it disappeared in an instant.

She didn't comment any further.

Valarie sniffled just as her father made his appearance back into the living room. He didn't even take a second glance at Valarie. It took a moment for him to settle in, before he began stuffing his face with food.

"Can you turn that *stupid* thing off Cindy. It's fucking annoying." Matthew muttered with food still stuck in his throat. His words sent a clear message to his wife, who quickly obeyed and switched off the phone that had been dinging on and off for the past five minutes.

"Who's messaging you anyways?"

His question came off as confused, like he couldn't believe someone wanted to talk to *her.* Valarie raised her eyes ever so slightly, but only at her mother. It was then she noticed how tense her mother's body seemed. Her shoulders were up high, and her bottom lip was curled in between her teeth.

It wasn't an unusual sight. To be honest Valarie couldn't remember the last time she'd seen her mother *not* look so heartbroken.

But this was the first time she saw guilt behind her eyes.

"Just the girls trying to organise a date to host book club."

Valarie's father nodded, humming through his tongue as he pulled another big bite of steak off his fork.

The room fell into silence once more. The scraping of knives and forks against the plate made Valarie internally wince. She wasn't hungry. In all her years Valarie had never *not* been hungry but as of that moment, she had no appetite.

"I don't particularly like you reading those books those women get you. Too gory for you."

Something in Valarie's brain flickered—like someone had just switched it on. She dropped her fork onto her plate, loudly, but without a care as she moved her hands down onto her lap, clenching them both into a fist.

She could feel his eyes move to her.

Valarie didn't look up.

"What's wrong with you?"

You and your fucking loud breathing and chewing. I can hear your pig-like mouth moving and it fucking irritates me. Fuck you, goddamn it! Why don't you go choke on a fucking dick.

A hand fell into her lap, and then squeezed. It was her mother, and Valarie didn't need tarot cards to decipher what her mother was trying to silently communicate with her.

Don't make him angry.

"Not feeling the best."

Her father blinked once. Then just shrugged his shoulders and continued on with his meal.

"Actually, can I please be excused?"

She didn't wait for her father's approval, nor did she look for it. She instantly stood up, grabbing her plate still full of food and dumping it into the bin before heading off to her room and closing the door shut.

Enjoying the sweet silence of her bedroom, she dropped onto her bed. But just as she closed her eyes to try and relax her body and mind, the ding of her phone made her quickly open them back up.

And just like that, another switch flicked on in her brain, and for the first time since Human Biology earlier in the day, a smile came onto her lips.

'Ruel_Diego1 wants to send you a message'!

10. PARTNERS

The weekend was lengthy and painful. Valarie spent the entire time caged up in her room, luckily not having to go out for anything during the day as midnight seemed to be the perfect time to grab whatever food and drinks she needed from the kitchen.

But the past two days she spent in her bedroom were nothing but boring. It was a repeat of the same thing each day, each hour. Her playlist of Lana Del Rey and Sufjan Stevens played through her headphones until they ran out of charge. She'd then buy some time by doing any homework or studies that needed to be completed before the second week of school began. But Valarie knew the teachers never checked, so realistically she didn't have to.

But it was better than doing nothing.

And then if that got too boring, the iPad she was given as a present years ago still had some games like Minecraft. They entertained her for a while, but eventually got boring too.

And then there was the beautiful distraction named Ruel Diego.

Saturday morning came around. It was around nine o'clock when she awoke from her slumber, and one of the first things she did was check her messages. Just in case Ruel had messaged her.

Not like she cared, of course. It was just more out of general curiosity.

The night before he had messaged her a simple *'hey'*. It made her head spin.

Did he want something? Was it an accidental butt text? Or had he possibly messaged the wrong person? Did he mean to send it to someone else? Maybe another girl with a similar name to hers. A *girlfriend*...

That same night, she replied with a '*hello?*'

Deciding not to read too much into it, Valarie turned her phone off and went back to sleep.

The next morning, he had replied with a '*Who's your favourite Avenger's character?*' Which then turned into a full-blown argument about who the best *Avenger* was.

By lunchtime, Ruel suddenly stopped replying. It was a few hours at most, but it was the longest few hours of her life.

She wondered during that time if she'd done something to annoy him? To make him stop replying. It made her nails chip against her teeth and her head spin in confusion.

But she didn't care, she tried to convince herself. Truly. She was just... curious.

Her questions were answered later that day when she saw he'd posted a photo of himself in a dirty jersey and tight shorts, his arms around the shoulders of people she assumed were his teammates. The caption clarified he had just won his first footy game. And she received a private message sent by him not even seconds later.

She pretended her thighs didn't rub together when she saw the photo.

"For today's lesson, we will be learning the art of doing everything *but* talking. I expect you all to take this seriously, as this exercise will assist you with your future assignments. Including our class play." Miss Apple-Berry clapped delightedly, a large smile painted on her face like always as she stood in front of the Year 11 Drama class. "Let's all stand up."

She lifted her hands as the class followed on. There was soft chatter between students who were confused about what was happening.

"Silence!" Her voice echoed throughout the room, silencing the students instantly. "As I said before, this is a *silent* activity. So, there *must*," The teacher took in a big breath before continuing, "be silence."

Valarie watched as Natasha mocked the drama teacher to a few of her friends who all giggled in response. She just rolled her eyes.

"Our production this year will be Romeo and Juliet." Beside Valarie, Layla began bouncing on her feet in excitement. "And something that makes Romeo and Juliet so… passionate is the way the characters can show their emotion, instead of saying it."

Valarie raised an intrigued eyebrow. "To become a successful actor, you need to be able to *show* a story, show your emotions and thoughts without saying them. We, as the audience, must be able to understand just from looking at you what picture you want us to imagine. What we're supposed to feel just by looking into your eyes. So, with a partner of your choice, you will both come up with a story, a short one that is, about anything you'd like and any topic you both agree on. Once you've come up with an idea, you will be required to present your story to the class, through only your actions and movements."

"So, no speaking?" A girl asked, her held tilted to one side. "At all?"

"None at all," the teacher smiled joyfully, clapping her hands together once more before turning away from the class and looking up at the whiteboard hanging from the wall. "You all have twenty-five minutes, starting from… now."

Quickly, chatter started up throughout the classroom, with students grabbing their friends' hands and finding a spot around the room.

"So, I was thinking…" Layla's arm linked with Valarie's, pulling her along softly. "We could do something really depressing."

"Sounds like fun." The sarcasm rolled off Valarie's tongue easily.

Layla laughed, "Super fun! But anyways," she shook her head, plopping herself onto the floor and flicking her hair behind her ear, "I was thinking we could do something about someone being blinded by love, or something along those lines."

Valarie nodded in an approving hum, taking a seat in front of Layla. "That sounds good. But if we want to make it *more* depressing, maybe we could have one of us wanting to jump off a building or something and then *oh!*" Valarie's eyes widened, "the other person could be behind them, begging and pleading for them not to jump but they do… or maybe they don't."

Layla blinked slowly as her lips curled.

"Just a thought." Valarie shrugged slowly, awaiting Layla's answer.

"Let's do it!"

The drama activity ended in complete disaster. People either didn't take the task seriously or didn't understand what they were supposed to be doing. One pair of boys decided to act out *Magic Mike,* which prompted the teacher to cut in halfway during their 'strip-tease'.

The only group that took it seriously other than Valarie and Layla were Natasha and her partner Jason, who both acted out a domestic violence scene with the ending being the woman (Natasha in this case) *killing* the man (Jason) in a slightly gruesome way. The teacher, for the second time in that lesson, had to cut in and stop it.

But Valarie and Layla's performance was the best out of everyone's, to quote Miss AB. She had complimented Layla's performance the moment it ended, and Valarie swore she saw Layla nearly break out into tears.

Later, in Human Biology class, Valarie was still basking in the praise. She was startled when Miss AB suddenly came to stand beside her, placing a piece of paper on her desk. "Please write your name on the hand-out I've just given you all, and make sure to keep it in a safe place as you *will* need to give it to me when you've finished the assignment!"

Valarie gulped, her hands skimming through the ten-page assignment her Human Biology teacher had just given her.

"This assignment has been split up into two parts." Miss C said. "You and your partner, who will be the person you sit beside," Valarie looked over to Ruel, "will work through this together. It will be due by end of this term. I know this may seem like you have lots of time as it is only the middle of February but *trust me* when I say you will need to use every spare second to complete this assignment."

Valarie pushed the hand-out onto the table face down.

The teacher continued. "The first part of this assignment is actually in preparation for the second part. You and your partner will need to answer the series of questions on the hand-out. You can either do that together or separately, I don't particularly care, as long as they're complete. The second part is a little bit more… hands-on." The teacher smiled sheepishly. "One of you will need to pretend you are a doctor and the other a patient, though you will both eventually swap roles halfway through the assignment. And whoever is the designated doctor will need to examine," the teacher used air quotes, "'the patient' in regards to different medical situations."

Murmurs echoed around the classroom. The teacher went on.

"The different medical situations will be written on your handout. Each partner will have different situations and there are four that need to be completed. Preferably, each partner will do two scenarios." Valarie bit her lip. "How this would work is the patient would know of their medical condition beforehand and the doctor would need to examine them and explain their diagnosis. Afterwards, the doctor would find out if they were correct or not. Any equipment needed will be provided by the school."

The teacher took a deep breath before continuing. "You *must* write a conclusion as to how you got to your answer and *why* you believe that your answer is correct. Without any evidence or written statements, you will *both* fail this assignment which by the way, is fifteen per cent of your overall grade this semester."

Murmurs started up again around the classroom, and this time the tone was a lot sharper and more anxious. Valarie's eyes met Ruel's once more.

"You will have no time during school to work on this." The class burst into a flame of rage. "Class, quiet *please!*"

It took a good minute or two before the class calmed down. "I understand you are all frustrated, but there is other work that needs to be completed during class. That's why you've been given so long to do this. If you cannot keep up with that, then you shouldn't have chosen Human Biology ATAR as a subject."

The class turned deadly silent. "As I was saying… no time will be given during school, meaning you and your partner will need to find some time outside of school to do this."

Valarie let out a soft sigh, her fingers pressing against her forehead as she leaned forward on her elbows.

"But just for the next ten minutes, I want you all to face your partner, and discuss the topic of the assignment. Read through it, and if you have any questions or concerns, please speak up. After that, we will be moving on."

The teacher gave a nod to the class before sitting down and instantly began typing away on her laptop, while the class simmered in rage. It was blatantly obvious no one wanted to do this outside school hours.

Valarie couldn't say she was too happy about the situation either. "So, when are you free?" Valarie raised an eyebrow.

Ruel laughed gently.

"You know, for this assignment thing?" She sucked in a harsh breath. "You want to catch up outside school hours to do this?"

Ruel hummed, then spoke nonchalantly. "That's what the teacher just said."

"Not at mine," Valarie said swiftly, eyes flickering away from his. He raised a curious eyebrow. "Just… not at mine."

"*O*-kay," Ruel laughed half-heartedly. "Well, I was thinking more a library or café or something… if that's alright with you."

"Yeah, no that's perfectly fine," she nodded, her arms squeezing around her stomach. "There is this quite new café, it's like a five-minute drive from my house. I can message you the address, if you want to meet there…?"

"Friday at four works for you?"

Valarie nodded. "Yeah, that's fine. For the assignment only."

"Obviously," he drawled. "What else would it be?"

Nothing, Valarie reminded herself, shaking her head. "Nothing," she laughed nervously, "obviously."

Ruel just grinned and nodded along, his body leaning back in his seat as he let out a low whistle and Valarie felt her body tense up.

And it wasn't because she was uncomfortable.

11. DATE?

He was wearing a black shirt, denim jeans and a silver chain around his tanned neck.

Valarie had been staring at Ruel from outside the café's window for the past five minutes. It was Friday, and surprisingly the week had gone by quickly.

It hit Valarie earlier in the week that she had to move on—forget and move on from the *incident* involving her father the week before. Because she couldn't sit there waiting for an apology from her father, or for her mother to check in.

If her parents wanted to forget about it, she'd do her best to follow suit.

She fell back into her normal habits, not sneaking out the back or missing dinner. She even began talking to Harmony, Addison and Tessa like normal too.

But here she was, feeling stupid as she stood outside the café with her backpack held against her stomach and a frown on her face. Ruel Diego was attractive. She knew she found him attractive too.

It made her head spin every time she thought too much into it.

"Hey," she coughed awkwardly, fumbling with her bag as she shoved the heavy thing beside her. She quickly slid into the space across from Ruel, who finally decided to look up at her, a small smile crossing his face when he made eye contact with Valarie.

She suddenly felt the overwhelming urge to dig herself into a hole.

"Hi," he said, nodding at Valarie, his smile only growing as he brushed his hand through his brown hair. "You ready for this assignment?"

Valarie only laughed. "Nope."

Ruel grinned. "Do you know what you want to eat?"

"I'm not hungry, thanks though." At that same time, her stomach growled in hunger, and a small laugh came out of Ruel's mouth. Valarie's cheeks broke into a rosy blush.

"You're not hungry?" He raised a teasing eyebrow. Valarie rolled her eyes but laughed half-heartedly.

"Maybe…" She shook her head. "Okay, I'll just get an, er…" Valarie quickly grabbed the menu that was laid out in front of her, her fingers skimming through the hot food section briefly before saying, "A small bowl of chips. Thanks."

"Anything else?" Ruel questioned. Valarie shook her head with her lips between her teeth, a sheepish look painted on her face. He smiled, nodding his head, before swiftly sliding himself out of his seat and walking towards the front counter.

A minute later Ruel walked back, with a number held in his hand and the other holding his credit card. Valarie blinked in realisation, and she felt guilt settle in her stomach.

"Shit," she muttered, staring at Ruel as he promptly pushed himself back into his seat, "I forgot to give you money for the food, here…"

Ruel let out a soft laugh, his tanned skin glowing from the lamp settled above their table. "Don't worry about it. And anyways, a man always pays on the first date."

"Date?" Valarie eyes nearly jumped out of their sockets.

"No," he tensed up. "Sorry I meant just like, y'know, study date. I was just being nice."

"Okay, sorry." She felt dejected.

"Don't be," said Ruel. Both seemed to find the floor or ceiling more interesting than one another.

Miss Candlewood wasn't joking at all when she said the Human Biology assignment would take a long time to finish.

Fifty minutes had gone past, and Ruel and Valarie had only finished *two* out of the fifteen questions, as each question required a whole page answer. Once the café began closing its doors to the public, Valarie and Ruel made the decision to call it a night.

Ruel pushed the café door open, moving his body to the side and nudging his arm through the door, indicating for Valarie to go first.

She smiled up at him, turning to look.

"Well, I'm off. So, I'll see you Monday, yeah?"

Ruel hummed. "Yeah. How're you getting home?"

"Bus," she nudged her head towards the bus stop that was across the road, right in front of a car park. Ruel didn't seem too pleased with her answer. His eyebrows creased together slightly.

"No."

No? Valarie gave him a confused look.

"You're not taking the bus home," he shook his head. "I can take you."

Valarie's eyes widened. "No," she shook her head while letting out a small uncontrollable laugh. "Thank you, but I'll be perfectly fine taking the bus."

"You live not far from here, right?" She nodded her head reluctantly. "Then driving you home won't be a problem."

She hesitated to answer.

"Just let me take you home Valarie."

Home.

She didn't want to go home.

"Okay. Thanks."

She gulped. Gulped at the way Ruel's face twisted into relief and *happiness*? Gulped at the way he began cheekily grinning when he unlocked his car door and his hand wavered behind her back while he held the passenger door open for her to hop inside. Gulped at the tingling feeling she got when his hand did brush over her back while she was sitting in his passenger seat.

She was stuck in his car, stuck beside Ruel, and stuck in this never-ending tug-of-war game of guilt and *whatever* feeling she got every time she thought of him.

And suddenly, Tessa Reed didn't exist; and neither did common sense.

12. TRUST ME

"**D**id you know that turtles can actually breathe from both ends of their bodies?" Ruel perked up suddenly.

Valarie blinked. She'd only been sitting in the passenger seat of his car for a minute before the silence was finally filled with words.

"What?" She said, confused.

Ruel laughed. "It's true, I read somewhere that turtles can breathe from their ass."

"How is that even possible," Valarie snorted, her hand squeezed at her thigh.

"Science," he shrugged again.

Valarie let out a puff of air, glancing at his face. The streetlights cast down over one side of his face, making him glow like some sort of angel.

She sighed with a small smile. "How do you even know about these weird facts?"

Ruel licked his lips.

Valarie forced herself to look away from them.

"Just do."

Her eyes narrowed on him but didn't comment on it any further.

"So, tell me about yourself."

Valarie was stunned for a moment. "What?"

"You say that a lot," he stated, meeting her confused eyes for a moment. "The word 'what.'"

"Oh." Her hands automatically covered her stomach.

"And that too," he nudged his head downwards.

"No, I don't," she tugged the top of her hoodie up again, a fiery look in her eyes.

Ruel raised his hands for a moment, looking slightly taken aback. "Sorry, I didn't mean to make you uncomfortable."

"You didn't," she shook her head. "I'm sorry, I'm just…"

"Going through some stuff?"

She turned her head away from him.

"I'm not here to fuck with you Valarie. I know you don't want to talk about it, and I know you think this is all some sort of prank. I can see it in your eyes every time you look at me. It's like… you don't believe me when I tell you I genuinely do care."

"I don't know what you're talking about."

"I think you do."

"I don't want to talk about it."

"Okay," he nodded, "that's fine. But one day, I'm determined to know. I'm determined to win your trust."

She huffed, pretending to be annoyed by his persistent attempts at caring.

"My favourite subject is Math, but only general Math." He said suddenly. "Because my brain can't handle anything harder. I like it because numbers come easy to me. I'm a dog person and for the longest time I've asked my parents for a dog but my mum's allergic, so that will probably never happen." Valarie's lips twitched into a smile for a moment. "And lastly, I have a huge birthmark on my left ass cheek and my mama thinks it's because she dropped me on my ass when I was younger."

He chuckled. Valarie snorted.

"Now it's your turn." A reassuring tone laced his open question. "If you want."

Valarie drew in a breath of air, speaking slowly. "I love history. I love everything about it and for the longest time, I've wanted to be a history teacher. But I hate kids so that'll never happen."

Ruel threw his head back in laughter.

She smiled blissfully, leaning back in her seat and allowing her shoulders to relax slightly.

"I prefer winter over summer, but realistically autumn is the best season. And um… lastly… oh I don't know. I think I was dropped as a child too, though I don't have any birthmarks." She scratched at her head. "Yeah, that's it."

The familiar sight of her driveway came into view, and the loud sound of Ruel's engine and car rolling into her bricked driveway drowned out any silence that lingered in the car.

The moment the car was put into park, Valarie unlocked her side door and jumped out, shutting the door behind her.

"Thank you." She coughed, rolling onto the heel of her shoes. "For the ride."

He nodded. His lips curled more upwards the longer she stood looking at him.

"Trust me, Valarie, unless you say the word, and truly mean it, I'm not going anywhere."

And that's what she was afraid of.

13. SHOPPING TRIP

"There is a sheet of paper being handed around now, please take one and pass it along. And *don't* lose it! Keep it somewhere safe, preferably in your school bag." Valarie Dale watched the students around her get handed the piece of paper in question.

"The reason I ask this is because it has all the information you'll need for your upcoming river cruise. Your parents or guardian must sign off on it. If they don't, you can't go." Miss Candlewood informed her homeroom class.

Valarie peered over Harmony's shoulder, trying to get a glimpse of the paper in her hand. But just then, her own piece of paper fell into her lap. Instantly, she scanned it.

"Fifth of April..." She muttered under her breath, her eyebrows creasing together. "That's the last day of school for this term."

"And it's about a month away." Layla piped up, feet tucked under her chair.

Valarie gasped. "Jesus, we're nearly halfway through the term."

Harmony hummed while nodding her head, pocketing the hand-out paper into the side of her shorts. "We've got a month until holidays."

Addison let out a joyful sigh. "I'm so excited."

"I'm not," Harmony muttered. Addison gave her a confused look. "Because, once term two starts, we only have six weeks before exams start."

Valarie pulled out her phone, clicked on the calendar app and instantly frowned at the dates. "Are you fucking joking me!" She shoved her phone into her pocket. "My birthday is on the first day of exams?"

Harmony burst into laughter, as Layla gave her a sympathetic look. Valarie only rolled her eyes, throwing her middle finger up at Harmony who sent a cheeky wink back.

"Are you going to have a party?" Layla asked with a tilted head.

Valarie shrugged. "Not sure. Probably not."

"Aw why not?" Addison pouted. "Your house would be, like, *perfect* for a party."

But my parents aren't.

She shivered at the thought of her father. "Actually, I might just go bowling instead."

Addison didn't seem too happy, probably more upset about there not being a party for her to attend than about Valarie missing out on having a birthday party, but she didn't make another comment. She instead turned her full attention to Harmony, whose body twisted in her seat. Her back to Valarie.

Valarie just rolled her eyes and turned her attention to Jenny and Layla.

"Maybe I should come in my blow-up dinosaur costume instead. Y'think the school will let me?" Layla said cheekily.

Jenny giggled, shaking her head. A small smile grew on Valarie's lips, and she quickly scooted her chair closer to the two, pushing herself closer into the conversation.

Both the girls noticed. "What are you going to wear to the river cruise?" Layla asked Valarie.

Valarie shrugged, leaning her elbows onto her knees, and propping up her chin onto her hands. "Haven't thought that far ahead to be honest. Probably just wear something comfortable. Like trackies and a hoodie."

Jenny frowned, "You always wear that though, why not go in a dress or something?"

Valarie shook her head. "Nah," she waved off as nonchalantly as she could, her hands moving into the large front pocket of her jumper, "I don't have any dresses anyway. And anyway, what's wrong with wearing hoodies and trackies all the time?"

Jenny shrugged, throwing her hands in the air. "There's nothing wrong with it, just... it's a river cruise and you would probably be expected to come in something formal." Valarie sighed. "But also if you've got no dresses then we could..."

"Go shopping!" A squeal from Addison made Valarie wince, her nose scrunching up.

"No, *absolutely* not." She shook her head, peering into Addison's eager eyes. "I'm not going shopping." *With you.*

"Aw, why not?" Harmony butted in, a pout on her lips. "It'll be fun."

"Fun for you maybe," she muttered, crossing her arms over her chest with a huff. Her eyes fell on Layla and Jenny who were already looking at her, small grins on both their faces.

"Oh, *come on,*" Jenny moaned, "we'll have a great time."

Valarie exhaled.

Valarie was going shopping this weekend.

She gave in, not willingly though, and not without a fight. Once homeroom was over, she was bombarded by Jenny. As the two of them made their way towards their next lesson, which just so happened to be History, Jenny insisted Valarie join the rest of them on a shopping trip.

She pulled her pouty face until Valarie complied.

And listen—it wasn't like she hated shopping, not at all actually, she found it kind of fun when she was alone. But the wonderful experience of shopping wasn't something Valarie liked to have with other people.

Because they just wouldn't get it. Understand that out of the one hundred and fifty clothing stores available to her in the shopping centre, probably only ten stocked her size. It was more humiliating than anything when she would catch retail workers staring at her as her hands hurriedly looked through the backs of the clothes racks, spending an unusual amount of time at them as she tried to find her size.

Being a size sixteen to sometimes eighteen was difficult. And even more difficult when she was small-chested but big everywhere else—when her shoulders and back were square like a box and her legs were thick like a large loaf of bread.

She couldn't even find rings to fit her fingers.

And while her friends could walk into any store and find their size instantly, half the time Valarie couldn't even find an outfit that would fit her. Part of the reason why she wore hoodies and trackies everywhere was because they were the only things that fit her. Unless she wanted to buy those floral dresses and shirts, which were the only available plus-sized options, she was stuck with the same type of clothes.

So yeah, you could say she was dreading shopping with her friends because she just *knew* they'd go to all the popular clothing stores that only sized up to a fourteen (if even that).

It sucked, badly. And it was something that she was used to. She had *had* to be fine with it.

But it wasn't something she was prepared to make her friends aware of yet.

So, for the rest of the week, that's all she thought of.

Shopping.

Not even Ruel could distract her, even if he tried—which he did. Every time they saw each other, which was usually just in Human Biology class, he tried to ask her what was 'up' but she just shrugged him off, faking a smile and a laugh when she was secretly dying on the inside.

He would message her at night, sometimes while she was awake, other times when she was fast asleep, and by the time Wednesday had hit, Valarie had begun forcing herself to stay up a little later than usual, just to see if he would message her.

Just to see if he'd gotten bored or not.

By the time Friday rolled around, there were two bits of good news that came out of the week. One, she survived! Both school and home. Her father was becoming more and more distant, and don't even get her started on her mother's behaviour. Her phone seemed to be stuck to her fingers for more hours than existed in a day.

And the second thing—the bruise on Valarie's neck had begun to heal and was barely noticeable. Finally, Valarie didn't have to wake up extra early in the morning to try and cover it with some sort of makeup.

She just made sure her hoodie was still covering it.

And speaking of Friday, when Valarie turned up to the café for her assignment meeting with Ruel, she found herself struggling to keep her eyes on her work when every few seconds she just felt the need to look up. To look at him.

He offered her another ride home afterwards, and it went similar to the week before.

"Tell me more about you."

But this time, Valarie was the one to ask it. She'd learnt his favourite band was The Backseat Lovers, he hated bugs, and he loved a custard scroll from Baker's Delight, which piped up Valarie's interest quickly as she butted in, "Me too!"

For the rest of the car ride the two argued about which was better, the custard scroll with or without the coconut icing.

But she couldn't think of Ruel. Not when she was sitting in the back of Harmony's car on a windy Saturday morning, with Tessa and Layla beside her, Addison up front while Jennifer found her own way there.

"Where do we want to go first girls?" Harmony smiled, her voice a pitch higher than usual and Valarie nearly rolled her eyes at the sound. "I'm thinking something like Cotton On or possibly City Beach."

And while most of the girls in the car hummed in agreement at the idea, Valarie was squirming uncomfortably in her seat.

"What do you think, Val?" Layla's voice came from beside her, a content smile settled on her lips; her fingers toying with strands of her box braids.

"Er," Valarie pulled at her hoodie. "Yeah… whatever you guys want." Layla's eyes narrowed slightly, clearly confused, but she didn't comment any further.

Valarie held her breath when her friends stopped in front of the popular clothing store. Loud music could be heard from metres away but the ringing in her ears was louder. She stopped just at the entrance, eyes trailing after Addison and Harmony who had eagerly rushed inside without even a look back to see where the others were.

"You, okay?" Layla came up beside her, titling her head innocently.

Valarie hummed shortly, not looking away from the store. "Yeah."

She didn't seem too convinced with her answer but left it as it was. She walked inside the store, with Jennifer following directly beside her. Once they got a few steps inside, Jennifer looked back over her shoulder and smiled at Valarie, her head nudging to the side as if to say, "Come on!"

And though Valarie put on a smile, one that she hoped was believable, on the inside, her guts were all twisted.

As she wandered somewhat closely behind Jennifer and Layla, with Harmony and Addison nowhere to be seen, Valarie swore she could feel eyes following her. She'd walked past a worker and it felt as if they had looked down. A group of younger teenage girls, all giggles and smiles, had instantly quietened down once Valarie looked at them.

Was it that obvious? The stomach she carried. The face that wasn't clear. The thighs that were huge.

Was it funny she was there, obvious that she was roped into something that wasn't designed for someone like her?

Could they tell she didn't belong?

Her arms went to cover her stomach.

Again.

"Do you think something like this would be too provocative?" Harmony asked no one in particular, coming back into sight of the group, holding up a tight black dress against her chest, a grin on her lips.

Addison shrugged her shoulders. "Knowing the school, they'll probably have a tantrum about the shoulders, but it should be fine."

Harmony grimaced, quickly putting back the dress. "I don't feel like getting into trouble, ugh."

"It doesn't say anywhere you have to cover up," Jenny perked up, encouraging the others to look over her. "On the paper we were given, it only says that our ass and tits basically can't be showing."

"Are there any restrictions for the boys?" Harmony snapped, though her sudden burst of anger was not towards Jenny.

"Nope," Jenny frowned.

Harmony rolled her eyes, following behind Jennifer who'd just started pursuing after Addison. "Of course." Valarie hung back for a second.

"You, okay?"

Her eyebrows creased, a small, tight smile settling on her lips as she nodded and replied. "Of course."

"Are there any clothes that you want to try out yet?"

"No," Valarie's voice tightened, "I probably won't buy any clothes, to be honest."

Layla's nose scrunched up, "Why not? The whole point of going shopping in the first place was to help you get some nice clothes for the river cruise."

She heaved a sigh, rolling her stiff shoulders in a circle. "They still would have gone with or without me. Harmony and Addison will use *any* excuse to go shopping. And anyways, my mum only gave me like fifty bucks. I can't even afford jeans with that."

Simultaneously, Layla and Valarie looked over to the other two. Watching Harmony wrap a jacket she'd just pulled off the rack around Addison's shoulders, giggling to one another as they whispered under the loud music playing from the store's speakers.

"And if this shopping trip was really for me," Valarie whispered with a lump in her throat, "they wouldn't have chosen this store."

"Why's that?"

Valarie stilled for a moment, before responding with a tired sigh. Her body turned to look Layla dead on. "Look at me, Layla."

And Layla did, with a look of confusion. Their eyes made contact, and instantly, Layla noticed the little trickle of a tear beginning to pool within Valarie's blue eyes.

"*Really* look at me Layla," she murmured, slowly dragging her right index finger down over her body. Layla's eyes followed the finger.

"And now. Look at everyone else."

Layla's eyes followed Valarie's finger which was now pointing to random people standing in the store, all innocently minding their own business.

"Notice it?"

Layla gulped, her head slowly turning back to meet Valarie's disheartened face.

"That shouldn't matter." She shook her head, wearing an expression of sadness. "Really, Valarie. If it's what I think it is …"

"It is," she said sternly, with a hint of dejection in her tone. "And it's fine," Valarie grunted. "I'm just pointing out the difference and pointing out the *truth*. Which is that this store isn't for girls like me—people like me. It just is what it is."

Layla shook her head firmly. "Doesn't matter if it's 'the truth', you can still enjoy shopping and can still go find a nice dress or something."

"It's harder than that for me Layla. I can't just walk into any store and find something that will fit me y'know, the stores I usually shop at are shit like Target or Kmart, stores that Harmony and Addison *certainly* wouldn't be seen in even if hell froze over. I don't have the luxury of choosing cute outfits and planning different things to wear. I'm stuck with, well, what I have on now."

She shrugged.

"And the last thing I want is to have to mention this to them," Valarie's eyes peered over to Harmony and Addison. "It's embarrassing."

"If they were true friends," Layla began softly, taking a step forward to Valarie, "then they wouldn't judge you and what you wear, or where you get your clothes from. If they were *true friends*, they would *help* you instead."

Valarie wiped a finger under her eyes. "But it's not that they aren't *true friends* per se, it's just more… that it's difficult to understand when you don't experience it. It's different when you're the big girl. And frankly, I don't want them to understand."

"I'm so sorry you feel like that," Layla frowned. "If I knew this was how you felt, about shopping and stuff, I would have *never* pushed that on you. I'm sorry."

"It's not your fault," Valarie replied instantly. "Honestly, I didn't tell you this to make you feel guilty or anything I'm just—I don't know. I trust you. I guess that would be the best way to explain it."

The silence that came after Valarie's confession made her insides twist.

"How about this," Layla perked up suddenly. "Let's go shopping, just us two, and well, maybe Jenny if you want. But just us, going to stores that *you* want to go."

Valarie licked her lips, nose scrunching up as she shook her head, "What about Harmony and Addison, won't they ask questions?"

"Let me deal with them," she waved off, her smile still painted on her lips. "You start thinking about where you want to go first, okay?"

Valarie's breath got stuck in her throat, so her only response was a small nod. And with a large smile, Layla skipped over towards Harmony and Addison.

She returned moments later and took Valarie's hand before dragging her along and out of the store.

14. CRUSH?

"**W**hat are you hiding?"

"Didn't know it was a crime to hold a bag behind my back." Valarie Dale was indeed, hiding her shopping bag from her father.

"Don't be a smartass Valarie, give me the bag."

She took a step back subconsciously. He took a step forward.

"It's nothing honestly, just clothes."

"That's what they all say."

Who's they? She wanted to comment.

"Just trust me."

"I don't trust shit." Matthew spoke, taking another step towards Valarie whose body stilled against her front door. "Give me the bag, girl."

"Fuck you."

She stepped sideways as he took a leap forward.

"Matthew." A tired voice spoke from behind him suddenly. Cindy looked defeated. "Leave it be."

"Don't tell me what to do, woman." Matthew sternly pointed at his wife. "What this little shit brings into *my* house is *my* business. What food are you sneaking into the house now, cow?"

"It's clothes!" Valarie cried out, shoving her bag out in front of her. "If you want to fucking know so desperately. It's a dress."

101

His eyes narrowed. "Even worse. Dressing like a slut just like your mother."

Valarie clenched at the fabric in her bag, throwing it at his face. His cheeks blew up into the colour red.

"Here! If you wanted to wear it that bad you could have just asked."

Matthew let out a roar of anger, and just in the nick of time Valarie snatched the fabric off the floor and ran to her bedroom.

"I swear to God, girl."

Valarie slammed her bedroom door shut.

For the next ten minutes all she could hear was the sound of her father shouting at her mother, screaming profanities, nothing unusual, talking shit about his own daughter.

It should have bothered Valarie. Should have stuck a knife in her heart when she heard the way he called her a cow or threatened to put a shovel through her head.

But it didn't.

April was in a week. Valarie couldn't believe how fast the term was flying past, how quickly the year was going. She swore it was only yesterday she was celebrating the New Year. Nonetheless, it was reality and something Valarie had to come to terms with.

Something else she had to come to terms with was the growing feeling in her chest every time she thought of Ruel. Yes, *thought*. Not even being with him—just thinking about him. And it was becoming quite difficult to not think about him because well, he was everywhere.

In her phone, from the time he had secretively taken multiple photos of himself.

In her messages. He was always messaging her and no, she wasn't annoyed he was sending her random photos of himself or whatever popular cat meme was available to him, it was just—well she got flustered every time she heard her phone *ding* and was even becoming desperate to see what he'd sent her.

And then school. Well obviously, she would see him at school, she wasn't oblivious to that, but it was like every corner she took he was there, like he was at the end of every hallway.

But she couldn't stop the feeling, and nor did she want to.

Miss Apple-Berry was her usual self, as always. A great big smile on her face, and her eyes wide as if there was sticky tape holding them apart.

"Thirtieth of July…" Miss AB spoke, her hand dragging through the air slowly as she leisurely walked back and forth in front of the class. "A date for *all* to remember. As it's the day we perform our class production of Romeo and Juliet!" Layla clapped once, straightening up happily as a grin broke out on her lips. "Another reminder that the play has been altered and shortened to fit school rules and the time frame we have been given which is an hour. Now, as for who will play which role in the production, *I* have already chosen. I have done this based on my observation of you all during our past few weeks together in class."

Murmurs began around the class.

"Shh," she pushed her index finger against her lips, scanning the class. "Now, I do not want to hear any complaints from *anyone* about which role you are given. What you are given is what you have."

Layla was practically jumping out of her skin.

"Scripts will be handed out to you all, please take care of them and begin practising your lines as of next week. Then, we'll have rehearsals."

Valarie gazed at the papers Miss AB handed down to Natasha, who rolled her eyes and chewed on her gum loudly before taking a script and handing it along to the kid beside her.

"Now for the roles..."

Names began to be called out. Most were all the smaller roles, with no one complaining. But when the larger roles came into place, Valarie started to become confused about why she hadn't been called out earlier on.

"Oh, I hope I get Juliet," Layla whispered in her ear, a near squeal of joy and nervousness in her tone.

Valarie smiled softly, knowing how much Drama meant to her. "I hope you do too." Her hand linked with Layla's, grinning lightly when Layla squeezed her hand.

"James Sheri!" She called out, pointing to a tall Japanese boy; he grinned and perked up when the teacher called up his name. *"You* will be playing *Romeo!"*

The black-haired boy beamed, nodding his head eagerly and then looking down at the script held in his hands.

"Valarie Dale!"

Layla nudged Valarie, a large smile on her face for her friend. "You, my dear, will be playing *Juliet's Nurse!"*

Valarie let out a shocked laugh. Layla nudged her once more, smiling. "That's amazing!"

"Natasha Campbell!" Natasha smirked confidently, leaning back on her hands as she waved her hair to the side. "You will be playing *Juliet's Mother, Lady Capulet!"*

Natasha's jaw dropped.

"What?" Valarie's nose scrunched up, her ears ringing at Natasha's high-pitched voice. "How did I *not* get *Juliet*?"

"What did I say about complaining Miss Campbell?"

"But…"

"No buts!" The teacher snapped, sending daggers towards Natasha whose shoulders dropped as her lips curled tightly together, steam coming out of her ears. "Now, as for who gets to play Juliet, I find it obvious as there is only one girl left… *Layla* my dear, congratulations."

Layla squealed out loud, her arms flying around Valarie's shoulder as she brought her into a tight hug. One that Valarie wasn't expecting. "I did it! Oh, thank *god!*"

Valarie laughed sweetly back, patting her friend's back. Layla's smile was so bright Valarie swore she was seeing a star.

"How is it *fair* that someone with little to no experience gets the lead role, yet someone like *me* who's had outside experience gets a smaller role?"

The class fell into silence, eyes flickering between Layla and Natasha who was staring at her. Valarie could feel Layla tense up beside her.

"Life's not fair Natasha," Valarie shot back. "Suck it up, sweetheart."

Natasha huffed, arms crossing against her chest. "But my experience is obviously higher than *Layla's,*" she said her name like it was toxic, "so why does she get the bigger role?"

Valarie quickly cut in angrily. "Shut your gob, Natasha. This isn't Broadway, it's a high school production. Get over it."

Natasha rolled her eyes, shooting daggers at Valarie before turning around with a huff. The happy energy that was once present within the room had now become hostile and quiet.

Valarie's hand slipped into Layla's, squeezing it. She squeezed back harder.

And just as the teacher was about to speak up the bell went off, indicating the school day was over and the weekend had begun. The students stood up, some already out the door. Two of them being Valarie and Layla.

"Don't listen to her," Valarie whispered to her friend. "You'll do amazing, okay?"

Layla nodded, giving a small *thank you* before walking off.

The Human Biology project was due in just under three weeks. Luckily for Valarie and Ruel, they had finished the hardest part of the assignment, which was answering the questions in part one. Now they were onto the second part which included a roleplay of a doctor and patient.

Valarie's hands didn't move from where they sat comfortably in the pocket of her hoodie once she walked inside the library, a new spot Ruel suggested to meet at instead of a café for a change of scenery.

She took a seat across from him. They were sitting on a small, rounded table near the back.

"Afternoon." He spoke, his eyes meeting hers.

"Hi," she smiled tightly.

"So, um," he began. "Do you want to be the doctor or patient first?"

Valarie let her eyes wander at the equipment the school had provided sat on the table. "I'll be the doctor, if that's okay with you?"

"Of course it is." He chuckled.

Valarie laughed half-heartedly as his shoulders dropped and a content grin settled on his face. A sense of comfortableness fell between the two of them as they organised their positions so they were beside one another.

"So, what first?" She asked innocently, peering down at her sheet.

"Well, you basically have to do a check-up, kinda like how a doctor does." He spoke. "You'll have to figure out what is wrong with me and give me a diagnosis. I already know the answer, but you don't. So, you need to figure out what's wrong with me by asking questions. And through asking me questions, hopefully you give me the right diagnosis. But if you don't, I wouldn't be thinking about becoming a doctor when you're older."

Valarie let out a snort, one that made Ruel chuckle and smile as if he were happy with himself for making her laugh. Her cheeks turned a shade of pink.

"Trust me, I *know* I won't be a doctor when I'm older."

"Why's that?" He asked, tilting his head.

Valarie huffed with a laugh. "Have you *seen* my grades? I'm stupid as fuck, you think I'd be able to even get into a university?"

She was laughing softly, finding her negative comment towards herself hilarious, but when she heard no noise come from Ruel her eyebrows furrowed.

"You're not stupid though."

Valarie blinked.

"Okay," she blinked again. Awkwardly coughing at the silence that lingered in the air. "Let's just get started, yeah," she muttered, changing the subject as she plucked the stethoscope given by the school. Valarie's hands tightened against the two connected cords and pushed the ends into her ears.

She heard Ruel's breath get stuck in his throat when Valarie moved her chair even closer to him. He spread his legs wide, seemingly to allow Valarie to get as close as she needed.

"I'm just going to check your heart, listen for a moment… if that's okay?"

She was hesitant, something Ruel seemed concerned about. She watched him nod, swallowing a lump in his throat. She wondered why his heart rate was so high, but wasn't able to ask the question as the scent of his cologne made her blank, and all thoughts of the project disappeared when his hands accidentally brushed against her shoulders.

Her body felt on fire. Literally, like someone had lit flames beside her body.

It took a moment for her to gain her thoughts back, and when she did, she made the mistake of looking up. Just to find him staring down at her.

Her lips parted in surprise, and she found herself losing balance on her chair. She instinctively put her hands out in front of her. Landing right in his lap.

"Shit!" She leaned back immediately. "God, I am so sorry."

"She'll be right," he shrugged nonchalantly, though if she were to look up to meet his eyes, she would have seen the way he was blushing too. "Honestly, it's okay."

She shook her head swiftly, gulping down the embarrassment her heart was feeling.

"I—" she took a deep breath in. "Sorry."

Ruel nodded as his throat bobbed.

The remainder of the time they were together, both made sure not to get too close to one another—a silent agreement they both made.

And, like an embarrassed schoolgirl, Valarie Dale didn't bother waiting around once they finished up for the day. She didn't want to risk embarrassing herself more in front of her crush by being in his car.

Her crush?

15. BREATHTAKING

"**H**e's just so *dreamy!*"

Tessa leaned her back against the fence as she let out a loud sigh. Valarie refused to look at her, keeping her gaze on the small patch of grass she was playing with. Perth decided to bring out its usual westerly wind, causing a bit of an issue every time she tried to look anywhere but forward.

"We get it, Tessa."

Addison quickly shut her mouth as Harmony nudged at her side, giving a warning look to shut up. Valarie rolled her eyes, not bothering to comment on Addison's irritated mood towards Tessa, being in no mood herself to get in an argument.

It was lunchtime, Monday the twenty-eighth of March. The river cruise was next Friday, her assignment in Human Biology was due in seven days and Valarie was, well—stuck in a bit of a predicament.

The weather had started to cool down, and finally, Valarie was allowed out onto the ovals. She'd lost her school hat a while back and hadn't been bothered to pay fifty bucks for a new one, so every time she'd tried to enter the grassed oval, she was denied. But now that the UV wasn't above four, and the teacher who usually supervised the oval was currently on leave, there weren't any issues.

Well, except for *him*.

"So not only is he hot, but he also plays *footy!*"

Valarie couldn't help it, she looked. And she kept looking.

Ruel Diego. Tall and lean, dressed in the summer school uniform of shorts and a polo shirt. School uniforms weren't designed to make the students more attractive, yet with Ruel's long-sleeved shirt rolled up against his tanned arms, his brunette hair messy in a *very* attractive way and a large smile on his lips showing his near-perfect teeth; Ruel was a man of wonders to look at.

And it seemed Valarie wasn't the only one who noticed.

She glimpsed Natasha and her group of friends all huddled against one of the side footy posts, chatting among themselves while Ruel and a group of boys continued with their game of AFL, none of them noticing the watchful eyes of their peers. Or should we say group of girls.

Tessa sighed dreamily once more, her head falling onto Valarie's shoulder as she pulled up her knees to her chest, eyes following Ruel. "What team do you think he goes for?"

Valarie shrugged, not knowing the answer. Although she'd been messaging him on and off for the past few weeks, all she knew was he played for their local football club. "Better be West Coast," she grumbled, arms crossing over her chest.

"What if he goes for Freo?" Tessa asked innocently, looking up at Valarie from where she lay on her shoulder.

"Then you aren't allowed to ever talk to him again."

Tessa gaped, pushing her head off Valarie to look her dead in the eyes.

"You're joking, right?"

Valarie shook her head snappily. "Not at all. No supporter of Fremantle will be dating my best friend." A sour taste grew on her tongue the moment those words left her lips. "Everyone knows the Eagles are the better WA team, *come on.*"

Harmony laughed from the other side of her. "I wouldn't recommend saying that in front of my P.E. teacher."

Valarie shrugged and leant back against the fence that cut off the outside world to her school and moved her gaze to the group of boys in her year level. But as much as she tried to keep her gaze on the yellow football being passed and kicked around, her eyes kept going back to the one boy she knew her friend beside her was also looking at.

Ruel must have finally sensed eyes on him, as he turned his head from the game and moved to look straight at Valarie; a small grin formed on his lips as they held each other's gaze.

God, he was gorgeous.

Valarie looked away first. Hoping no one noticed the small blush that had appeared on her cheeks.

The last day of school had come around. And all that was on people's minds was the river cruise.

Valarie managed to sneak out of adding into the conversation regarding Ruel when Tessa began explaining how she was going to try and dance with him. Possibly even make some moves on him. Valarie just busied herself with watching a group of Year 8s play four-square.

Harmony would be picking up Valarie around six p.m., meaning by the time Valarie got home from school she had just under three hours to get ready.

She put on a bit of makeup, just some concealer, mascara, lipstick, and a bit of blush. Nothing crazy, nothing over the top. And then she slipped on the dress Layla had found with her all those weeks ago while shopping, and instantly smiled.

The dress was something she never would have bought in the first place if it weren't for Layla.

It was scandalous, and not in the Kim Kardashian way, but in a Valarie Dale way.

It was revealing, but nothing over the top. Fully black, with a v-cut down her chest but due to how small her breasts were, she had to bobby pin the end of the v-cut, so it didn't fall. The dress wasn't tight, but more flowy. It covered Valarie's body while showing her curves (that's what Layla said, anyways).

The dress was long-sleeved and stopped a few fingers above her knee, not halfway up her thigh but just below that. She was tempted to wear some tights, to cover the pale fat that was her legs, but decided against it when she realised she didn't actually have any black tights, only navy. And she knew Layla would have a fit if anything she wore didn't fit the outfit she had hand-picked herself.

But once Valarie slipped on her black high-heels, ones that weren't overly tall but just gave her that extra height, she looked at herself once more in the mirror and actually *smiled*.

She didn't look half bad, she thought.

Her head tilted off to the side, her hands came down to brush down her flowy black dress and for a split second, Valarie didn't feel disgusted with herself, she felt *nice*. She didn't actually mind what she saw in the mirror at that moment.

Her hair was straight, hanging over the front of her shoulder and her lips looked slightly pinker with the lipstick she was wearing.

She liked it.

And with that in mind, Valarie picked up the small black purse she had stolen out of her mother's cupboard and walked through her house, a small grin on her lips as she caught sight of Harmony beginning to pull into her driveway when she peered out the front door.

Perfect timing.

And for the rest of that car ride, Valarie felt completely content with herself and how she looked.

Valarie hated how she fucking looked.

With her arms wrapped tightly around her stomach, she felt herself wanting to burst into tears as she took in her year group, all stood huddling together, laughter spilling from everyone's lips and smiles on teachers' faces.

It was all innocent. Completely fucking normal. She knew that.

Boys. In suits and nice buttoned-up shirts, with clearly expensive pants and outfits. Standing there with confidence oozing out of them, while they talked with their friends. And the girls, the girls stood in *also* expensive dresses. All skin-tight and pretty. High heels that made them taller than *her.*

Valarie could *smell* the money, could smell that the clothes weren't bought from Target. Could see they took time and effort into perfecting their outfits. All the while she stood there in a flowy black dress, one that she managed to get for a bargain of thirty bucks from Target and some high heels that had obviously had a life before her.

And as her eyes fell on Harmony, she could see she also wore something similar to everyone else. A tight red dress, one that she had to keep pulling down every few steps as it would roll up her thighs due to how fucking *tight* it was. Valarie watched Addison bring her into a hug, commenting on how *hot* and *gorgeous* she looked.

Some were even wearing dresses fit for a ballroom.

Valarie couldn't believe she thought she would fit in.

Of course she fucking didn't. She never did.

"Lovely dress, Valarie," Miss Candlewood smiled sweetly. She had clearly seen her standing alone and probably came over to give her attention. Was it that obvious she was alone? That she didn't want to be there? "Where did you get it from?"

Valarie gulped, tears stinging in her eyes that she desperately tried to blink away. "Target, Miss."

"Oh," she smiled, her voice dropping the *tiniest* bit, but Valarie noticed. She always noticed. "Well, it's very nice."

"Thanks."

Valarie gulped again, turning her head to the side slightly and moving her chin lower to the ground. Miss Candlewood took that as a sign to move away, walking towards a group of boys who began complimenting her in a probably too-friendly tone.

A sour taste lingered on her tongue.

And she quickly came to the realisation that she was jealous. Jealous that Addison was getting kisses on her cheeks and bright gasps of awe as girls alike complimented her.

"You're such a stunner!"

"You look amazing!"

"You look gorgeous in that dress!"

Giggles and hugs, wandering eyes and lips wrapped up in a truthful smile. And like a bucket of ice water hitting her face, Valarie Dale suddenly felt like the whole world was looking at her.

Could they see how pale her thighs were? Could they see beneath the fabrics on her skin like some type of x-ray machine had been placed in front of her body?

"You look *absolutely breathtaking*, Valarie."

She almost choked.

Her eyes dilated as they fell onto the voice of the person who had spoken. Ruel was standing there with a soft yet gorgeous smile, looking at Valarie's face as if she'd grown a third eye.

It was a look Valarie didn't truly understand, couldn't comprehend. Because he wasn't looking at her in confusion, or sympathy, not even a flash of disgust. He was intrigued—awed, if she may say.

But she was thinking too far ahead of herself, she knew that.

"Do you understand that, Valarie?" he whispered, taking a step forward towards her. "Do you understand how fucking *gorgeous* you are?"

Did Ruel not see the rolls on her stomach? Did he not see how thick her thighs were, how they rubbed together every step she took? Did he not see the fat around her neck and the way her arms looked like cucumbers? Did he not see how pale she was, and the stupid little pimples she had spread out on her chin?

"Do you understand?"

Valarie's breath hitched in her throat, and she blinked up to look at Ruel as he peered slightly down at her.

"Get over here mate, what's takin' so long?"

Valarie peered over Ruel's shoulder to see Oliver Lynch grinning, standing there beside Natasha and the rest of her friends. *The popular kids.* But when she looked back to meet Ruel's eyes, she noticed he didn't even look at him, didn't make any movement or indication that he was going to respond to Oliver.

He just kept staring at her.

He didn't say another word. Instead, he titled his chin lower, his eyes shifting around her face as if he was trying to read through each insecurity she had, every freckle on her pale face, every little bit of extra skin that her friends didn't have.

And with a small nod of the head and a little grin growing on his lips, he began to walk backwards, slowly, with his eyes still on her. After a few steps, he smiled once more, making the inside of Valarie's stomach flip and then spun around on the wooden decked floor, making his way towards his friends.

Her eyes trailed after him, in a trance-like state as if she couldn't believe what had just happened. Suddenly her gaze met a bewildered Natasha's, who gave a sneering glare before flipping around and giggling with her friends once more.

And for the rest of the night, Valarie Dale spent more time looking at him than talking with her friends.

16. ANOTHER ONE

Valarie spent most of her time in her bedroom. Two and half weeks. Of staring at white walls, her ears never getting a break from her headphones and her mouth always chewing on some sort of food item that she'd managed to sneak into her room from the kitchen.

It was tedious, long and painfully boring. Except for him.

Ruel Diego. Always full of surprises. Like how he apparently was in New York City.

Well, not 'apparently'. Valarie knew he wasn't lying, it was just that he hadn't bothered to mention it.

Or the fact he had two mums.

Not that it bothered Valarie or anything...

His trip to New York was sudden, and he explained it with a short thirty-second clip he'd sent her once he'd touched down in the state, telling Valarie he was meeting up with his parents. They were currently backpacking around the USA, and he wanted to surprise them.

And as sweet as it was, Valarie was saddened by his sudden departure. Because unrealistically, she had dreamt that she would be able to spend the school holidays with him.

She had dreamt of him turning up to her house with flowers, a big smile on his lips and a huge sign that said, *Go to prom with me!*

Okay, maybe she'd watched a little too many American high school movies, but she just wanted a friend. To experience hangouts and late-night drives, all the shit she knew everyone else in her year did, except her.

But no, she was too busy wasting away the days wishing upon a star someone would come to save her from the hell that was her life.

A Prince Fucking Charming to be exact.

Harmony's face popped up in her head.

And though Valarie never got to see Ruel during the break, she got to talk to him, a lot. He'd message her at ungodly hours of the night, seemingly not picking up on the fact time zones were a thing until Valarie pointed it out.

And it turns out, the yellow school buses that Valarie always had seen in American high school movies were real. Ruel sent a picture as proof to her once she began to argue with him on the fact, because she didn't believe it.

But overall, the break wasn't anything special. And if there was one thing Valarie could be grateful for, it was her parents leaving her the *fuck* alone.

Ruel: I miss you.

Valarie's feet kicked up in the air late Monday night—a day before school started up again.

Valarie: I miss you too.

Friends. She missed her friend too.

And there was nothing wrong with that.

Nothing at all.

"Did you sleep *at all* last night?"

Valarie let out a long puff of air. She shrugged at Layla's question and played with a small string broken off her hoodie.

"Why didn't you sleep? You *love* to sleep."

That was true. Valarie did love her sleep.

Well, except for last night.

Layla was currently standing right in front of James, the man who was cast as Romeo for the Year 11 drama play. Valarie was sitting against the wall, knees tucked to the best of her ability into her chest and her arms hugged tightly around them while she watched Layla and James practise their lines and scenes together.

In reality, Valarie should have been practising too, but she was too tired and caught up in her own thoughts to think about having to be someone else. Not while she was dealing with being herself.

"Wanna talk about what's causing you stress at the moment?"

I would if I had the words to explain it.

"No. I'll be okay."

Layla stopped what she was doing, shifting all her attention onto Valarie whose head was hung low, eyes droopy like she'd been taking drugs.

"Babes," Layla whispered, sweet like an angel. She dropped her script beside James before kneeling in front of Valarie. "It's okay if you want to talk about it, whatever is on your mind. I'm here to listen."

Valarie's bottom lip quivered, and that was all Layla needed before she turned to look at James.

"James, please take my script and go to someone else to practise for a little while. I'll be back a bit later, 'kay?"

James nodded eagerly, a bright smile on his lips as he snatched up Layla's script off the ground and rushed away from the two girls.

"He so likes you."

Layla burst out into laughter. A small giggle followed straight after when she looked towards James who was now busy with another student. He must have felt someone watching him, as his eyes met Layla's and instantly a smile came across his lips again.

"Okay, whatever." Layla moved closer to Valarie. "So, what's up?"

"The roof."

"I will kill you."

"Aggressive much," Valarie smirked.

"You haven't *seen* aggressive."

Valarie laughed. Layla rolled her eyes once more before her face dropped into a more serious expression. "Now, stop ignoring the question and just answer it. What. Is. Going. On."

Valarie pulled her bottom lip in between her teeth. "I need advice. Desperate advice."

Layla gave a comforting smile.

Valarie took a deep breath in and out before starting.

"So *hypothetically* thinking okay, if you had a crush on someone…" Layla perked up but didn't comment, "and the person you have that crush on is *also* your friend's crush. What do you do?"

"So, you're saying you have a crush."

"*Not* me," Valarie cut in swiftly, "it's a fake scenario, okay? Just imagine this is happening."

"Okay, sure." Layla said, clearly not believing Valarie. "So, what I'd do is tell the friend. And then ask him out."

"W-what?" Valarie perked up, lifting her head and shaking her head instantly. "No way, that can't happen!"

"And why not?"

"'Cause, it would end badly."

"Would it?" Layla's eyebrows raised. "Would communication really be that bad? That friend can't get mad at the girl because technically she hasn't done anything to upset her. No one can control their feelings. It's not like the best friend is dating this guy, right?"

"No," Valarie said gloomily. "But that's not ideal! I shouldn't have a crush on him in the first place! And what if Tessa doesn't take it well if I confess? Huh? I have close to no friends as it is, I can't risk losing her over a *boy*. I mean, he's not *just* a boy," Valarie rambled, "he's Ruel fucking Diego and he's gorgeous and nice and smells really good too…"

Valarie's lips swiftly sealed shut.

"You like Ruel?" Layla gasped in excitement.

"No."

"But you just said—"

"I didn't say anything. You heard nothing!"

"Don't try and gaslight me, Valarie Dale. I know what I heard." She gasped again. "I cannot believe this. My little Valarie all grown up. I should have seen this coming."

"Shh!" Valarie pushed her finger up against Layla's plump lips. "Shut up."

"No, you shut up!" she squealed. "Oh my god this is so exciting. I'm so happy for you!"

Valarie's eyes narrowed.

"Have you asked him out?"

"No?" Valarie scoffed. "Why the fuck would I do that?"

"I don't know." Layla mocked. "Maybe because you *like him?*"

"Get fucked, mate, if you think I'm going to ask him out. Who do you think I am?" Her eyebrows furrowed.

"I think you're a strong and kind woman who deserves a little lovin' from a nice-looking man."

"Stop." Valarie pushed her finger onto Layla's lips again. "Seriously. Stop."

"Why?" Layla licked at Valarie's finger causing her to pull back in disgust. "Seriously. What's wrong with you asking him out?"

"Did you not hear what I just said, like two minutes ago, about *Tessa?*"

"Who cares," Layla shoved her braids behind her back. "Honestly, Tessa's not dating him. It's not cheating."

"But it's rude!" Valarie sighed heavily, leaning her head back in defeat. "What if she hates me for life? What if I ask him out and he doesn't even like me—wait I take that back, I *know* he doesn't like me back. I'll lose two friendships and probably more. Including my ego."

Layla stayed silent for a moment. "It's up to you, but you only live once and who knows, maybe you'll get your first boyfriend?"

Valarie turned her head to the side. "I don't know if I'm even ready to date yet."

Layla's hand patted Valarie's thigh in comfort. "Why not?"

"Er," Valarie looked anywhere but her eyes. "I don't know, I just—I've kind of convinced myself love is something that's only given to pretty people. Girls who have the bodies boys like to look at."

"Oh babes," Layla frowned sadly. "Don't believe that shit. You know it's not true."

"Isn't it?" Valarie's eyes stung with tears. "Look around Layla. I'm the odd one out, I've *always* been the odd one out. Is it so hard to believe Ruel would choose someone like Addison over me?"

"Yes, it is unbelievable. Because you're fucking Valarie Dale and you're kind and strong and beautiful."

"And fat." Valarie muttered. She stayed quiet. "You know, I've accepted the fact I'm unlovable because of my weight. I'm fine being alone for the rest of my life. But Ruel," she stuttered for a moment, "he treats me like he sees something no one else ever has in me. And frankly, it fucking scares me because …"

Valarie stopped herself for a moment.

"Because I think I'm falling for him. And when the day comes that someone else grabs his attention, I'm scared I'll never recover from it."

She sighed.

"I've seen what heartbreak and relationships can do to someone. And I have enough issues going on as it is, I don't need another man to break my heart. But it's so difficult to stay away. And I don't know what to do."

17. DRIVING TEST

"He loves me, he loves me not… he loves me, he loves me not…" Flower petals covered Valarie's school bag. It was lunchtime, and her head hadn't lifted from its spot for the past twenty minutes.

Tessa, Addison and Harmony were busy talking about school, boys, sisters, brothers, Drama—whatever was going on in their perfect little schoolgirl lives.

It frustrated Valarie. She felt green with envy every time she looked at them.

And it wasn't fair. It wasn't their fault they got everything Valarie wanted.

"I know it's only recent we got together, but I really feel like he might be the one!"

The squeals coming from Addison's mouth made Valarie want to throw her laptop at her face.

"Harmony, that's amazing to hear. I know your previous break up was difficult for you. So glad you've moved on, girl."

Valarie rolled her eyes.

She wished it was that easy for her. To date someone without worry of judgement. Without worrying you'll come out looking like a fool because of your appearance.

"So, Valarie!"

At the sound of her name, she looked up at the group of girls. "Your birthday's next week, are you excited?"

"Not really."

"Why not?" Addison pouted.

"'Cause, I'll probably be spending the day studying for exams."

"Are you having a party?"

"I swear I already told you this," Valarie muttered under her breath, though quickly let out a sigh and said loudly, "No Addison. I am not. I'm taking my driving test on my birthday."

Harmony grinned excitedly. "Make sure to check all your blind-spots, like over-*exaggerated* looking. They mark you down if they think you aren't looking correctly."

"And remember to check your mirrors regularly—they'll fail you if you don't." Tessa said.

"*Oh, anddd* when you're parking make sure to check both sides as yet again—they'll fail you."

Valarie licked her lips swiftly, a short laugh leaving her lips. "Thanks guys, really appreciate the advice."

"No problem," Addison smiled widely, her unnatural perfectly straight white teeth coming out for air.

"Have you even done all your hours yet?" Harmony asked.

"No," Valarie grimaced internally, "but I need like two more and then I'm done. I'll get it finished in the next few days."

"Just fake it? It's what I did for like half my hours," Tessa snorted.

Valarie laughed. "No wonder it took you three times to pass."

"Oi! You promised you wouldn't bring that up again!" Tessa threw a piece of carrot she was chewing on straight at Valarie who ducked her head while letting out a loud laugh.

"And you promised you'd stop throwing your food at me, dickhead!"

Tessa only stuck out her tongue teasingly, winking at Valarie when they made eye contact.

"I've never actually asked before, but how do you do your hours? Who do you drive with?" Harmony cut in, ignoring Tessa and Valarie's antics and bringing them to a halt.

Valarie suddenly gulped. "Er, my grandparents pay for my lessons as my sixteenth birthday present."

Harmony gaped. "A lesson's like seventy bucks each though! And fifty lessons to do the fifty hours needed…" Her face morphed into shock. "That's a lot of fucking money."

Valarie only shrugged. "They've put money aside for me every day since I was born. They were going to give it to me when I was eighteen, but due to er—circumstances, they gave it to me earlier."

"Damn," Tessa muttered.

"Yeah," Valarie smiled, her hands twisting together where they laid against the top of her knees.

"Is big ol' Valarie Dale going for her driving test or do my ears deceive me?" The voice of Oliver came from down the corridor. Harmony and Addison grinned happily, already offering seats for him and his mates to join.

Some boys from her homeroom came into sight and took seats around them as well.

"Fuck off, Oliver."

He only laughed loudly, throwing his hands in the air as his smirk grew larger. "Such a naughty mouth for such a big girl."

"Yeah, *fuck off Oliver*." Ruel Diego suddenly butted in. Taking a seat beside Valarie.

"Just a joke man, calm down," Oliver snickered, wrapping his arm around Harmony's shoulder. "Ain't that right Val, that's what friends do, joke around with one another."

"Sure," she shrugged.

Ruel looked over at Valarie, frowning slightly but not commenting anymore.

"Where are you taking your test, Valarie?" Brady Solomon asked.

"Mirrabooka."

Justin let out a loud whistle, drawing all eyes onto him. "Good luck, mate."

Valarie frowned, and so did Ruel. "Why good luck?" asked Ruel.

"'Cause, rumour has it they don't let a lot of first timers pass so you'll have to re-do and pay 100 bucks."

"That's a load of dog shit then," Ruel scoffed from beside Valarie.

"Tell me about it," Justin snorted, leaning back on his hands. "Though, if you're going on a Monday and you're one of the first comers, you're more likely to pass."

Valarie's lips curled up. "I'm going around ten in the morning on my birthday, do y'think I'd have a chance?"

"Oh, definitely then," he nodded, tilting his chin up. "Just don't fuck up and you'll probably be fine, yeah."

Valarie grinned happily, leaning her head against the wall. But her eyes turned to look at Ruel's who was already watching her. "I'm so excited."

"I'm excited for you," he whispered back, grinning widely. "How are you getting there?"

"Probably just get Harmony to take me or something," she shrugged nonchalantly.

Ruel's eyes narrowed ever so slightly. "Want me to take you?"

Valarie's breath hitched. "Huh?"

Ruel let out a soft laugh. "I'll take you to your test and back, if you'd like."

"Why?"

He shrugged calmly, a slight hesitation to his voice. "Because I want to—and it's your birthday. I'd love to see you."

Don't say yes. Don't say yes. Don't say yes...

"Don't you have an exam?"

He shook his head. "No, my first exam is on Wednesday."

She hesitated for a moment before responding. "Fine. Yeah, thank you."

"I'll take you out if you want," he spoke softly. "Lunch will be on me?"

"Are you asking me out on a date?" she said jokily, nervously laughing.

His shrugged his shoulders. "Only if you say yes," he said.

She didn't respond at all, and it wasn't that she didn't want to. It's just that she couldn't find the words to.

18. HAPPY HALLOWEEN

"**H**ey, Mum. I—I don't know if you can hear me or not. The doctors say you can, you just won't respond. Or can't, is maybe the better word. Which I mean, is fine I guess, 'cause at least you're not in pain right? Or are you? I don't know, I don't really understand how this whole thing works. But I hope you're okay. God I really hope you're okay."

Ruel Diego stilled for a moment.

"Mama thinks I should go back to school, but I don't know. There are two weeks left until the end of the school year, so I don't know if it's worth it or not. Everyone will probably ask questions." He let out a sigh, leaning back in his chair. "And I just don't think I'm ready for that.

"God!" Tears suddenly sprung into his eyes. "Everything's a mess. A big fucking mess."

"Language, Ruel!"

"Sorry, mama!" He let out a breathy chuckle, looking away from his mum Caitlyn, who laid still on her bed—machines provided and paid for by her partner, Vanessa Diego, and St. John's hospital.

She'd been like that ever since May.

Vanessa rolled her eyes, tenderly squeezing one of Ruel's cheeks as she walked past him.

"Do you think she can actually hear us?"

Vanessa sighed, running a tired hand through her short brunette hair. "We've spoken about this already honey. The doctors said most patients in her type of condition can hear us but there's always a chance they... can't."

Ruel breathed out softly, leaning forward in his chair, elbows on his knees. "When will she wake up?"

"Again honey, we don't know for sure."

"Sorry."

Vanessa frowned at her son's saddened expression. "Don't be. We all want her to wake up, but—it's about patience."

"Maybe give her a kiss, Vanessa, and she'll wake like *Sleeping Beauty*."

Mr Diego, better known to Ruel as Uncle Dion, muttered from where he laid on the couch behind Ruel.

Vanessa threw her head back in laughter, continuing on with folding the laundry.

"I wish it was that easy."

Ruel swiftly stood up, "I'm going to bed." He turned his head so neither his uncle nor mother could see the tears he had started producing. "Night."

"Night! And oh, Ruel," Vanessa perked up quickly, he stilled for a moment. "Happy Halloween."

19. LEARNING CURVE

School was back, for two more weeks. Valarie Dale had just come out of exam period, which ended a week before Halloween. She though it was stupid they were still required to come to school for another two weeks even though there was nothing to do or learn.

It made life miserable for Valarie, but it was better than being at home. So at least there was that.

Ever since Ruel disappeared, with no communication as to why, leaving Valarie to miss her driving lesson on her birthday, she'd been in a mood. One that neither her father nor friends took lightly.

Her school life reflected her head—all messed up and tired. By the end of the first page of her history essay she stopped writing and walked out without a glance in the teacher's direction.

Let's just say, the trip down to her head of house's office became somewhat familiar by the end of July.

"Thank you for meeting me here today, Valarie," said Mr Lynch, the head of students and curriculum. "I asked you here because I wanted to discuss your future. Specifically, your future schooling with us. I am not sure if you're fully aware of the grades you're required to have to be able to choose ATAR subjects, but I'm here to explain that to you and just discuss some options of how we can get the best outcome to your schooling next year."

"What is this about?" Valarie cut in, shoulders hunched.

He smiled timidly. "Unfortunately, because of your grades slipping once semester two started, below the average we require for the subjects you have chosen for next year. Those have now become unavailable for you."

"What do you mean?"

"It means that the classes you've chosen as ATAR next year will now either have to be dropped to general or be dropped entirely. So that is your History ATAR, Human Biology ATAR as well as English ATAR." He looked up from where a sheet of paper sat in front of him. "Both English and Human Biology offer general classes for students which I think will be a great fit in your situation, but unfortunately with History there was only ATAR classes available so you will not be able to attend that subject."

Valarie opened her mouth to speak but quickly shut it.

"I also just want to check in and see how you're doing? You were going wonderfully at the beginning of the year, specifically in Human Biology where you ended your first semester with nearly an A+, but now… you've barely scraped over the average."

She blinked. "I'm doing bloody fantastic."

"Valarie," he sighed softly. "Listen, I can understand the disappointment you may be feeling. Your history teacher has spoken very highly of you and even tried to fight for your place in his class, but the rules are the rules. This isn't the end of the world Valarie, don't take it personally, take it as a learning curve."

"How can I take it as a learning curve if you won't let me learn?"

He stilled for a moment. "Good point. But I don't make the rules unfortunately, I only enforce them. Now, here is a list of subjects you can choose from instead. Please let me know if you have any questions."

He slid a piece of paper towards her.

Valarie stared down at it.

"You're kidding," she gaped. "P.E. General, Outdoor Ed. General, Accounting and Finance General."

She looked back up at him. "Piss off."

"Language," he frowned disapprovingly. "But yes, I am serious. Human Biology general is there for you to choose. I will assume you're still wanting that class?"

She nodded.

"And Drama ATAR is still available—I heard you did pretty well in the Romeo and Juliet player earlier in the year," he smiled.

She wasn't amused.

"Listen, I know it's not what you wanted, but you've got to choose something. Think of it this way Valarie, you have three terms next year and then you're out. You're done. Never have to do it again. So, is there any way you could suck up doing P.E. for that length of time?"

She stared blankly at him.

Mr Lynch smiled awkwardly.

20. BEACH CHATS

"**I**'m so fucking sick and tired of you being glued to that device twenty-four seven! What's so fucking important you need to be on that thing all day huh?"

The booming voice of Matthew Dale echoed through the house.

"It's nothing, Matthew! It's just the girls talking—"

"Bullshit, woman! Don't fucking lie to me."

Valarie closed the front door behind her with a sigh. She made her way to the bus stop two streets over from her house.

She used to love being in her room, even though she could hear every sentence her father spoke whether he was behind her door or on the other side of the house—it was her safe haven.

Well, until he snapped her door off its hinges and hadn't bothered to get it fixed.

And surprisingly enough, even though the past few months she hadn't been well in the head she'd managed to snag a job down at a café. The same one she used to go to with Ruel, funnily enough.

Taking her normal bus route to her job, Valarie was dressed ready for work. It was only a three-hour shift, nothing too crazy for a Saturday afternoon.

The time went by fast, and at five p.m. Valarie had locked up the doors and made her way back to the bus stop.

Well, until someone called out her name from outside her place of work. "Valarie?" The man's voice was soft, timid. It made the hairs on Valarie's back stand up tall.

She turned to the voice, eyes connecting with Ruel Diego's.

"Ruel?" Her jaw dropped.

He hummed. "Yeah, er," his hand came up to his hair, ruffling it as he tried to find a comfortable position from where he stood meters away from her. "Hi."

Valarie blinked. Taking in the sight of him in front of her. He looked… well, he had looked better. "Hi?" She questioned, her voice laced with frustration. "That's it? Hi is the best you've got."

"No—no," he stammered, shaking his head. "Can we er, talk?"

"You want to talk?"

He nodded his head. "Yes, please. I think it would be best."

"You don't say," Valarie sighed, eyes scanning the area around her. "Well, you can start with where the fuck you've been the past seven months?"

"I can explain."

"Please do." Her arms crossed over her chest.

"Just let me…" In frustration he ran his hands through his hair again, his cheeks red. "Please just let me explain, but not here."

"I don't want to go anywhere with you."

"I get it." He looked hurt. "Trust me. I'd be pissed too, but just give me a chance. I want to make it up to you."

His hand held out towards her, she stared at it for a moment before meeting his eyes again. "How did you know where I was."

He shrugged, not dropping his hand. "If you come with me, I'll tell you."

A small smile crawled onto her lips. "Have you been stalking me, Mr Diego?"

"Only if you wanted me to."

His hand nudged closer to her. "Come on. Please."

She hesitated before allowing her hand to softly fall onto his. Blood rushed to her cheeks at the warmth. Ruel tightened his hand around hers, as if he was making sure she wouldn't let go—wouldn't disappear on him.

But as confused as she was, she wasn't planning on letting go.

He took her to the beach.

Valarie Dale wasn't too sure what to think seeing him in person again. She never believed the rumours that spread around the school. That he was dead in a ditch in the middle of Kalgoorlie, or he'd suddenly run away from life.

She knew him well enough, or liked to believe she did, to know that Ruel Diego wouldn't just disappear without a word or a reason.

But by the seventeenth message she'd sent a month into his disappearance, Valarie stopped caring about the why and just became frustratingly sad as to *where*.

Where was Ruel Diego? It was a question she didn't spend a day not thinking about. It had been seven months, two weeks and two days since she'd last seen him.

Valarie didn't realise how much you could miss a person until they met again.

But now, now she was just confused. And upset, because she cared too much. And there was no one else to blame for that but herself.

"I realise you've probably got a million questions, but if you let me explain I promise you I'll answer all of them."

Valarie's mouth became dry, and not just because of the smell of the salty water.

"Sure."

He hesitated for a second, as if he needed a moment to collect his thoughts and words.

"You know how my parents were travelling through America earlier in the year." She nodded her head. "Well, something happened to my mum—an accident. She fell off a cliff while hiking in Nevada and got hurt pretty badly. So bad she's still in a coma."

Valarie's mouth slacked as tears sprung up in her eyes. "Oh, Ruel."

His hand landed on her knee softly. "It's okay—but I guess it was just so tough for me and my mama, especially my mama, that I just couldn't mentally handle leaving her alone and going to school. Trying to pretend everything was okay. I couldn't do it."

His head shook, "I couldn't Valarie, I…" he stopped speaking.

"It's okay," she leaned over and began rubbing her thumb over his knee, giving a comforting smile. "You don't need to say anymore if you don't want to."

His breath hitched in his throat. "I want to tell you. You deserve the truth."

"But not if it's hurting you in the process," Valarie said. "Ruel, listen to me. You don't need to tell me *shit* if you don't want to. I'm not your therapist, I'm your friend. All I need to know is you're not doing okay, and I'll come running to wherever you are."

"Even if I'm in the middle of nowhere."

"Even if you're in the middle of nowhere," she repeated, smiling up at him.

Ruel leaned back against the headrest. "I want you to know how sorry I am though. For just leaving you, especially on your birthday, without any excuse as to why."

"You were dealing with something, Ruel, it's not your fault."

"I should have at least messaged you," he grunted. "Or called, or done just something!"

"Agree to disagree," said Valarie. "I'm sorry I was angry earlier, you didn't deserve it."

He opened his mouth just to be cut off by Valarie. "Don't try and argue against me on this, it wasn't fair. But I can't change how I acted. And neither can you."

A small smile grew on his lips. Warmth bloomed into Valarie's cheeks, a sudden wave of heat running through her body at his eye contact.

"So, what have you been doing for all these months? Anything exciting?"

"If you consider rotting in your bedroom exciting, then sure."

A laugh escaped his lips. "Tell me about it."

"You don't want to know."

"I think I do."

"You really don't."

He stared her down. She stared right back with the same amount of force. "I really *really* do." His hand curled around her own, squeezing at it.

It was an odd feeling, Valarie thought. She'd never had a man hold her hand, let alone want to. Frankly, the last time someone from the opposite gender showed her affection was… never.

Valarie wasn't one to like affection either, so part of it was her own fault, which she could acknowledge, but something about Ruel's touch—it was soft, gentle, treating her skin like fine china.

She loved it.

"Well, like I said, nothing too exciting." He nodded along to her comment. "But I did pass my driving test! Your girl's officially on her reds."

He grinned. "I'm proud of you."

Blushing, she responded, "Thanks."

"What else?"

Her shoulders shrugged. "Nothing, honestly I've been doing nothing."

"How's school going?"

"Let's not talk about it."

"Let's."

"No, seriously Ruel. I don't want to talk about it."

"Okay," he said. "No worries."

She sighed, thumbing at her forehead. "I'm sorry, again that's me being an asshole. I'm just not doing well at the moment with school, and it makes me frustrated when I think about it."

He nodded in acknowledgement.

"But I, er," Valarie's body stiffened for a moment. "There's this party… it's Harmony's eighteenth birthday and anyone's invited if… I don't know," her hands rubbed up and down her thighs, "if you wanted to come."

"With you?" he asked.

She licked her lips. "Well, it doesn't *have* to be with me exactly. I'm not asking you to be seen with me or anything if you don't want to—it's more an invite to the party if you wanted to come," she rambled. "But if you're busy that's totally fine too, no stress!"

"Do you want me to come with you?" he asked, again.

"What?" Her eyes widened.

"Do you want me to come with you?" Ruel repeated.

"I mean… only if you want to."

He laughed, "Valarie do *you* want me to come with you, yes or no?"

"Well—yes," she said finally. "Yes, I do."

"Great, I'll pick you up."

She nodded her head ferociously. "Okay, cool. Yeah. No dramas."

The blush on her cheeks didn't disappear for the rest of the day.

21. BIRTHDAY PARTY

Twentieth of November. Harmony's birthday. The big one-eight. And *big* was the right word to explain the crowd of people entering Harmony's house.

Valarie had been sitting in her mother's car parked across from Harmony's house for the past five minutes.

Ruel did offer to pick her up, and originally, she was going to let him. But her mum had been nice that day surprisingly. She'd not only offered her car for Valarie to use, but also bought her lunch and gave her money for dinner.

It was the first time her mum had ever let her use her car.

And it had been a while since she showed any sort of acknowledgment Valarie even existed.

The sight of Ruel's car pulling up against one of Harmony's neighbour's curbs caused her to grin. Without another thought, she jumped out of her car and walked straight towards him.

"Hey, Ruel."

His right hand clutched against the top of his car roof as he stood up. "Hey gorgeous."

She didn't have a moment to respond or react before he came rushing over to her, grinning down at her. "I got you somethin.'" Ruel pulled out a small box from the pocket of his pants.

"What's this?" she laughed awkwardly, not knowing what to say.

"Look and you'll find out."

And so, she did. Opening the lid of the box, a gasp escaped her lips when she saw the glimmer of a silver necklace.

"Oh wow… Ruel." The pendant was smaller than the tip of her finger. It was a white teardrop.

"Just as a little sorry gift, for you know," his hands rubbed at the back of his neck. "Everything."

"You didn't have to…" Valarie continued to stare at the jewel. "I don't know what to say."

"Say you forgive me?"

She pushed the box to her chest, looking up at him with adoration. "There's nothing for me to forgive."

"Well then, I guess I can take this back." He went to snatch the necklace out of her hands, but she playfully pushed him away.

"Hey! No need to do that," said Valarie. "I'm sure I can find something wrong with you that requires forgiveness."

"But I'm perfect."

"And I think I just found something wrong with you," Valarie drawled.

He wrapped his arm around her shoulders, but at the feeling of her tense up from the sudden affection he went to pull away.

"It's okay," she said shyly, "I—I don't mind."

He stared down at her.

When he didn't reply she nodded once more in confirmation. Slowly he settled back down around her shoulders, and when he once more received confirmation it was okay, they both made their way into Harmony's house.

Valarie thought they'd blend in with no issues. She wasn't wearing anything shock worthy and yes, she expected some sort of commotion about Ruel but nothing like *that*.

Stares, lots and lots of eyes fixed onto them. Was it her? Did she smell bad? Was there something funny on her face?

Instinctively her hand came to the small necklace hung around her neck, still not used to the feeling of it.

"You okay?" Ruel had led her towards the outdoor area, past the crowd of people dancing in the middle of the living room, the kitchen, as well as the other living room, and the upstairs part of her house.

It took a few minutes to finally get outdoors.

"Is it just me or does it feel like everyone is staring at us?"

He looked around the area. "Well, kind of."

"Fuck me," she muttered under her breath, removing herself from the comfort of his hold to wrap her hands around her stomach.

"Ruel," she turned to him, and only then did she notice his dejected look. Instantly she stepped closer to him, grabbing a hold of his hand. "Oh, wait—I didn't mean …"

"You made it!"

A body suddenly clutched itself onto Valarie. A cluster of blonde hair had made its way into her mouth. "Oh my god—I can't believe you're here!"

The smell of alcohol made Valarie's insides shiver in disgust.

"Hello to you too, Addison."

She finally let go. "We made a bet on when you were coming," she slurred, smiling giddily. "Harmony said six but I," she pointed at herself, "thought you wouldn't make it at all."

"That's … nice," Valarie muttered.

"Oh … you!" Addison's finger went to push at Ruel's chest, eyes wide, "I didn't know you were alive."

"As I'll ever be," he joked.

Her head titled to the side as she took a few steps towards him. Ruel took a step backwards unconsciously.

"I forgot how hot you were," Addison licked her lips, "Do you want to—"

"Addison," Valarie cut in, "do you know where Harmony is?"

"Oh—*oh!*" Addison's head whipped around. "Harmony." A big grin curled over her lips. "I love Harmony."

Valarie hummed, "Sure you do. But do you know where she is?"

"Over there," she pointed. "With oh—her boyfriend."

Valarie looked at Ruel. "Do you want to come say 'hi' with me?"

He wordlessly nodded, clutching onto her hand as the two walked towards Harmony and the group she was with.

"Hey Harmony, happy birthday!"

Harmony's eyes connected with Valarie's. "Hey, Valarie and *Ruel*?" At the sound of his name, the people Harmony was talking to before made their way over and all at once, questions started getting thrown his way.

"Where have you been?"

"How are you?"

 "What are you doing here?"

Valarie felt like she was invisible at that moment, not that she was complaining but she was just… shocked.

Shocked that so many people pretended in that moment to care about Ruel. The same people asking questions, with worry written on their faces, talking about how much they missed him, were the same ones who had been making jokes about the rumours of his death.

"I just had some personal things I needed to deal with…"

"No, I didn't get resurrected." Ruel laughed it all off awkwardly.

A few minutes had passed, and Valarie hadn't moved. It seemed the longer they stood there, out in the middle of Harmony's backyard, the more people made their way over to see what the commotion was.

Mostly the questions and glances were directed at him, but every now and then Valarie would catch someone looking down at their connected hands, and an eyebrow would be raised before moving on.

Five minutes turned into ten, and then twenty. By the time the sun had fully set her hands were sweating from how long she'd been holding Ruel's hand.

But then suddenly her phone began vibrating against her leg. Her eyebrows furrowed together when she noticed it was her mum calling and unconsciously, she dropped his hand.

"Mum?"

Ruel's head snapped around the moment her hand left his, a concerned look on his face when he watched Valarie still.

"Okay, *okay*. Yeah, give me ten minutes and I can be there—no, I can't be any quicker, do you want me to get a speeding ticket?" Her hand came up to rub at her forehead. "What's the big rush for? You told me I didn't have to be back until midnight … fine, yeah fine, see you soon."

"You okay?" Ruel asked the moment Valarie took her phone away from her ear, placing it into the pocket of her pants.

She turned back around to look at him. She skimmed over the crowd of people that stood directly behind him—most had begun to mingle with one another.

"Yeah," she pulled at her shirt, "It's just, well, my mum wants me home. Like immediately."

"Do you know why?" Ruel asked in concern.

Valarie shrugged. "No, she didn't say, just that I need to be home as soon as possible."

"Okay," said Ruel. "Let me walk you out."

The two walked side-by-side inside the house after saying their necessary goodbyes—Harmony didn't seem to care that she was leaving. They headed towards the front door, narrowly escaping beer being poured onto their heads.

"So, I wanted to ask."

"Ruel!" A hand came to grab at his bicep, "I didn't realise you were here. How are you?"

Valarie would know that voice anywhere. Natasha Campbell, blonde waves tumbling down her upper body while the remainder was covered by a short skirt.

"And I didn't realise people paid you for your time." Natasha gazed down at Valarie.

Valarie rolled her eyes. "Nice to see you too Natasha."

She smiled sweetly. "Why don't you come with me, and I'll introduce you to some people," Natasha said to Ruel.

"No thanks," he said coolly, stepping away from her touch and causing her to frown. "We were just leaving actually."

"Well, why don't you stay," her finger twirled in her golden locks. "There's a little surprise I want to show you—it'll be really funny, I don't want you to miss it."

Valarie's eyebrows narrowed when Natasha yet again glanced her way, a mischievous grin on her lips.

An unsettling feeling bubbled within Valarie's stomach, but she didn't have a moment to clarify what it was as a bunch of her schoolmates, who were all friends of Natasha's, made their way over to the three of them and began to crowd around Ruel. Asking the same type of questions he'd been asked all night.

Valarie could see the frustration growing on his face.

"I'd love to chat but…"

"I appreciate the questions and concerns, but I've actually got to go, something important has popped up."

"Yeah, I am well thanks."

His words kept getting cut off by the drunken crowd, all pushing their way towards him and around him.

Natasha's hand had somehow made its way back to settle against his arm and just as Valarie went to speak someone pushed her to the side. Whether it was accidental or not, she couldn't tell.

It was just then Valarie could feel her phone vibrate against her thigh again, and without looking she knew it was her mother.

The music was too loud for her to be heard anyways, so without a second glance she waved at him when his eyes finally found hers, pointing to her phone and from the quick nod of acknowledgment he gave she swiftly made her exit, jumping into her mother's car and driving off.

22. SPOT THE DIFFERENCE

Something was wrong.

It was unnatural for this many people to care about Ruel Diego. He considered himself a loner. He didn't have friends, only companions, people he'd sit with at lunch, and occasionally see outside of school.

He was fine with it, though. He didn't really have a lot of time to grow some sort of strong, worthy relationship with someone since he, well you know, left school not even halfway through the year.

But something in Valarie Dale clicked for him. She was all he needed to get through the week.

Being at Harmony's birthday party, with a crowd of people he couldn't remember half the names of—it was unsettling.

It was weird.

But what was weirder was how Natasha was treating him. Looking up at him with doe eyes like she was trying to invade his mind.

Again, weird.

He watched Valarie walk away. The pit in his stomach told him to follow her but what good would that do? For one, he couldn't even escape if he tried, not when everyone had apparently decided it was time to shine the spotlight onto him and two, what would he do? What would he say?

All she was doing was driving home. Nothing out of the ordinary, and it was clear she was in a rush, he'd only be holding her back.

So, he gave up. Gave up trying to fight against the questions and the sudden care people were showing.

He let them drag him over to a couch in the living room, with a perfect view of everyone. They had only been there a few minutes before Ruel started noticing the people around him had begun side-eyeing one another, all with a glimmer of excitement.

And suddenly, phones lit up around the room. Murmers of laughter followed not long after.

"Look at this!"

"Fuck, she really does look like a whale."

"A pig more like it."

"Hey, look at this picture!"

Ruel's head swivelled to where Natasha sat next to him, and like a bomb had just exploded, his knees began to turn weak.

"She's so fucking *ugly*."

Ruel couldn't think rationally—he grabbed at Natasha's phone and began scrolling through what was making her grin.

What everyone around him was laughing at.

"Hey!" she went to grab at her phone but from the death stare Ruel gave her she pulled back.

It took ten seconds of scrolling before bile began crawling up his throat. Throwing the phone back into Natasha's lap he stood up. "What the fuck, Natasha?"

"What?" She looked genuinely surprised at his outburst. "It's just a joke."

"Did you do this?" He pointed at her phone. "Did you post those?"

She side-eyed her friends either side of her, all of them with amused smiles. Natasha finally responded. "Yeah, I did. But like I said, it's just a joke."

"A joke is when both sides are laughing," he said sternly. "Does it look like I'm laughing?"

"It's not about you, Ruel," she spat. "Valarie knows how to take a joke. It's just friendly banter."

Ruel couldn't believe what he was witnessing, what he was seeing. His jaw was slack with shock.

"Well, I don't find it very funny."

She giggled, wiping her arm under her nose, red drunken eyes gazing up at Ruel. "I think it's fucking hilarious actually. Tell me, Ruel," she shoved her phone into his eyesight, the screen lit up with a picture of Valarie and a pig. But not just one—multiple photos, all posted on an Instagram page that was dedicated to her. "Can you spot the difference?"

Laughter sprang up from the crowd surrounding them. Harmony was one of them.

His jaw clenched.

Silence was the loudest sound of them all.

Silence was supposed to calm people down, but instead, all it did was send a shiver up Valarie's spine. As much as she loved the silence, loved the peace and quiet that came with it, something about *this* silence didn't feel right. Didn't feel right one *fucking bit*.

Every step Valarie took, every breath she inhaled and exhaled, the clock was ticking. As she got further and further into the house, through the hallway and into the large kitchen and dining area she saw two things.

Number one, a duffle bag; black like the midnight sky, usually something Valarie would enjoy looking at. The bag was full of something, Valarie didn't know what exactly, but she could see outlines of objects all squeezed and jumbled together, not organised at all.

Clearly packed in a hurry.

And the second thing Valarie saw? Well, she heard it first; the tears leaking out of her mother's eyes, her sobs muffled against her hand. And then she saw *her*. Her mother sat there, curled in a near ball on a chair as she cradled herself. Like a mother holding her newborn baby but instead, she was holding herself.

"Mum?"

Cindy sniffled, her whole body jumping at the sound of Valarie's voice. And when their eyes met, Valarie nearly burst into tears herself.

"C-come sit," she whispered through hiccups, nudging her head towards the empty seat in front of her.

Valarie did so quickly, eyebrows furrowing in confusion.

"Listen Valarie," her mother spoke softly, shakily, eyes barely open. "I–I'm leaving, okay. I've been kicked out, by your father."

Valarie's breath hitched in her throat.

"He, um…" Cindy took a shaky breath in, tears spilling from her eyes. "He went through my phone. Managed to get into it somehow, I don't know… I don't know…" Her head shook violently side to side. "He saw some things… some messages."

"Messages?" Valarie muttered to herself, "Wait—what *type* of messages?"

Her sobs grew louder.

It was the most emotion Valarie had seen her mother express in her seventeen years of living.

"I'm sorry," Cindy cried out, standing up and wiping the tears off her red cheeks, "but I have to go. Now, before your father gets back."

"Where is he?"

"Out," she said coldly, picking up her duffle bag and holding it under her arm. "He requested for me to leave before he got back. So, I appreciate you coming so quickly." Cindy took one last look at her daughter. "Goodbye Valarie."

She then began walking off.

"Whoa, whoa, whoa." Valarie quickly grabbed at her mother's arm, causing the older Dale to still. "Hold up, where are you going to stay?"

"I—just a friend's place."

Valarie blinked. "What friend?"

"Why do you want to know," Cindy answered in a defensive tone.

"Why do I want to know?" Valarie repeated sarcastically. "I don't know, maybe because you're my mother? And I want to know where you're going because I'm worried about you."

Cindy's shoulders tensed. "You won't know them."

"It doesn't matter. You know what," Valarie let her hand drop. "Just message me when you're there okay, I want to make sure you're okay."

She nodded.

"And when you settle into your own place, let me know and I can come meet you or something."

"Sure. Now are you done questioning me? I have to go."

Valarie flinched.

"I—okay, sorry. Yeah," her hand scratched at her neck. "Sorry."

Cindy didn't respond.

"What about me?" Valarie spewed. Cindy once more stopped in her tracks. "What will happen to me?"

"Nothing, everything will be fine."

"No, it won't," she said, "None of this will be okay. I—I'll be alone, with him in the house."

"Like I said, it'll be okay."

"Promise?"

Cindy's eyes met Valarie for the last time, "It'll be okay. I promise."

But if promises were meant to be kept, why did it feel like Cindy Dale just broke hers the moment the front door slammed shut?

Valarie's heart felt hollow, like someone had grabbed it out of her chest and left an aching gape not even love could fix. The hairs on her back tickled and she had a deep unsettling feeling in her stomach.

It felt like this was just the beginning. Of the feeling in her chest. The sadness in her eyes. The deep set of worry stuck in her heart.

A beginning to an end to be more precise.

THE DURING

"It's a woman's worst fear.
No one wants to be the fat girl."

23. MESSY

We are taught to pick up after our own messes from a young age. Messes are messy, as said in the name. If you dropped something, your teacher or parent, babysitter or grandparents would remind you to *pick up after yourself.* Fix your mistakes and clean up after yourself.

But it seemed, at his grown age of forty-eight, Matthew Dale had yet to learn that skill.

Food was rotting away, dishes left to clean themselves in the sink, broken glass still against the wall. Everything had changed in the Dale household.

Valarie's life was a cycle, a numbing cycle that ever since her mother left, all those weeks ago, hadn't changed.

She would wake up, after a long sleep, to make her bed, slip on a pair of the same trackies she'd been wearing for the past month and then walk out into the kitchen to find her father dead asleep on the counter, head tucked into his crossed arms which laid on the white countertop. Valarie's next move would be to brush past him, pulling a glass out of the near-empty cupboard and filling it up with water, sipping on it until it was empty.

Afterwards, she'd face her sleeping father and just *watch.* Sometimes she'd stand there for hours, sometimes minutes, but he *always* woke up before the sun set to walk out of the house and begin *his own* cycle, leaving Valarie to rot away in her room with nothing but the same five books she'd found in her mother's closet when she began cleaning her stuff out after she'd left.

And once the clock struck eleven p.m., and the next day was crawling up on them, Matthew would stumble through the front door, a bottle of whatever drink he felt like that night held in the palm of his sweaty hands. He would walk past the same wall, each night, throwing the bottle in the *exact* same spot before stumbling away.

All the while Valarie Dale sat in complete silence, a dustpan and brush held in her hand, waiting for her father to walk away.

Silence.

What a silly little word. Valarie loved silly little words. It was silly how silent the house was, silly that Valarie was beginning to forget what her own voice sounded like, silly that her mother had yet to contact Valarie.

Silly that the promise she made had yet to prove itself truthful.

Promise.

Another silly word.

Valarie giggled to herself as a piece of shattered glass cut her finger.

24. VOICEMAILS

"Hey Valarie. Er, I haven't heard from you in a few days, and well—I've been kind of getting worried... I don't know if you wanted me to have your number and I'm sorry if you didn't, but your friend Layla gave it to me after I asked—er, because she just gave it to me. Yup.

And um, you—you weren't answering me on Instagram, and I thought maybe you've deleted it or something which I totally don't blame you if you have, but if you haven't and just haven't gone on the app that's—that's great. Maybe just don't, um, not that I'm trying to control you or anything," he took a breath. "Please just get in touch, even a one-word message will work. It's Ruel by the way, if you didn't know."

"Hi, me again. You're probably sick of hearing my voice, so sorry—I'll stop messaging and leaving these voicemails if you'd like. But um, I'm just really worried about you Valarie, it's been over three weeks since I last saw or heard from you and I'm beginning to really freak out. If you need to talk to someone, or just need some company I'm always free, always will be for you—um, anyways, just let me know, okay."

"Are you getting these voicemails? If not, that would be kinda awkward. Or maybe I've been sending these to the wrong number and that would be very embarrassing. But I don't think so, I double-checked with Layla and she said the number was right. Well, I just wanted to wish you a Merry Christmas. And I got you a present, so if you want to open it, I can come over if you'd like... just let me know!"

"Please—please Valarie, I'm begging you to answer me. I'm really getting worried now..."

"Happy New Year Valarie. Hope you're okay."

No new voicemails from this number.

25. BROKEN GLASSES

Her glass of water was empty. Her plate of food was not. There was no cutlery; Valarie forgot to pick up a fork after she finished putting an old frozen container of pasta she found in the back of the freezer, probably dating months back into the microwave. Maybe forgetting her cutlery was a sign she shouldn't eat it. Or maybe it was a sign of stupidity. Either or, Valarie didn't pay much attention. She only stared at the plate, eyes dropping from the lack of sleep (and food), throat dry from the tears that seemed to never stop falling down her cheek and unbrushed and unwashed hair falling past her shoulders.

She picked up her plate.

Deciding she was sick of it all she threw the pasta straight into the over-filled bin, the smell not quite reaching her nostrils before she closed the lid. Her plate got piled on top of the tall tower of dishes and once she flipped around on her cold feet her eyes narrowed on the empty glass sitting on the kitchen counter. She didn't waste much time, storming over to the glass and clutching it with her shaky palm.

The pile of glass her father had left was against the same wall where Valarie had found herself in the confines of her father's hands months ago and without a second thought, she threw the glass at the scratched white wall, the pieces smashing against it.

Her breathing came out harshly, too fast to be counted at the normal rate. Her eyes stayed glued on the spot where her glass had smashed and for only a second, she hesitated against her thoughts, but her feet seemed to have a mind of their own as she began walking towards the broken pieces. Her bare feet tippy-toed swiftly through the pile, pain shooting up her spine, but she ignored it as she bent down to pluck a large piece of glass.

She stood up and observed the glass between her fingers, eyes dropping instinctively to her cut-up wrists before looking back up.

Tears began streaming down her face; the realisation that she *wasn't okay* hitting her so hard blood began dripping from her palm where she'd begun unconsciously squeezing the glass. Her legs were wobbling so much she bent forward from the struggle of holding her shaking body together and her knees landed harshly on the floor.

Valarie could barely see, the salty tears free falling from her eyes blurring her vision. Her hands were shaky, her mind was unhinged; everything was wrong.

She had broken her promise.

Three years, sixty-two days and twenty-three minutes.

She'd gone *that long* without thinking the worst, *doing* the worst to herself.

But now, *now* she'd broken a promise—one she had made to herself all those years ago: that she wouldn't fall back into that headspace, the one where every night she wished she wouldn't wake, every morning she'd find her small stash of knives and sharp objects in her drawer and an empty spot on her stomach that wasn't already filled with cuts. Valarie Dale was okay; she was doing good.

But now. She'd never make the four-year mark of being clean.

She had tried her best, truly.

She promised.

26. MISS TURNER

"**D**o you hate yourself?"

"Depends on what you mean by *hate yourself.*"

"I'll re-word it. What do you *dislike* about yourself?"

Her chapped lips curled between her teeth, hands tightening around the pillow stuck to her stomach, holding it tightly. "There are a lot of things... I dislike about myself." Valarie's blue eyes darted from the older woman who sat opposite her, flicking up to the small painting of a kangaroo hung up above the older woman.

"But what *specifically*?"

"You really know how to ask the difficult questions don't you?" Valarie's laugh was harsh but soft. A sob began crawling up her throat, but she did her best to push it back down. "Haven't even been here for more than five minutes."

"You don't have to answer if you don't want to," Miss Turner smiled softly, and for a tempting moment, Valarie nearly wanted to spew *everything*. "But the whole point of this session is for you to talk, and through your talking I can support you."

"I don't *need* your support," Valarie muttered, toes curling in her shoes. "I was perfectly fine being alone, doing it alone. I helped myself and got myself better, I don't need anyone."

"Then why are you here?" The therapist said softly, head tilted slightly as her eyes continually stayed on Valarie. "If you are so determined to do it alone, why did you organise a session with me?"

Because I need help. I need someone to understand, to hear, to listen. Because I'm losing my mind, and no one cares, no one is noticing.

"I don't know." Her hand instinctively came to play with the necklace around her neck.

A pregnant pause.

"I hate everything about myself." Valarie took a deep breath. "I know hate is a strong word or whatever but it's honestly just how I feel. And I mean it. I hate how I look, how I talk, how I breathe. I hate how my friends act like they care or understand when I try and explain my problems. I hate my mother, I *hate* my father, I hate everything and everyone."

"Do you hate me?"

Valarie's breath hitched in her throat. "No."

Miss Turner smiled. "So, then you don't hate everything and everyone."

"I guess," Valarie shrugged.

"Tell me more about why you hate yourself, Valarie."

Her lips parted, and the inside of her mouth began to dry out. "Um," she coughed suddenly. "Well, I'm *really* pale. Like *ugly* pale. I look like a fucking ghost all the time and *no* I can't just *tan*, my skin doesn't work like that. I just fucking burn and gain freckles or some shit. Unlike my friends."

Her therapist hummed in curiosity.

"All my friends tan like it's the easiest job in the world, it's so unfair. And freckles. I have *a lot* of them, and they're really annoying and ugly. Though I find freckles super cute, I have like *too* many freckles you know?"

Miss Turner nodded once more. "And let me guess, your other friends *don't* have freckles?"

"Correct," Valarie nodded. "And don't even get me *started* on my fucking body in general. I'm fat okay."

"You are not—"

"Don't," she snapped. "*Please,* I know I am, and it's fine."

Miss Turner nodded swiftly, crossing her right leg over her left.

Valarie's head dropped slightly. "I'm big, that's fine, I always have been but it's so fucking annoying because everyone just treats me differently. I have big thighs, and not the attractive kind either—they're beefy and pale and heavy. My stomach is the same, with stretch marks all over it. I have a huge chin, I have broad and big shoulders, a big back, thick pale arms and..." She took a big breath in. "*Everything* about me is big and ugly, and pale."

"And my friends, *oh don't even get me started,*" Valarie scoffed to herself, "Addison, Harmony and Tessa are like fucking *models.* Literally. Harmony actually does modelling and Addison has been asked by companies in the past. They are all fucking gorgeous, skinny bitches who can do or get with whoever they want without any second glances. But if *I* wore what they did or tried what they've done then I'm the fucking issue and get judged for it."

"You seem to hate them for something they can't control," her therapist said. "Don't you think that's a bit unfair?"

"Yes. It's fucking unfair," Valarie scoffed, her nails digging into the fabric tucked into her chest. "Why do they get treated differently? Why do they get attention from boys when all I get is a scoff and a teasing tone? Why do I get laughed at when I eat? Why is it funny to ask me out for a date or embarrassing to be seen out in public with me? Why is it *fucking funny* to make comments about how I look and call me a whale only to turn around and say *it's a joke!*"

Her cheeks were burning red.

"Why can't I fit into the clothes everyone else wears? Why can't I shop at the shops they all fucking go to? Why can't I just *live* without being reminded every, single, *fucking day* that I am bigger than everyone else? When I walk into a store the first thing I see is mannequins standing there looking like they haven't eaten in weeks." Valarie's voice broke for a moment. "And when I think I find a nice piece of clothing I find the store only goes up to a size fourteen, while I need a stretchy sixteen, sometimes eighteen depending on the fabric and style. And at school, during P.E. class I have to wear the bibs around my neck or wrist because they don't fit over my body, and I'm just expected to continue playing through the teasing laughs and pointing fingers from everyone."

Valarie's breath hitched.

"So, you say it's unfair for me to *judge,* to be rude and hate someone for how they look? Be jealous for something they cannot control?" Valarie scoffed in an airy laugh. "Well now they can maybe understand how I feel and have felt for the past seventeen years of my *life.* Because they can't control their bodies, and neither can fucking *I.*"

Valarie quickly wiped a tear off her cheek, her knees curling into her chest to the best of her abilities.

"You have a lot of hate, don't you?"

Valarie's lips curled together as she shamefully looked down to the ground.

"I don't blame you," Valarie's eyebrows perked up at her response. "Society treats bigger people, women *especially,* disgustingly. If it isn't social media causing the damage, it's your peers. It's a dangerous cycle, one you, Valarie, have sadly fallen into."

"How could I not?" she spat, growing defensive. "When my whole life I've been treated like complete fucking *shit* because of how I look, how much I weigh. How can I not be obsessed when my body affects my life and how it plays out? I'm never chosen by anyone, whether it's my friends, strangers, teammates when I used to play netball, teachers, employees, *or boys,* I'm never chosen, never looked at other than as a piece of fat meat and no one fucking cares."

"I don't hate being fat," Valarie's voice was monotone. "Though it might seem like it—it's kind of true, kind of not. I just hate the so-called 'consequences' that come along with it. Because *no one* wants to *be* fat; it's a woman's worst fear. No one wants to be *the* fat girl."

"People do like bigger girls Valarie," Miss Turner smiled, nodding her head. "Trust me, when you get older, when everyone around you begins to mature, they'll want you."

"I'll believe you when I see it."

Miss Turner frowned.

"You do know that your worth isn't any less just because you are *bigger*, correct?" Valarie's lips curled tightly. "You do know that, right? That you're beautiful no matter what. And though society might say otherwise I can guarantee you someone out there will see you for *you*, not how much extra weight is on your skin. You do know this, right?"

She didn't respond.

"Can I ask something from you?"

"Depends on what it is."

Miss Turner just smiled. "Can you describe to me what your friends look like? Physically?"

Valarie blinked.

"What?"

"Could you please, to the best of your memory, describe what your friends look like?"

Valarie licked her bottom lip.

"Er, well Tessa has short brown hair, kind of like a sandy colour. She has these beautiful like honey-golden eyes, brown, but not like *brown*. Do you get what I mean?"

"Hmm, go on."

"Um," Valarie breathed out, lips puckering, "and she's really sporty. She's played every sport known to humankind I swear." She laughed to herself. "But she's super fit, like thick thighs but not the same as my type of thick thighs. Like the shit you see on those people who go to the gym all the time. And er, she has a few freckles, but not like mine. More just like small cute little dots on her face.

"And Addison—she's like a fucking model or something I swear." Valarie's shoulders dropped, taking a deep breath in. "She's short, but not like too short, and men love that. Because she's smaller than everyone else but not under four feet. She has long blonde hair, like sunny, golden, beautiful hair; like the chick from Tangled type hair. Her jawline is to die for and to this fucking day I wish I could have her jawline."

The therapist made a small understanding sound.

"She's tan as fuck, her stomach is literally flatter than a piece of paper and I swear that girl had breast implants or something because no one can be that fucking skinny and have that big of a chest." Valarie stopped for a second.

"And Harmony," Valarie groaned dramatically. "Don't even fucking get me started on that gorgeous woman. Clear-ass skin, perfect lips, perfect body, long legs, thigh gap, and the literal definition of a model."

Miss Turner nodded once more, her mouth opening to only shut when Valarie began speaking once more.

"How is it fair? That all my fucking friends are gorgeous and smart?" Valarie's lips curled. "Have you ever seen that movie *The Duff*? The main character is me; I feel like I'm the Duff in this situation, in every situation to be honest actually. And the guy she gets with in the movie is super-hot and he looks like the guy who played Scotty from Prank Patrol on ABC 3. But he's not. *Fuck,* I had a *huge* crush on Scotty—anyways," Valarie chuckled to herself. "Off topic."

Her fingers came to rub at her chin. "Er," Valarie cracked her head to the side. "Shit man, I'm an asshole. I didn't mean to come off so *hateful,* I'm just ..."

"Frustrated?" Miss Turner finished for her. "I get it. And it's okay to feel that way. But Valarie, the reason I asked you to describe your friends is because I wanted to see if my theory was correct."

Valarie's eyebrows jumped.

"Every single person you described is the complete opposite of you. And I believe that you don't hate them, you just wish to be something—someone different. And this isn't uncommon."

Valarie stayed deadly silent.

"Take this example," Miss Turner leaned in, plucking two different coloured pens from the small desk beside her. "If this blue pen were to look in the mirror every day, every hour, every minute for the rest of its life, there would come a time where they would get tired of what they see, what they're forced to live with. But, if this red pen," she held the pen in her other hand, "was to come along, and join beside them in the mirror, the blue pen now has something to look at, *something different.*"

Valarie's eyes widened in realisation.

"It's why plastic surgery has become so popular, why wigs and makeup are one of the most leading products bought by women. It's because they want a change. They want to look at something *different.*" The therapist put down the two pens before curling her hands together and leaning her elbows on her knees, eyes locked on Valarie's.

"You, Valarie Dale, wish for something different, for something to change. So, you look at your friends and wish you were them, wish you looked like, acted like, *became* them; and not because you're jealous of them in general, but more that you want something *different*."

Miss Turner leaned back in her seat, a small comforting smile on her face.

Valarie nodded slowly. "You're wrong about one thing though," Miss Turner raised a curious eyebrow. "I don't want to be them, my friends that is. I just want people to *treat* me like how they treat *them*."

27. LIKE DAUGHTER LIKE FATHER

Walking into her cold house, for the first time in a while, Valarie Dale had the sudden urge to scream at the world. And, as if the world was giving her what she wanted, at that moment her father Matthew Dale drunkenly stumbled his way onto the living room couch.

"What have I done to make you to hate me so much?"

His drunken glossy eyes refused to meet his daughter's.

"Did—did I do something to hurt you? Have I embarrassed you in some way?" Her voice was high-pitched, a sob finding its way up her dry throat.

"I don't *hate* you, Valarie." His voice was rough and dirty. A whiff of alcohol filled Valarie's nostrils. "Where'd you get that stupid thought?"

She scoffed lowly, her stomach shakily expanding as she took a deep breath in, staring daggers at her poor excuse of a father. "I don't know, Dad. Maybe the shit you've thrown at my face for the past seventeen years of my life? Or—or maybe the lack of care and affection from you, the angry screams of blame thrown my way when your life became too difficult? Just a few things in my life that made me come to the realisation that my father, the man who's supposed to protect and love me, actually hates my guts."

"You're overreacting."

"Overreacting..."

Her voice was soft as she repeated his words. She curled her arms around her chest, moving a step forward towards the always ever-hungover man who sat on the living room couch, his eyes struggling to stay awake.

"I'm overreacting, yeah?" She laughed through the pain. "Well, if I'm overreacting then you are too. With mum that is."

She watched his face drop.

"Mum cheated, yeah? Well, maybe you fucking *deserved it*. Maybe you're overreacting and the shit you dealt with when you were growing up isn't as bad as it seems. You know, the stories you shove down my throat about the abuse you had to handle while growing up, and the bullying you experienced at school as a child. And your mother's *death*—it's a bunch of bullshit and you need to *grow* the *fuck* up."

"You will shut your goddamn fucking mouth, Valarie," he pointed a stern finger at the girl. "If you know what's good for you!"

His eyes finally met hers. And all she did was stare back.

"How does it feel, Dad?" She took another step forward. "Someone telling you how worthless your trauma is, how you need to *grow up*? Does it feel good inside? Or does it feel like your heart is being ripped into shreds? Because that's how I *felt* when you put your hands on me all those months ago." She watched him physically gulp. "When you couldn't even look me in the eye afterwards. When you tell me how worthless I am, how much of a cow I am. When the only time you talk to me is when you're angry."

"I didn't realise it was that bad…"

A tear rolled down her cheek. "You can't even take responsibility for what you've done. What you've caused this family to become. Mum cheated because of *you*."

"I never pushed your mother to cheat." His voice was low, his bottom lip quivering. "*She* did that herself."

"No—it's because *you* didn't give her any love. You *failed* as a father, a husband, a son." Her voice was monotone, her face was stone cold but, on the inside, she felt her heart breaking and emotions swirling as she watched her father break down into a pile of sobs. "You became just like your father."

"D-don't say that," Matthew's voice was shaky. "I...I didn't do what he did to me to you. I...I'm not like him. You think I'm bad. You don't even know the half of it."

"Am I supposed to be grateful for that?" Her laugh echoed in her ears. "Say, 'Oh, thank you, Dad, for abusing me my whole life but not enough for it to be as bad as you had growing up!'"

He turned his head away from her, looking to his side.

"Say sorry," she demanded. "Say sorry for abusing me, sorry for putting your hands on me, for pushing Mum away. Say it!"

He shook his head harshly. "I...I'm sorry."

"For what?" She tilted her head up, trying to stay physically strong, but the wobble in her knees and the breaking of her heart were only getting worse. "For what, Matthew!"

"For everything," he fell forward, his hands over his face. "I...I know I was bad. D-don't you think I saw the fear in yours and your mother's eyes? Or the hesitation in you two girls every time I came home? Don't you think I knew how much you despised me?"

"Then why didn't you stop?"

"I didn't know how..." He sniffled, wiping his cheeks as he made eye contact with her once more. "I...I hate myself Valarie, more than you'll ever know. All I see is anger, like the world is just *red*. And by the time I realised I was too far gone was that day— when I...I *assaulted you*." Valarie curled her lips slowly. "I tried to give you space but—but... I don't know."

Valarie took a small deep breath in, lowering to her knees to allow herself to be level with him. "Get help, Dad. I go to therapy once a week, and you can too. I know a great therapist who would be happy to work with you."

"I tried it once already, it didn't work." He shook his head in defeat.

"But did you *actually* try?"

His head only dropped lower, until his body fell over and his head landed in his daughter's lap; an awkward position for both but neither cared as he broke down into another sob, large echoes of his agonised screams hitting Valarie like never before.

And for the first time in her seventeen years of life, Valarie Dale was hugging her father.

Just like how Matthew Dale had hugged his mother's dead body at the age of seventeen.

28. BEING TRUTHFUL

"**H**ow are you today, Valarie?"

She shrugged nonchalantly. "Alright. You?"

"Good, thank you for asking." Valarie gave a quick smile. "So, Valarie, have you ever... harmed yourself in any way. Intentionally?"

If water was in Valarie's mouth at that moment, she would have spat it out all over the floor.

"Huh?"

Miss Turner only smiled softly. "I apologise if in any way I am making you uncomfortable or distressed. I can stop at any point if needed—but for me to help you in every way I can, I need to know *everything*. No holding back."

"So, Valarie," her voice was sincere, careful, considerate, "have you ever harmed yourself?"

"Yes."

Miss Turner's eyes turned soft. "Recently?"

"I was clean for nearly four years."

"When?"

Valarie's mouth turned dry. *No holding back.* "A few weeks back, just after New Year. I-it was an accident in a sense, with a piece of glass and..."

"It's okay," she smiled in reassurance, "you're not going to get into trouble. And you don't need to go into full details either, I am not expecting you to, no one is but I am here to listen if you want me to."

"I…I don't really want to get into it, sorry." Her voice turned quiet, soft, timid. Her hands twisted together where they lay in her lap and she let out a deep sigh.

"That's okay. Thank you for being honest."

Valarie nodded with a small bashful smile. "Sure."

"How is your mum?"

She shrugged. "Don't know, haven't heard from her."

Miss Turner's eyes widened. "She left last year in November. She hasn't contacted you once?"

"Nope." Valarie shrugged as if the thought wasn't hurting on the inside. "It's okay though, she's probably just super busy finding a place and stuff."

"It takes one minute to send a message." A frown was evident on her lips.

"Oh well."

"It shouldn't just be *oh well*, Valarie." Miss Turner sighed, running a hand through her thin brown hair. "How is your relationship with your mother?"

"Lonely, emotionless, distant."

"And how's that?"

Valarie shrugged uncomfortably. "My whole life the only thing I could remember was my mother just *being* there. But it was more like she was physically there, but emotionally and mentally—not at all. I can't remember the last time I got a hug from her, or any sort of affection. But I get why she's like that, I don't blame her."

"And why do you think she's like that?"

Valarie deeply sighed. "Because my dad isn't nice to her, and probably hasn't been their whole relationship which is longer than how long I've been born. She's probably switched off her emotions to survive."

Miss Turner's face paled. "And when you mean survived, do you mean abuse?"

Valarie's lower lip went under her top teeth, bitting down on the muscle, her shoulders tensed. "Well, I mean—I think it's abuse, what my dad had been doing to both me and my mum, but it was never physical. I mean once..." Valarie quickly cut herself off. "No, it never got physical. But my dad... He wasn't emotionally there *either*. Or it seemed he could only produce one emotion and that was *anger*. Which then created *fear* which then led to us creating defence mechanisms to survive. Such as turning your emotions off."

Her voice was monotone. "It's why she always worked extra shifts and made sure to stay clear of the living room or bedroom when she could. It's why she stopped coming to my netball games as a kid or school plays. She just shut herself down and hasn't switched back on."

"But that's not fair on you." Miss Turner frowned. "A daughter *needs* that affection from a mother, no matter what is going on in their life. Have you tried reaching out to her?"

"No," Valarie shook her head. "Well—one time I did, it was way back when she just moved out, but I gave up after the third message when she didn't respond."

"Okay," Miss Turner nodded, "and how about school? It's your last year, I know you mentioned something about that last session. Do you care to go into more detail?"

She sighed. "I have my school ball on the twenty-seventh, meaning I have to see everyone from school earlier than expected. School doesn't start for the Year 12s until the third of Feb. And usually, I don't care about school and the people in general you know, because most of them are a pack of cunts anyways but um..."

She titled her head up, watery eyes looking up at the ceiling, "On the night of my friend's eighteenth party, Harmony's her name, I found out my mum cheated on my dad, as I kind of mentioned before," she heard the lid of a pen pop, and the sound of scribbles, but she couldn't find it in her to care. "And that same night, an Instagram account was created dedicated to *me*. By whom, I don't know, but I could probably guess. And on the account were some things about me…"

Valarie squeezed her hands together. "There were photos of me, comparing me to a photo of a cow or pig. One was even a whale. There was over ten *at least*." A shiver ran down her spine. "And there were comments, *lots and lots* of comments laughing at them—me. Me. They—they were all laughing at me."

She sniffled loudly, wiping her nose with her sleeve. "The account stayed active for no longer than a week, but by the time it was deleted or taken down my whole Year had seen it."

"That's very messed up Valarie, I'm so sorry." Miss Turner frowned heavily, deep in thought.

"Don't be," she waved off, shrugging like it was the easiest thing to ignore in the world. "To be honest, it could have been *a lot* worse. And also, the posts were kinda right in a way. Like this one post, I think it was the third one or something, compared me to that principal from Matilda, you know her? I think she's called Miss Trunchbull or something—well anyway, it was a photo of me from Year 8, one from school photo day and it just so happened that year I found out what *makeup* was, so I had this full face of like *orange* foundation—" Valarie snorted, "—that was *not* blended at all. It literally stopped at my eyebrows."

Miss Turner's lips curled into a small smile, but sympathy still lingered.

"But anyways, yeah. The post was kind of funny, but it still hurt."

"And it would," her therapist said in full confidence, eyes boring into Valarie's. "Don't disregard what's happened to you. Valarie, that's bullying, serious bullying that isn't something you should be treating as a joke."

"I know, but if I don't laugh, I cry. And I'm fucking sick of crying."

"Did the school do anything about it? Say anything?" Miss Turner said in a worried tone.

"No," Valarie shook her head. "It was off school property as well as during school holidays. They probably don't care."

"Okay," she nodded.

"You know, the photos all had one simple goal in mind and that was just to call me fat and ugly. Which, by the way, very fucking original," Valarie scoffed. "But I won't lie, there was one post that got to me. Badly. It was the night of my Year 11 river cruise and er," Valarie let out a deep sigh, "I was wearing this dress, something I usually wouldn't wear but um, for one of the first times in my life that night I…I felt *pretty*. There's this boy in my year, and I really like him—or liked, as a friend. Or maybe more, I don't know anymore."

Valarie looked down at the floor, her hands coming up to play with her necklace. "But anyways, he came up to me that night and complimented me. And me being me, I freaked the fuck out because never in my life had I been complimented in the way he complimented me, and by a boy *especially*," she rambled.

"I mean I've gotten the, *you look nice*, type compliments but he-he made me feel… *wanted. Loved* even. I thought he was joking at first, to be honest," an airy laugh left her mouth, "but he wasn't. I don't think so anyway." Her eyebrows furrowed.

"But he called me so many things, so many nice things, that my whole life I-I've wanted to hear. My whole life I've heard and watched people say the things he said to me that night, to my friends."

Her feet curled within her shoes. "And in the post the Instagram account had compared that night, a photo of me in that dress was next to a picture of an over-sized cow. And out of the sixteen posts, that one had the most comments."

A tear fell down her cheek. "It really got to me y'know, when I saw that post. Because now, every time I think back to that night, instead of seeing all the good memories, the happiness that I experienced, I only see and feel all my classmates judging and laughing at me."

"Oh, Valarie…"

She shook her head, "It's okay. Honestly. It's just that I had hit rock bottom when I found my mum was kicked out, and then *that* happened. It was like, the world decided to make my life a literal shit hole for the summer holidays so they jampacked a whole lot of trauma and shit for me to deal with all in the span of a few months."

"Did something else happen too?" Miss Turner asked. "As in were there other events that had caused you to 'hit rock bottom'?"

Valarie nodded shortly. "Yeah, I found out I might not be graduating school because I'm basically a dumbass. I can't continue doing the subjects I love and that guy I was talking about earlier, who complimented me—yeah, he left, for seven months. Just after my seventeenth birthday. Without a word to anyone. He just disappeared."

"Oh, do you know where he is now?"

"Yeah," Valarie nodded. "He came back, last year after Halloween and explained what happened. Actually, thinking back on it now, I think that was the only good thing about last year."

Her therapist smiled.

"And then my friends. Harmony and I used to be really close, but in the past six or so months she's kind of been quiet with me.

Or maybe I'm overreacting but she just seems to be busy. All my friends seem to be busy... all the time."

"Have you talked to them about that?"

She shook her head. "No. I haven't had the energy, to be honest. But it kinda just hurts that I haven't heard from really anyone in the past few months. Well, except for Ruel, he's not stopped messaging me, it's overwhelming."

Valarie laughed softly to herself, a smile growing on her lips.

"Why haven't you answered him?"

Her smile dropped.

"I don't know."

"Why don't you do it now?" Miss Turner's eyebrows raised. Valarie only shook her head.

"No. I—I think the reason why I haven't answered him is because I'm scared. Scared he'll—he'll leave. And I'd rather force him away than watch him walk away on his own."

"And why are you scared?"

Valarie looked down to the ground.

"Because I don't want the one good thing in my life to get ruined because I'm an emotional trainwreck."

"Don't you think he deserves to make that decision on whether he wants to stay friends or not?"

Valarie let out a large sigh. "Ruel deserves better. A lot better than me, someone who can treat him with care, love, and attention. Who won't ruin him or let him get dragged down because of their family or own personal issues. He deserves the fucking *world,* and I can't give that to him."

"It sounds like you're explaining a situation that is a lot bigger than just *friendship* Valarie."

Her bottom lip quivered. "I...I don't... I don't know." Her fingers came in between her teeth, crunching down at her short nails.

"And it's okay to not know," Miss Turner smiled comfortingly. "But it is also okay to admit you like him. Love him even."

"I don't *love* Ruel," Valarie scoffed in a quick laugh. "That's— that's just not correct. I can't love him," she blinked a few times quickly, shaking her head from side to side as she leaned back in her chair.

"I...I've known him no longer than five months and he was gone for six. You can't love a person you don't know. I mean I have no *idea* what his favourite colour is or who is his favourite artist. Or what his go-to ice cream flavour is—actually I know that because when we were out together this one time at his uncle's ice cream shop, he got himself chocolate and I remember watching him also buy chocolate milkshakes every time we hung out at this café back when we had a partnered assignment due," she rambled on. "And now that I think about it, he loves Bruno Mars because I saw him on his Spotify account as his number one artist when he let me use his phone to play music in his car."

Valarie's face dropped. "I don't love him."

"Okay." Miss Turner shrugged, a cheeky and knowing smirk on her lips. "Whatever you say."

"Fuck you and your sly smirk!"

Miss Turner laughed loudly.

"I *don't*. Seriously. I do not have feelings for Ruel Diego! Not anymore anyways..."

"Okay. *Okay*, maybe—a little crush still. But I'll get over it!" Valarie let her head drop back in a loud groan. "I have to."

THE AFTER

"Who could ever love
someone like you?"

29. NO JOB, NO MONEY

Valarie didn't know what to think.

With a budget of four hundred dollars that she'd been saving up from her work hours, *that* was the best she could get. It was too big—how could a size eighteen be *too* big on her?

The sixteen wasn't available so she tried the size fourteen, and she thought it looked way too tight. However, the store employee said otherwise.

Apparently, the tightness of the dress showed off her curves gorgeously.

Valarie nearly let out a huge laugh. *Curves, what fucking curves?* But when she noticed the employee was being serious, her laughter died out.

"It's—it's too tight," Valarie repeated quietly, looking into her own eyes in the large mirror. Green covered her body, from top to bottom. There was a cut down the middle of her chest, dark green with a hint of glitter wrapped around her small breasts. The dress then panned down, a small patch of tight fabric just below her breast area before it curved out into a large fluffy green ball of fabric that floated around Valarie.

It was the *perfect* dress. It was glittery, but not *too* glittery. It covered nearly her whole body except for her arms and upper chest area, and the colour brought out her eyes.

But it was just *too* tight.

"It's not too tight, Valarie," said Alyssa, the store employee who was helping Valarie. She stood against the corner of the large dressing room, staring at Valarie's dress in the mirror. "You can fit fingers through the middle of the dress."

Valarie sighed as she stared down at herself, pulling the fabric against her chest out before letting it go. "I guess it's not tight…"

And it wasn't, she was just *worried*. Because to her, it was too tight. Her usual style of clothes consisted of things that would allow a bowling ball to fit between her stomach and the fabric.

She played with the dress, running her hands over the fabric.

If she wore this, if she managed to convince herself to buy this dress, it meant people would be able to see her arms. They would notice how small her breasts were and the tiny little patches of acne on her chest. They'd be able to see it all.

"Can we add sleeves to this dress?" she asked Alyssa, raising a hesitant eyebrow.

Alyssa nodded, "Yes we can, but it would cost extra."

"How *much* extra?" Valarie asked.

Alyssa continued to smile. "You're looking at around a hundred dollars, and an extra fifty if you need it done within the week."

Valarie's eyes nearly popped out of her head.

"Would that be a problem at all?"

Valarie gulped. She looked at herself in the mirror once more. "Not at all," she smiled with as much confidence as she could muster up. "That'll be fine, can we organise that?"

Alyssa nodded once more before walking off, leaving Valarie to her thoughts.

"*Please,* I'll do anything. I just really had a rough month, well few months, dealing with some personal issues … but I'm okay now."

Dean, Valarie's boss, *or seemingly ex–boss now,* let out a small sigh, settling his glasses down on the table where he sat in the manager's chair. "Listen, Valarie, you were a great employee. You had an amazing work ethic and were always on time. But I'm sorry, I can't give you any more shifts. We've got someone else now."

"But you didn't fire me," Valarie shot back, "and I didn't leave. So technically I'm still employed right?"

Dean shook his head, "Valarie… you were gone for nearly *two* months. Without a word of communication. We just assumed you quit… I'm truly sorry. But there aren't any available positions for you at this moment. I'd be happy to give you a call in the future if anything pops up."

She bit at her bottom lip. *"Please.* I really need this job."

"Valarie, I'm sorry, there is nothing I can do," said Dean. "But I'm more than happy to act as a reference if you need one?"

Blinking, Valarie stood up, gave a half-smile and walked out the office, brushing past a family of four as she sped through the front door. Outside, the brisk walk turned into a near run, her head bowed against the sting of unshed tears, a quiet sniffle breaking the silence of her swift departure.

"Valarie!"

Her heart dropped.

She knew that voice.

"Valarie Dale?"

She snapped around at the sound of her full name, her glossy blue eyes meeting Ruel Diego's and like a tsunami, her heart dropped out of her chest.

He took three steps forward, his hands shakily coming out as they patted down her body; his eyes following suit. But once

Valarie took one stumbling step back his hands snapped to his side, his eyes swiftly meeting hers once more, and for a moment Valarie swore she saw tears forming.

"Are you here right now?"

Valarie snorted softly. "What type of fucking question is that? Of course, I'm here."

His shoulders dropped as his head tilted, a sigh of relief leaving his nose as he took another step closer to her, until they were right in front of one another. He could see the dark clouds that hovered over her eyes, the dark circles under her eyes.

But while he was examining Valarie, her hands unconsciously began curling around herself.

"How are you?"

Valarie gulped. "Brilliant."

"Yeah?" Ruel smiled timidly, eyes refusing to leave hers, refusing to let this moment go. Refusing to let *her* go. "Where have you been?"

"At home." Valarie muttered. "Busy. Really busy."

He only nodded, not commenting any further. "Alright. And what are you doing *here?*"

"Getting fired," she rolled back onto the balls of her feet. "You?"

"What?" His eyebrows furrowed, worry settling onto his face. "What do you mean you got fired?"

"Well," she coughed. "When someone is employed and does a shit job at their job, if the company decides they don't need them anymore they can do this thing called…"

"Valarie." His tone was raw. "Talk to me."

Tears. That's all she wanted to do. Cry *again*. Act like a crybaby *again*. Valarie was fucking sick of crying. But as one tear fell down her cheek and she wiped it away, Ruel sprung into immediate action.

"Hey, look at me."

Her eyes met his. "Do you want to talk about it?"

"I'm sick of talking about it."

"Okay. But if you wanted to, I'm happy to hear you talk about it."

She stood there awkwardly for a moment. "Well, I'm going to go…"

"No!" he backtracked, "Sorry—just, don't go. I… I don't want to lose you again."

She peered up at him. "You never lost me. Why would you think that?"

"You tell me."

She took a deep breath in. "Listen, Ruel—I've just had a really difficult few months."

"You said that last March."

"Well, then a difficult whole fucking year."

"Okay." His hand went out in front of him, apologetic. "But do you want to talk about it?"

Valarie stared at his open palms. "I won't judge. And I'm not even mad that you didn't answer any of the messages I left for you. I get it, trust me."

I do trust you. That's the problem.

"Come on, let's talk."

Her hand slowly slipped into his, and at the light touch her cheeks flushed red. She followed behind him to his car, taking her familiar spot beside his driver's seat, and the words poured out nearly instantly.

She explained how fucked she was for the school ball. How she just signed herself up to pay an extra two hundred bucks by the end of the week, but had no money to begin with, especially now she had lost her job. She explained that her parents were separating but didn't go into too much detail why.

And Ruel, well, he just *listened*.

His hands were tucked in his lap, though, as the minutes went by, the sun began setting and the moon came out to play. His right hand moved closer and closer to her until the tips of his fingertips were playing on the top of Valarie's thigh.

Ruel's eyes didn't once waver from hers.

And the entire time, Valarie didn't notice the look in his eyes: the worry, the confusion, the sympathy, the *love*.

So, the only logical thing to do, because for Ruel, he would do anything for the people he loved, was to turn around and ask three things. "Just out of curiosity, where is this place you got your ball dress from?"

The second question, "Do you want to work for my uncle at his ice cream shop? There is an open spot if you'd like it?"

He lied. There was no open spot, but he knew his uncle needed the extra help.

And finally. "Do you want to go to the ball with me?"

But Ruel never got around to asking the third, finding himself too nervous to speak another word.

30. SUCH A CRUEL WORLD

Ruel Diego dropped Valarie home.

She stood at her door for a few moments while she allowed herself to be happy. To let the bubbling feeling in her chest settle and just savour the feeling of *hope*.

Valarie stopped caring about trying to control her feelings for Ruel about half an hour into being in his car.

She decided it was worth possibly getting her heart broken; she couldn't deny any longer the tingling feeling in her chest when he was near.

Her cheeks hurt from smiling so much, and she knew any neighbour who looked her way would be concerned. Valarie's fingertips came to touch her thigh, where his hand had been not long before, goosebumps arising after each touch as the feeling of his warmth crawled up the back of her neck.

But then she stopped, her once upright shoulders falling with the weight of gravity when she walked inside her house, scanning the mess on the floor and the mess she called her father.

"Do you know why I throw my bottles at the same wall each day Valarie?" Matthew Dale slurred through his words. He was seated in the same seat her mother had left from.

Valarie didn't move a muscle.

"Do you?"

She gulped. She shook her head once as her hands began folding themselves into her pockets.

"No?" He tilted his head, his left elbow leaned on his leg as the other hung over the top of the chair. "Wanna know why?"

She didn't answer him.

"Because…" he sniffled. "Every time I look at that place, that wall—all I can see is you." Valarie did her best to hold back her shock. "I hear your screams, you begging me to let you go, I see your face and the way your eyes began to drop from the chokehold I had on your neck. The sobs your mother produced as she watched me assault my own daughter."

His head dropped. "What have I become?"

A lone tear fell on Valarie's left cheek.

"I'm a letdown. I've failed you, Valarie, as a father. I've failed your mother as a husband, a friend. I failed my own mother—the promise she made me make days before she died about *breaking the cycle*. About not becoming my father. But look where I am, look at *me*." He shook his head, tears flying from his cheek onto his lap, his fingernails digging into the fabric of his chair. "I am not a good man. I don't deserve you or your mother. I don't even deserve to… to *live*."

"What do you mean, Dad?" her voice dropped.

But he kept silent for a moment, and the silence seemed to answer the question for him as Valarie's bottom lip began wobbling, "What do you *fucking* mean, Matthew!"

"I don't deserve to be here!" he shouted through his sob, raking a hand through his buzz-cut hair, "I…I should just *die*. Everyone's life would be so much better right—*right?* I mean," he stood up suddenly, eyes boring into Valarie's, "you're fucked up because *of me*. I fucked you up, just like my father fucked me up—and your mother—*Cindy*…" he sniffled. "Cindy doesn't love me, because

I... I treated her like *shit!* Like my father treated my mother like shit. So I should die, right? Everyone's life would be better, I know that for a fact."

"Dad, *stop*," she tried to sound stern, but the tremble in her voice only grew bigger. "You're scaring me!"

"Why do you care about me, Valarie!" He took a step forward, towards the unsteady girl whose eyes burned with salty tears. "Why do you care if I die or not? You *shouldn't*. You should be *happy* that I'm going to die."

Her feet crunched over bits of glass, the sting of physical pain subsiding the deeper pain she felt in her heart.

"Help me, Valarie," his voice murmured. "Help me die. You... you could get the rope and I could start setting it up."

"You need *help!*" she cried out. "Serious *fucking* help, dad!"

His shoulders hung low, his feet dragging across the wooden floor towards her as Valarie backed herself up against a wall.

"I'm sorry," his head lowered so he could make level eye contact.

A beat of silence echoed. After three painful, silent moments, Matthew moved himself away from his daughter, his eyes dragging along the floor as he slowly made his way toward his bedroom.

But Valarie didn't move. Not even when the birds began chirping, the sun began rising, or her foot began throbbing where glass was still stuck in the skin. She just stayed there, eyes never wavering from the closed bedroom door of her father's room. Sleep didn't come to Valarie the entire night.

And only, *only* when Matthew Dale walked out of his bedroom, eyes wide awake and a small content smile on his face, did Valarie move, did Valarie speak.

"Fuck. You."

His smile dropped. His brown eyes scanned Valarie's broken state and it was then his face twisted into confusion and concern.

"Why are you standing there? Are you okay?"

Valarie licked her chapped lips, laughing nearly manically. "Do you even remember what happened last night?"

His face twisted into fear. "What did I do? If I did anything or said anything I'm sorry," his voice became uncertain. "I didn't mean it, probably. And—and today is my first therapy session," he smiled timidly. "So, whatever happened last night I *promise* won't ever happen again. I'm getting help I promise. I'll be better for you and your mother."

Valarie tiredly spoke, eyes droopy, "I wish you meant every *fucking word* you said last night."

And with that, Valarie dragged herself to her bedroom, collapsed onto her bed and picked up her phone to call the one and only person who she gave an inch of a shit about.

She didn't care whether or not it was selfish, or wrong, dangerous or reckless. She just needed out—she needed him.

"Could you pick me up now? Please."

Ruel Diego arrived in front of her house in less than five minutes.

The last time he dropped her off, it had taken longer than ten.

31. ONE DAY

Ruel Diego had just slipped on a pair of black shorts when he got the call.

For the past two months, every time his phone went off, he had a glimmer of hope. Hope that the notification on his phone would light up with her name and she'd be okay. She'd be safe.

"Could you pick me up now? Please."

Seven words, twenty-five letters and the sound of her exhausted tone—that's all it took for Ruel to grab his car keys off the side table in his bedroom and rush towards to the garage, wasting no time.

She didn't give him any time to ask questions, hanging up nearly instantly afterwards.

The moment the four wheels of his car stopped dead in the middle of her driveway his hand went to honk the horn, indicating to Valarie he was outside, but something inside him stopped his hand from going further. Something deep within his stomach was telling him not to—that making that type of noise, of making himself known to *whatever* or *whoever* else was inside with Valarie Dale was not the best idea.

And that only made his head hurt more. Because he didn't understand why his instinctive thought was that she was in danger. And the danger was inside. But he just had a feeling.

So quietly he plucked his phone from his pocket, flicking up Valarie's name in his messages and sending a quick, *'I'm here'*.

Every second that passed he became more worried, and his mind began spiralling with thoughts of why she wasn't coming, why she wasn't outside yet.

But after nearly one minute of nothing, no communication, no sight of her, her front door swung open, and the first thing he caught a glimpse of was brunette hair.

That was until she turned around.

"What the fuck..."

He cut himself off, forcing his jaw to lock back into place.

Valarie Dale stood there in all her glory, with brunette hair that clearly hadn't been brushed and looking like she wore the same clothes from yesterday. Well, except for her shoes.

Because there were none on her feet. But there was blood.

Fresh blood.

His hands went to his door handle, swinging the heavy thing wide open before sprinting straight towards her.

Before he could even get his hands on her, Valarie's hands were wrapped around his stomach, and her tears began falling freely on his white shirt, cleansing the fabric.

"Hey, gorgeous," Ruel said unsteadily. "Breathe for me, okay? Slowly, in and out."

Valarie's eyes were squeezed shut.

"Breath in and out Valarie..."

And she did. With minutes passing the two didn't move nor did they make any effort to do so. Comfortable within their own space, his fingertips ran slowly over the skin of her back and shoulders.

"You did amazing for me, gorgeous," his right hand moved towards her face, thumb rubbing over her cheek softly as his palm held her face under her jaw. And with a small content sigh, Valarie leaned into the touch, not caring how desperate she looked for the skin-to-skin contact.

"I'm taking you to my parents' place for the day alright?" Valarie didn't respond, only licking her lips timidly. "And then we can chill, *you* can chill, okay?"

She didn't have the energy to disagree, and instead nodded her head along to his idea.

"Just wait here for a second," he rolled himself out of her arms, unlocking the back door to his car to pluck out a large jacket. Valarie's eyes widened.

"Here, wear this." He didn't allow her to answer, but instead walked behind Valarie, wrapping the jacket around her shoulders and rubbing the fabric down her arms and shoulders, making sure it was nice and tight around her. "There."

Valarie shuddered at the feeling of Ruel's soft breath on her neck.

"Now, get in the car."

She obliged instantly.

The soft breeze through the open window was somewhat comforting and soothing on Valarie's pale skin. Her left arm lay on the windowsill, her head laying straight on top. The wind blowing through her hair, her cheeks pushed back slightly and her eyes half-closed as if she would fall asleep at any moment. Ruel's jacket sat consolingly around her shoulders, and the sense of comfort at the smell of him only helped the soft state her mind had fallen into.

They were going slower than usual, but Valarie didn't question it.

Because of how slow Ruel was driving, the two didn't arrive at his house until nearly twenty-five minutes later. By the time they *had* arrived, Ruel had to shake Valarie awake with the tips of his cold fingers and a sympathetic smile.

"I'm sorry for waking you, but you need to get out of the car."

Valarie hummed tiredly, nodding her head as she lifted herself into an upright position. She rubbed her eyes, smiling drowsily at Ruel when she made eye contact with him.

"Come on, gorgeous, let's get you into a bath, yeah?"

His hand rubbed down the side of her hair softly just before he opened his door, rushing around the front of the car to help open Valarie's side. Once her feet had swung around, and touched the concrete floor she let out a small sob of pain and in an instant Ruel's hands wrapped around her waist and lifted her completely out of the car.

"Don't carry me," she muttered softly. "I'm too heavy."

Ruel shook his head, a frown forming on his lips as his arm moved to sit under her armpits, lifting her so the side of her body was leaning into his.

The walk into his house was quick, so quick Valarie didn't have enough time to even take in her surroundings before she was put down onto a toilet seat and the sound of fast-flowing water burst from the bathtub.

It was like she was having an out-of-body experience—her eyes were closed but she could still see what was happening. Ruel's hands rubbed her arms softly, his eyes never wavering from her, his voice whispering like an angel.

"I need you to take your clothes off for me. I can leave if you like."

Valarie gulped, shaking her head, her hand grabbing onto his wrist. "Don't. J-just maybe turn around."

He gulped, nodding his head as he turned around, eyes facing the bath that was quickly filling up. To busy himself while Valarie took off her clothes, he grabbed some bubbly soap and poured some into the bath.

"Fuck," she mumbled under her breath as she slid off her pants, the fabric crossing over the small pieces of glass that were still stuck in the bottom of her feet.

Ruel's shoulders instantly rose up stiffly. "You okay?" He held himself back from turning around, from facing the now naked woman in his bathroom.

He had no clue what to do, or how to react. He didn't know what would be pushing Valarie's boundaries but from what he could gather, Valarie seemed to trust him enough to be in the same room with him while in such a vulnerable position.

And like fuck would he ever try and ruin that trust.

"Yeah sorry, just the glass…" Her eyebrows furrowed as she took in the lower part of her body, wincing at the sight of dried blood on her feet.

"Okay, are—are you… ready?" Ruel tilted his head up towards the roof, internally cringing at himself.

"Yeah, um," Valarie coughed awkwardly, "do you want to just close your eyes as I get in?"

Ruel nodded quickly. "Yep."

Valarie scurried over, her arms twisting around her body as she slowly lowered herself into the bathtub. As she took her time, Ruel squeezed his eyes shut, so tight that he saw stars.

"Y-you can open your eyes now…"

Slowly, hesitantly Ruel opened his eyes and the sight he saw was something he'd *never* forget. Valarie, sitting there in *his* bath, using *his* shampoo in her hair, in *his* bathroom. She wasn't completely naked, as the bra straps on either side of her shoulders confirmed. She was clearly in pain though, from either the glass *still* in her foot or something else.

He would have done anything at that point to know what she was thinking.

"You don't need to be so awkward," she muttered, rubbing some water over her face. "I get this probably isn't the prettiest sight you've ever seen."

"No, it's not that…" he shook his head, "not at all." His hands went to move his shorts into a comfortable position. "It's just I don't know what to do."

"You've done enough, you don't need to do anything." Her eyes met his. "Thank you, by the way."

"Anytime." He gulped.

32. ALLOWED

Her eyes struggled to open. Once she had woken up, the first thing she did was curl up further into herself, from where her legs lay comfortingly under a warm blanket that was unfamiliar to her. Stretching out her legs, Valarie cracked her shoulders and allowed her neck to roll away from where it lay on a pillow that, oddly, smelt like Ruel Diego. Her body felt free of pain, and under the warm covers of the bed, she wiggled her toes.

Her eyes finally shot open.

Eyebrows furrowed, Valarie began looking around the somewhat darkened room. Light poured through the bedroom's window and closed curtains, finding gaps to fill the room with their brightness. She blinked once, twice and for the third, she pushed herself up into a seated position and began rubbing the exhaustion from her eyelids.

The room was bland but it also *wasn't*. There weren't any paintings or pictures hung up except one—a small picture of two women, one dressed in a suit and the other in a wedding dress. Valarie assumed it was Ruel's mothers. A few random fake plants sat around the room, and a bedside table next to the bed she was on was pushed into the corner of the room. A chair was in the opposite corner from where she was lying, with a large picture of the 2018 football grand final hung right above it but other than that, the room was just a room.

But it was also just *so* Ruel.

Her feet were cleaned of any remains from what happened the night before. She remembered sitting on the edge of Ruel's bathtub while he helped pull out the shreds of glass from the bottom of her feet. They counted twenty-six pieces in total.

Valarie had known he wanted to ask questions. He wanted to desperately know what had happened—she saw it in his eyes every time they made eye contact.

But she was just too conflicted.

She pushed the blanket off herself, moving her legs to sit off the side of the bed as her hands gripped the end of his white sheets, head hung low as she leaned forward. As she took a small breath in, she allowed both her feet to touch the ground, taking her time as she let the pain become comfortable.

Murmuring voices echoed throughout the house, causing Valarie's breath to hitch when she heard Ruel's voice.

He was talking to someone—*maybe his mum?*

Rubbing her hands up the side of her arms, she took another deep breath in before turning the doorknob. A whiff of hot food flooded Valarie's nostrils instantly.

"... deserves the world, mama, I don't know what to do..."

He isn't talking about me, is he? she thought, her body getting closer to the half-closed door, which she assumed led to the kitchen as the smell of whatever food was cooking was only getting stronger and stronger each step Valarie took.

"... I don't want her to go home..."

The door squeaked as she slowly pushed it open. Two faces instinctively set their eyes on her.

"You're awake!"

Suddenly, two arms were wrapped tightly around Valarie's shoulders, and instantly Valarie tensed up with the unexpected touch. Her body went into defence mode as her hands pushed outwards and into the chest of the warm body.

"Mama!" Ruel's hand landed on top of his mum's shoulders, pulling her back and off the shocked woman. "Ask before hugging people and *Jesus Christ* let the woman get to know you first."

Valarie let out a small awkward laugh, her cheeks flushing a bright red at the embarrassment that trickled through her body. Her arms wrapped around the shirt hung over her chest and her legs quickly squeezed together as Valarie reminded herself she was still wearing the shorts Ruel had given her last night.

"I apologise, Valarie," Vanessa said, sincerely. "I didn't mean to frighten you, but I've just been so worried about you. You've been asleep for a while; I was going to get Ruel to wake you up soon."

"Okay she gets it," Ruel said, his cheeks reddening. He softly pushed himself in front of his mother and came inches away from Valarie's face, a small smile settling onto his lips as his eyes began taking in the sight of the woman in front of him.

"Hey." Her head tilted to the side.

"Hey back." Valarie said.

"Ruel Alan Diego!" A hand slapped softly onto Ruel's shoulder making the two teenagers jump. "Why have you let this girl freeze to death? Go get her a jacket or *something* to cover her up."

"It's honestly fine, thanks," Valarie shook her head. "Don't worry, I'm not cold."

"Are you sure, my dear?" Her voice was kind, comforting, soft. "Ruel doesn't mind," she turned to him, "do you?"

Ruel shook his head swiftly, "Not at all." He turned to Valarie, "If you need a jacket or something I can happily give you mine."

"I mean if you don't mind …" she said.

He didn't let her finish before rushing to his room.

Ruel's mum smiled, taking a few steps towards the girl and lowering her eyes onto Valarie's. "Come sit down, dear. My name is Vanessa by the way," she said softly. "And I want to apologise if I made you uncomfortable earlier on, I'm big on hugs."

Valarie laughed sweetly, pushing a long piece of her hair behind her ear. "It's okay."

Vanessa smiled in relief. "Here you go, Valarie." A jacket suddenly wrapped itself around her shoulders, and a smile crept onto her face when she heard his voice. "Warm now?" He titled his head downwards, smiling softly at her.

She only nodded as he pulled out the empty seat beside Valarie, turning to face her.

"Will you stay for dinner, Valarie?" Vanessa asked.

Valarie's face dropped, looking bug-eyed. "Er, you want me to stay for dinner?"

"Well, I insist," Vanessa smiled sweetly, "and I would really like it if you would."

"What she's *trying* to say," Ruel cut in, a hand landing on her thigh softly, "is that if you *want* to you can. But there is *no* pressure to stay."

Valarie bit into her lower lip, her eyes flicking down to where his hand met her bare thigh, the paleness contrasting against his tan hand.

"Valarie?"

She blinked, her shoulders tensing slightly, "Um, well do *you* want me to stay?"

Ruel gulped, but quickly responded, "Yeah—I mean, I'd love you to stay for dinner…" *I'd love it if you stayed here forever, with me.*

She tried to hide her excitement.

"I'll stay," she nodded, locking eyes with Vanessa. "Thank you."

"Don't worry about it," Vanessa waved her thanks off with a motherly smile, standing up. "You can stay as *long* as you want. I'm sure Ruel won't mind either." She winked at her son before walking off into the kitchen.

Valarie and Ruel grinned at one another, like kids that had just been told by one another's parents they could have a sleepover.

"You alright with this?" Ruel titled his head quietly, "You can go home—I can take you home if you'd like... don't feel like you have to stay because mum's persistent."

"If you want me here, I will stay. For as long as you want me to."

33. DINNER WITH THE FAMILY

It didn't take long for dinner to be served. And by the time it was, Valarie had learnt three new things about Ruel Diego.

First: he couldn't stand bugs. Anything that crawled in the dirt scared the living shit out of him.

Second: in Year 3, he won fastest boy in the hundred metre sprint at their sports carnival. "But there were only six boys competing so… but still. I won it."

And last: Ruel Diego *hated* History.

"It's too *hard!*" Ruel groaned dramatically, throwing his palms into the air, "How am I supposed to remember all those stupid dates? And what good does it do to me and my future to know when *Alexander the Great* took a shit on the fucking—I don't know—twenty-fourth of May at exactly eleven at night?"

Valarie gaped at him. "That's not what History is!" she huffed and leaned forwards, hands entwined together as she narrowed her eyes at him. "History is about *understanding* life. Where it came from, how it started, who was there. Everything around us is and has history! Think about it, where we are sitting *right now* someone, and probably the tradies who built this house, stood here before you."

Ruel just looked at her.

"And that new Bunnings down the road, it was originally a *hospital* before they upgraded it and moved location. Think about all the people that had been there before! Someone had to build that hospital, then workers had to be employed, people got sick, people died, families cried and got reunited."

Ruel blinked. Valarie smiled.

"That's just sad," he spoke with a small pout. "Why would you want to know stuff like that?"

"Because it's fascinating!" Valarie exclaimed, nearly jumping out of her seat. "Everything has history Ruel. History is the reason for your existence, and mine. And everyone else's. And I'll admit what I just said probably wasn't the best example, but you get what I mean! History allows us to understand *why* things happen, *why* we are here, *where* we are. It answers all the questions that you may have about the past. It teaches you about people's past mistakes and allows us, as a world, to grow and learn from them."

Ruel smile was lopsided.

"Think about it. Nothing happens *just because.* Wars don't occur *just because.* There is *history* behind it. History behind why two countries don't like each other, or why our government system is the way it is. Why does it privilege some and not others? Or why is anyone the way they are? It's fascinating. Because everyone has history, *everything* has history."

Valarie was nearly out of breath when she finished her rant. "Sorry," she said sheepishly a moment later, her cheeks red.

"For what?" He tilted his head curiously.

"Er, *that,*" she laughed awkwardly, craning her neck to the side to stretch it. "I didn't mean to go into that too much. You were just stating how you feel about the subject, and I turned it into this massive argument, so I do apologise."

"It's fine," he spoke seriously. "Honestly. I loved hearing you talk about History. It kinda makes me want to take it now as a subject."

Valarie laughed, wide-eyed. "Well, I won't be in that class next year but do it! I'm sure they'd let you join."

"Wait, why aren't you doing History next year?"

"Well," she clicked her tongue against the roof of her mouth. "Since I didn't get good grades last year, I won't be able to take History because it's an ATAR subject."

"Oh, that sucks," Ruel frowned.

"Tell me about it," Valarie said sadly, pulling down on the sleeve of her—*his* jacket.

At that exact moment, the front door opened, and the familiar voice of Mr Diego came echoing through the house. She perked up in an instant, and swiftly turned in her chair towards where the voice was coming from. The light hung over the man's face as he came into view and the moment his eyes locked onto hers a great big smile came onto his lips.

"My favourite customer!" He dropped his bag off his shoulder onto the floor, walking towards her and Ruel.

"Mr Diego," she exhaled. "How are you?"

"Amazing my dear," he grinned, taking the seat Vanessa was once in. "How are you?"

Valarie turned to Ruel, smiling softly when her eyes met his. "Great, thanks. How are you? How's the shop going?"

"It's going really good, especially since summer is still at its peak and all," he grinned toothily. "But there just seems to be someone missing…" He raised an eyebrow, and Valarie didn't need him to finish his sentence for her to understand what he was insinuating.

"I'm sorry," she said guiltily. "Truly. I've been… *busy*. But I've been meaning to come on down, and definitely will make the trip sometime soon."

"And what about your other half?" he questioned. "Harmony? I haven't seen her around much either."

Valarie's head dropped, her fingers curling inside the warm jacket over her shoulders. "I'm not sure about her, to be honest, Mr Diego. I haven't really talked to her for a while."

She licked her lips, forcing a smile. "But I'll talk to her…" *If she wants to talk to me that is.*

"Dinner!"

Vanessa came scrambling towards the table, four plates full of pasta, salad and more in her hands. Instantly Ruel stood up and took a plate from his mother's hand, giving her a *'really?'* look with his eyebrows raised before setting it down onto the table.

"Take however much you want honey," Vanessa whispered to Valarie when she leaned down beside her to place the two other plates of food down. "Don't be shy okay?"

Valarie smiled shyly. "Thanks."

Vanessa only winked before walking away.

Ruel was walking past Valarie when she grabbed his wrists softly, his eyes looking down at hers. She swiftly moved her fingers off of his. "Sorry."

He just grinned. "Um, do you want me to help at all?"

She shook her head. "No, you're right."

Not even a minute went past before the four were all seated, with Vanessa beside her father and Ruel next to Valarie. Plates were handed around, and food heaped onto them. Ruel grinned at Valarie as he placed some mozzarella cheese on top of her Bolognese, a small 'thank you' coming from her lips straight afterwards.

"So, Valarie," Mr Diego scraped a piece of his food onto his fork. "Ruel here has informed me you are in need of a job."

An embarrassed blush crawled up her cheeks. Gulping down the food that was stuck in her throat she gave a tense smile. "Um, yes. I just lost my last one and I'm kind of in need of some money."

"Aren't we all," Vanessa laughed. "Well, how much do you need? I could surely chip in."

"Oh, I couldn't ask you to do that," Valarie cut in.

"I truly don't mind Valarie," the older woman smiled sweetly, leaning a hand on the table. "Any friend of Ruel is a friend of mine."

"Thank you," Valarie managed to choke out, "but it's okay, honestly."

"Then when are your available hours?" Mr Diego spoke up, looking at Valarie.

"Er, whenever, to be honest. I don't have any hobbies, and I don't get out much." She laughed.

"Could you start tomorrow morning, around eleven?"

Valarie's eyes widened.

"Yes—*yes* definitely," she smiled ecstatically. "I'll be there. Thank you."

"No issue," he winked, and looked back down at his plate.

Valarie turned to Ruel, who had a large grin on his face.

She smiled back.

34. QUESTIONS, SO MANY QUESTIONS

Ruel didn't want to let Valarie go.

Something in his gut was telling him that letting her walk back into that house wasn't a good idea. That the drive to her place should never have happened. He should have kept her there, with him, safe in his bed, his house, his room. And the unknown, the discomfort felt deep within his stomach of knowing he could not control what happened to Valarie stirred something within him. Something that made him stay still, not moving his parked car from her driveway for *minutes* as he stared at the front door.

Something about the whole scenario made his heart turn cold. *Is something happening inside that house?* Well, of course, something was going on—no young girl just walks out of their home with blood on their feet and pain in their chest without *someone* asking questions. Without *something* having happened. But what exactly caused that pain? What questions did he exactly want answered?

Because yes, Ruel believed Valarie lived in an unsafe environment. Anyone with a brain would put two and two together and see that something was happening to her in the place she was supposed to be kept safe. And it took every part of him to not call the police or lock her up in his home to make sure she never went back there. But the real questions he needed answered first were things he didn't have the courage to actually ask.

Because did he *want* to know? Did Ruel Diego *really* want to know the answers to his questions? Could he handle it? Would he be able to stay calm and mature?

And maybe—maybe he was reading too much into the situation. Maybe he was completely wrong. Maybe Valarie didn't even live in an abusive household. She may have just dropped a glass and stood on it by accident. Maybe she did it to herself… and instead of dealing with a domestic violence case he was handling a suicidal girl that was reaching out to *him* for help.

What should he do? Should he call the cops? Should he tell his family? Should he tell the school? Should he go into her house, guns blazing and demand her parents stop *whatever* they're doing to their daughter?

Maybe he was going about this all wrong and he needed to just leave it alone. Because if Valarie wanted help, she'd ask right? She'd tell someone, the cops or a trusted adult at school, right? Because that's what everyone does when they're in a bad state of mind, they find help. If Valarie was in an abusive household or was struggling to find reasons to stay alive, she'd tell someone… right?

He shoved his head into his hands moments after he had parked his car on the side of the road, far enough away from Valarie's house so it didn't seem suspicious.

So, what should he do now?

Should he ask Valarie straight up: *'Are you in need of help? Are you suicidal? Do your parents harm you?'* Or should he ask for help somewhere else? From someone who he can trust with his thoughts?

No matter his confused mind, he did know one thing—and that is no matter *what*, Ruel Diego absolutely *refused* to let Valarie feel alone.

And he was determined to find out more.

She peered at herself in the bathroom mirror. Dressed in black pants, a black polo shirt and a random red hat she managed to sneak out of her father's cupboard, Valarie Dale was ready to start her new job.

She'd pulled her hair into a ponytail, with only a few baby hairs stuck out to try and shape her round head.

And while she stared at herself in the mirror, she realised she missed him. She missed Ruel Diego, and she knew why.

Valarie was in love with him.

Funny.

He was perfect. With everything he gave her how was she not supposed to love him? Her heart had clung onto the man and now—now she was stuck. Stuck with the worry he didn't love her back. That she was interpreting his kindness for love. His sympathy for general care.

She licked her lips, forcing her feet to move across the floor and back into her bedroom. Picking up her backpack that consisted of house keys, a hairbrush, deodorant, her phone and headphones before walking out into the kitchen, fully determined to get out of the house as quickly as she could.

"Where are you going?"

She stopped in her tracks. Her eyes moved down to the floor as she replied as emotionlessly as she could. "Work."

Her dad huffed in confusion. "You work? Where?"

"Just a store close by," she said, eyes meeting her father's when she realised, he wasn't drunk. "Why do you care?"

"I care." He quickly said, taking a step forward and Valarie's shoulders instantly tensed. He must have noticed as his eyes dropped and he took a step back. "I can take you if you want. I've got nothing to do."

"No," she shook her head swiftly. "Don't worry I'm catching a bus."

"But—"

"I'm going to miss it, the bus that is," her hand tightened around the strap of her backpack on her shoulder as she walked towards the front door. "I'll be back later."

"Okay," he said timidly. "Have fun."

Valarie furrowed her eyebrows but didn't bother thinking any more about his odd movements before walking off.

Nearly half an hour later Valarie was walking through the door to Mr Diego's ice cream store, a smile across her lips as she caught sight of the owner.

"My favourite employee!"

Valarie laughed. "Not favourite customer anymore?"

He shrugged as she came around the corner of the store's desk. "You'll *always* be my favourite customer, but I think an upgrade was needed."

She smiled happily, walking towards Mr Diego but he quickly put his hand out and his face dropped into a serious look. Her eyes widened.

"Now. As your boss, you will only call me *sir* or *boss*. No jokes are allowed in this store and all phones must be thrown down the toilet each time you come into work."

Valarie's eyes widened and just as she was about to respond the lips on the business owner began to lift and a loud snort left his nose.

"I'm joking Valarie," he laughed heartily, patting her shoulder and then walking behind the store's counter. "Call me Alan, none of this Mr Diego shit anymore."

Valarie let out a relieved laugh. "Okay *Alan*, where do I start?"

His lips curled even more.

Since Valarie was starting school again in two weeks, her shifts would be from four to nine p.m. during the week, all day Saturday, and she would have Sundays off. Mr Diego ran her through how to use an ice cream scooper, the types of deals and ice creams they sold and the cup and cone sizes. Luckily, since Valarie had been going to the store since she started high school, she was pretty familiar with what type of ice cream and sizes they offered but still needed a bit of work to remember them all.

She was grateful the prices, types of ice cream and sizes were already programmed into the store till.

And by the time four o'clock came around, Valarie had begun serving customers.

The entrance bell rang at around half past five, and instinctively Valarie spoke up. "Hey mate, what can I get you." Her voice trailed off as she peered up from scooping a bit of the mint-chocolate chip ice cream. "Ruel?"

He smiled, hands in his pockets as he walked towards the front counter. "Hey gorgeous, how's the job going?"

"Yeah, great. I really like it. Can I get you some ice cream?"

"No," he shook his head. "I didn't come here for that. I actually wanted to ask you something…"

"Okay, what did you want to ask?"

"I was er, wondering if you um …" he pulled at the collar of his shirt. "I know this probably isn't the best timing, but do you want to come to the …"

Valarie's eyebrows furrowed when he suddenly stopped talking. As she looked up, she noticed Ruel was peering out the store's window. Curiously, Valarie followed his trail of sight and let out a small giggle when she saw two pairs of thumbs high up in the air and a large smile coming from Vanessa Diego.

Sitting in the passenger seat of Ruel's car, her eyes widened when she caught sight of Valarie and quickly, she pulled out her phone and began aimlessly scrolling through the device.

With confusion written on her face, Valarie faced Ruel once more and with a deep breath, he began speaking again.

"Um—shit, I forgot what I was going to say."

"It's okay Ruel, calm down." Valarie smiled. "Just spit it out. Whenever you're ready."

His breath caught in the back of his throat. *Spit it out,* he repeated to himself. "Yeah—okay, well er—Valarie, do you want to come to the—"

"Stop flirting with my favourite employee, Ruel." Alan Diego's voice came storming out from the back, a mischievous tone in his voice. "She's got a job to do."

Ruel's mouth opened only to close once more. His eyes looked into Valarie's blue ones, and with a disappointed smile, he finally spoke again. "Sorry. I will er—I'll catch you later."

Valarie watched him walk out the door, his feet kicking at a rock lying on the ground as he shook his head.

"Can you go get some more of the honey-comb ice cream from the back for me please?" Her boss's voice echoed through her ears. "And then you can go on your ten-minute break."

She only nodded, looking away from Ruel, and quickly walked into the back. With the sound of screeching tires and a car's engine getting quieter with each passing second.

35. NEED HIM

Valarie believed the gods had finally given her a chance to breathe.

With a week's wages from her new job at Mr Diego's ice cream shop, she was able to pay for her ball dress. And when the day of the ball came, and the green dress was wrapped around her body perfectly, she felt like she was on top of the world.

Her hair was pinned up, with soft, small strands of straightened hair framing her face, which felt heavy with the amount of makeup she was wearing, but she knew it wasn't over the top. She was just being dramatic.

Her hands came to her exposed chest, swirling the necklace between her fingertips as she stared at herself in the mirror.

She felt—*good.* And for once, she was determined to enjoy herself. To worry about something, *anything,* other than how she looked. She was just going to enjoy the night, letting all her worries and concerns float away *just* for a few hours.

"Can I come in?"

Valarie's eyes instantly widened at her father's voice coming from behind her closed bedroom door and quickly she turned around to face the door.

"Why?"

Her voice may have come out strong, stern, confident—but that was the opposite of how she felt inside. *Is he drunk? What does he want, money, an outlet for his anger?* Valarie didn't know what to do.

"I… I just want to talk."

He didn't sound mad or drunk. There was an emotion there Valarie had never heard come from his mouth before and for a split moment she wanted to drop her defences and let him inside.

"Go out to the kitchen, I'll be there in a moment."

He complied, and the sound of his feet against the wooden floor got softer and softer until there was nothing but the sound of her own breath coming from her slightly parted lipstick-red coloured lips.

She quickly rushed towards her bed, picking up the small black purse that laid there and putting the essentials inside: her phone, lipstick, comb. Quickly tying her silver heels over her feet, she slowly pushed open her door, checking to her left before walking out fully.

Her heels clicked against the floor, and every step she took, the closer she got to her father and the quicker her heart raced. Once she made eye contact with her dad she swiftly manoeuvred herself so there was a good amount of distance between the two.

"What do you want?" she asked.

For the first time since she last properly talked to him, Valarie noticed the darkness on the skin under his eyes, and the wrinkles that seemed to have multiplied in a matter of days.

"I… how are you?" He seemed nervous, almost as if he was scared of Valarie hurting him.

Valarie nearly scoffed out loud at the question. "Fine. You?"

"Good." He nodded. "I went to my first therapy session the other day."

If Valarie was shocked, she certainly didn't show it. "Cool."

His face seemed to drop slightly at her cool response but didn't comment on it. "And I... I realise I haven't been the *best* the past few months."

"Years," Valarie cut in, arms crossing over each other. "Seventeen years, dad, you haven't been *the best.*"

He sniffled softly. "Yes, *years.* And I just—I want you to know I'm going to be better. For you *and* Cindy."

At the mention of her mother Valarie gulped harshly, feeling tears beginning to form, but she quickly pushed them away. *I refuse to cry now.*

"I'll believe you when I see it." Valarie said unemotionally. "But I have to go. I'll miss my bus."

"Let me take you," Matthew Dale begged, his eyes widening. "Please."

Valarie hesitated, her eyes dropping and her eyebrows creasing. "You want to *drive* me to the ball?"

He faltered for a moment before nodding his head enthusiastically, and it was like a shock to her chest when she saw how determined and *excited* he seemed. "Yeah, it'll keep your dress clean and your feet, well y'know from the heels..." he jumbled his words near the end.

Valarie smiled lightly, her eyes fluttering faintly as her heart rate began slowing down to a normal rate. She thought for a moment, and with every second there was silence it seemed his enthusiasm began leaving and his face began falling.

"Fine. Yeah, sure take me to the ball."

And he did exactly that.

"Will you need a lift home?" Her father's voice echoed throughout the quiet car. They'd been parked out front of the venue for a while.

Valarie was struggling to find the confidence within herself to walk towards the crowd of girls and boys. All dressed to perfection.

Valarie shrugged. "I don't know."

"Okay, well if you want me to pick you up... I'm happy to. If you want."

She gulped. "Cool." Nodding, she lifted her dress hem and opened up the car door. Just as she went to close it, he spoke up once more. "You look nice by the way, green suits you."

She closed the door. As Valarie walked towards her peers, she began to notice how everyone looked... older. She hadn't seen anyone from school other than Ruel since last year, but with heels on girl's feet, and ties around boys' necks—she began to feel the pressure of standing out for all the wrong reasons.

She did her best to ignore the mothers crying as they looked at their daughters, all dolled up with a pretty boy around their arm.

Valarie wondered what her mum was doing at that moment. Did she even remember she had a daughter?

But what got Valarie to stop in her tracks was catching sight of none other than *Natasha Campbell.* Laughing happily with her mates in a baby pink dress tight around her whole body and all its curves. Valarie could only wish her curves looked like that.

And then it all came rushing back at once: the Instagram page, the photos, the comments, the captions... *How could I have forgotten?*

Valarie began shaking her head slightly, feeling tears coming. She turned away, hands rubbing up and down her arms as she crossed them against her chest, sucking in her stomach.

She peered down and as she let out her breath, she watched her stomach fall back into a comfortable position and now that she was looking at it her stomach *did* seem obvious. *What was I thinking. Dressing like this, in a tight dress, thinking I could look like all the other girls?*

She flipped back around, her bottom lip shaky now as she stared back at Natasha.

"They want a reaction out of you Valarie," Miss Turner spoke in her head. "Good or bad it doesn't matter. So don't give them what they want, act like you don't care."

But she did. Valarie Dale *did* care. She cared how people thought of her and what their opinions of her were. She *wanted* people to like her, to think she was pretty and smart. She wanted people to think she was a good person and believe that she could be a good friend if they tried to talk to her.

Natasha had hurt her. Her friends had hurt her. Her cohort had hurt her.

Throughout the two months Valarie stayed home during the holidays, not *once* did *anyone* message her asking if she was okay, not *once* was she invited out or checked on. Except for Ruel.

Harmony didn't even wish her a Merry Christmas or bother to check up on her *best friend.*

Because that's what Valarie was to Harmony right? Best friend?

Valarie had known Harmony since the age of *ten.* When they first became friends in Year 7. And they'd stayed together ever since. But now, *now* it had been two months and she hadn't heard a single word from her, not in person or online.

Natasha's laugh closed all around Valarie, like a bubble surrounding her. She couldn't stop it, couldn't get the sound of Natasha's laugh or the giggles her friends were making out of her head. *How is it fair she gets to live her life like nothing happened?*

Valarie wanted to go home.

No.

She needed Ruel.

Her new lifeline. Because *yes,* she'd clung onto the male who seemed to be the only one in her life that gave enough shits about her to message, to ask the question she'd always wished someone would ask—*are you okay?*

He cared, *he fucking cared.* It was all she ever wanted.

Valarie's eyes suddenly locked onto those of the very man she was thinking off. And when Ruel Diego's lips curled upwards and he silently, from across the road, began asking her to stand beside him, nothing, *nothing,* stopped Valarie from following his orders.

She was stupid to fall for a man who held too much power over her heart.

But as long as Ruel cared.

As long as he stayed. She'd risk everything to keep him.

36. NO EXCUSE

People talked.

Valarie wasn't surprised that people stared. What was surprising was that she didn't care.

How could she? When Ruel's thumb was slowly dragging itself across the back of her hand, her shoulders grazing over his arm as they stood side by side, heads turned to give each other their full attention.

But no words were said. Valarie thought the silence between the two would allow her ears to lock into any surrounding sound. Like Natasha's snide remarks. But it was like Ruel had tapped into her senses, controlling them from the inside out and forcing them to connect to one thing and one thing only.

Him.

She looked over his body, and maybe the definition of what she was doing was *checking him out.* But Valarie didn't feel like she was *checking him out* but instead was allowing herself to soak in the sight in front of her.

"You're fucking *breath-taking,* Valarie Dale." His eyes met hers and the thumb that was rubbing slowly over the front of her hand twitched like he wanted to move it further up. Her lips curled upwards from his comment, and if it wasn't for all the makeup on her face, he probably would be able to see the blush forming on her cheeks.

"I could say the same thing about you, Ruel Diego."

It was his turn to smile and from then on Valarie promised herself she would do *anything* to see that smile form again because of *her* own words. He was smiling because of *her*.

He took a step forward, both still smiling as he dipped his head down towards her and whispered. "Be my date, to the ball."

Giddily, she grinned. Valarie had to hold herself back from letting out a squeal. And nothing could stop her arms from moving around his waist, pulling him in for a hug and leaning her head on his chest. Ruel didn't hesitate with his response back. He wrapped his arms around her neck, a small breath leaving his lips as he leaned his chin on top of her straightened hair.

"I've been wanting to ask you for months, ever since I got told I could complete Year 12—but I never found the courage."

As Valarie's arms tightened around his body, her heartstrings tightened around her heart, squeezing it snugly. Her mind was all over the place, and she was struggling to convince herself this was real life, not one of her made-up dreams or her imagination playing with her emotions. Ruel Diego had *actually* asked her to the ball—at the ball.

"I would have said yes, no matter when you would have asked it."

Valarie felt Ruel's chest move up and down from the small laugh he let out his mouth.

Loud whistles suddenly echoed throughout the carpark. Cheers and shouts as if a celebrity had just turned up made them both curious enough to finally break their embrace. Ruel slowly unhooked himself from Valarie's hug and turned to face the loud voices of the crowd that were beginning to form outside a limousine.

But, just as Valarie went to follow what Ruel had done, he quickly pulled her back into a hug, curling his arms tightly around her and moving so her head faced away from where the noise of the crowd was.

"Hey."

"It's okay Valarie," he mumbled in her ear. "You don't need to look."

Valarie frowned against his chest.

"What—*why?*"

Ruel just sighed, his head shaking softly from side to side. "Like I said Valarie, don't even worry about it."

"I want to see," she said sternly. She made direct eye contact with Ruel as she titled her head up and after a moment of her intense stares, he nodded and let her go.

Her eyes landed on where the crowd had formed. Her heart fell out of her chest when she caught sight of the new attraction.

Addison Archer was making out with Oliver Arson, their arms intertwined together as people cheered and laughed around them. Layla Whitlock smiled as James Sheri's hand intertwined with her own, helping her out of the *black limo* she and Addison had stepped out of earlier.

Next came Jennifer Graham, with her hand holding onto her dress as she followed behind Layla and Addison, stepping out of the car with a man Valarie didn't know. Harmony and her boyfriend Connor came hand-in-hand out of the other door, and last was Tessa Reed and her date.

They were all together. Her only friends. And she hadn't received an invite.

And maybe it was karma. Possibly from the time Valarie stole twenty bucks out of her mother's wallet back in Year 6, or the time she had laughed when the teacher in Year 9 was speaking to the class about how *disappointed* she was with them and quote-unquote *'in her twenty-one years of teaching, she'd never experienced such horrid behaviour...'*

Valarie's heart felt stuck in place. Faintly, she could feel Ruel's hand rub up and down her back, his presence alone helping Valarie emotionally.

But when she watched Natasha Campbell walk up to Harmony with a great big smile and bring her into a *hug*—the tears that threatened to escape her eyes finally let loose. And Valarie swiftly turned away, wiping them away.

She let her lips curl into a smile as she met Ruel's worried and concerned eyes. "It's whatever."

"It's not *whatever,*" Ruel frowned. "You're allowed to feel upset. They're a pack of assholes, Valarie."

"But maybe—maybe it was my fault slightly," she shivered as she looked down. "You know, I've been complaining and upset about how no one gave a shit about me over the summer break and how the only person who bothered to check up on me was *you*. But how am I supposed to expect them to care for me or invite me to things or check in on me if I never bothered to ask for help? Or to reach out first?"

"But they're your *friends* Valarie," he stopped her, his hands holding onto both of hers and forcing her to look him in the eyes. "Everyone knew what happened *that* night. Everyone knew it was wrong and your friends should have checked up on you. There is *no* excuse for them to not message you. None at all. They were all there, they knew what happened."

Valarie's frown deepened.

"So don't say it's your fault. Because it *isn't*. And if they were your true friends, they would have stuck up for you. They would have shown they cared."

She looked towards the crowd, where Natasha and her friends were talking to Harmony and Addison, with laughter and smiles on every face. It only made the pit in her stomach grow bigger.

"You deserve better than them, Valarie," Ruel's finger curled under her chin, pulling her eyes away from the crowd.

"A lot better."

37. MIRRORBALL

The sun was setting quickly. By six o'clock the whole student Year 12 cohort had arrived and by six-ten teachers and staff had ushered them inside.

Valarie was ecstatic to walk in with Ruel. Not only was he her ball date (as of forty minutes ago) but he was also the only person who seemed to be *remotely* interested in her as a human being rather than just something to laugh at.

There was even a chance he may *like-like* her, because surely, he wouldn't just ask her to be his ball date if he didn't like her? Friendly or non-friendly. Or maybe, maybe he was just desperate, because from the looks of things Ruel didn't have a lot of friends either. *But what about that group of boys?*

As Ruel and Valarie walked hand in hand through the hallway that led to the entrance to the ballroom of the hotel, she could feel the hot stares of her peers on her, and maybe if Ruel's presence wasn't so distracting she may have been able to listen in on what the groups of students around her were talking about.

"Where do we sit?" Valarie mumbled in Ruel's ear as the students all stopped just in front of the door.

He peered down at her, smiling. "We're seated at designated tables." Valarie's face dropped. "But don't worry, we're seated next to each other."

"But who else is sitting with us?"

"Well, we had two choices," Ruel's face seemed to pale slightly. "Either sit with Natasha and her gang of cunts or sit on the teachers' table."

Valarie's face paled. "No please no—don't tell me we are sitting at the teachers' table."

"I'm sorry," he mumbled apologetically. "But I chose this after Harmony's party and there was no way I was going to let you sit near Natasha, or Addison, especially after the way she treated you at Davis's eighteenth."

"She didn't mean it," Valarie mumbled, remembering the cruel and drunken words she spat at her that night, before everything went downhill. "She was drunk off her ass, remember."

"Drunk words most of the time equal sober thoughts, Valarie," her lips had fallen into a frown. "I'm sorry but Addison isn't a nice person, and that night just confirmed it."

Valarie gulped. "She was my friend, though."

Ruel smiled sympathetically. "Friends don't do that. They don't treat their friends like how she treated you."

Valarie sighed sadly, her eyes closing as she leaned her head against Ruel's chest. She could hear his heartbeat and how it seemed to quicken as he wrapped his right arm over her shoulder and leaned his chin on top of her hair. Again.

This, this was home. This was safe. It didn't matter if people judged, looked or talked. It didn't matter that Ruel could feel her stomach against his flat one; nothing mattered when she was in his arms.

Valarie questioned herself as to why she had deprived herself of this affection for so long.

The chatter quieted suddenly, and the squeal of the two wooden doors opening started a rush of students walking inside. Valarie and Ruel were some of the last people to make it inside, and a small content smile came across Valarie's lips when she took in the sight in front of her.

Multiple round tables were scattered around the place, all in a circle around the dance floor in the middle of the room. The DJ was in the back corner and already the beating sound of a Taylor Swift song echoed through the building and room. Photobooths were beside Valarie where she and Ruel stood off to the side; already students were lining up at them with their dates or friends. There was an outside area, a long balcony that hung over the edge of the Swan River and from there, Valarie could see the iconic *Elizabeth Quay* bridge.

She smiled at the sight.

But the thing that really caught her attention was the large *mirror ball* dangling in the middle of the room. It was spinning slowly, and Valarie only looked away when her eyebrows began to furrow from the question that was suddenly on the tip of her tongue.

"Wait—quick question," Valarie asked out of nowhere. Ruel hummed in response, looking at her as she asked, "How did you know I would want to sit with you for the ball?"

Ruel smirked, his arm slinging around her as they began their movement towards their designated seats. "Well, I did it so it would give me another reason to ask you as my date to the ball and I want to be next to you."

She smiled up at him, leaning in hesitantly to only swiftly place a kiss on the side of his cheek before untangling herself from his arms and making her way quickly towards the teacher's table, her heels clicking against the floor as she waved through the large crowd of students.

Ruel's fingers lingered on his cheeks where Valarie's lips had just been. A giddy smile had crawled onto his lips, which he struggled to remove.

"You look absolutely fantastic, Miss Dale!" Her Math teacher complimented the girl, giving her a great big smile as she quickly took a seat at the table.

Valarie smiled softly back. "Thank you, Mrs Inch." Her eyes moved around the table, finding herself unfamiliar with some of the teachers. She quickly figured out a lot were teachers in subjects Valarie had never done before.

But one familiar face appeared and Valarie's smile grew. "Miss Candlewood!"

The woman in question turned around in her chair, her body now facing Valarie's. "Valarie my dear," she smiled softly. "How are you?"

"Good, thank you for asking." In this dress, the heels, the makeup, the hair, the area she was sitting in, Valarie felt confident.

She took a seat.

"How are you?"

Miss C. smiled, and the elegant red colour of her traditional Indian gown against the dark pink of her lips made her skin glow gorgeously under the lights of the room. "I'm well, thank you."

Just as Valarie's mouth opened wide to continue their conversation the seat beside her suddenly became occupied and an arm wrapped itself around her shoulders—pulling her into the side of Ruel Diego. A smile painted her lips and from the corner of her eye, she could see Miss Candlewood grinning.

"Lovely to see you again, Mr Diego." She nodded towards the man who had busied his eyes with the woman in his arms. He looked up to the teacher with a shy grin.

"You too, Miss. C."

The teacher only winked at him.

"Don't look now, but Natasha's looking at you."

As slowly and nonchalantly as she could, Valarie turned towards where the set of eyes was boring into the back of her head and made eye contact with the blonde.

Her lips twisted into a devilish smirk and all Valarie did was roll her eyes and throw her middle finger towards her before looking back to the man beside her. Valarie swore she heard an angry loud shock of disgust come from Natasha's direction, but she made no move to investigate further.

She leaned down, scratching her ankle with her fake five-dollar nails she'd brought from Kmart and put on herself, before whispering to Ruel. "I hate these fucking heels. They're giving me blisters."

It also didn't help that her feet were still recovering from the glass that had stuck in her foot just a week before.

"I *knew* I should have just worn fucking sneakers or some shit," she muttered angrily, pulling herself to sit upright. "How is it fair that I have to dress up and if I dare to dress or look the same as someone else, I'll get shit for it. While *you* and the male species can wear the same suit, same colour, same everything and get complimented all night?"

Ruel looked down at her, smirking. "Do you want me to wear your heels? We can swap shoes, I heard it's the new romantic gesture this year."

"Oh, piss off," she shoved him playfully, her lips fighting a smile. He only chuckled, his arm wrapping around her shoulder once more and rubbing the side of her shoulder before leaning down and kissing the top of her head.

Her lips spread open slightly in shock, eyes widening as she titled her head to look at him. "Ruel…"

"Class of 2022. Welcome, to your Year 12 ball!"

Cheers erupted around the room, whistles coming from some students' mouths and laughs coming from the teachers. Valarie peered over to the podium where the deputy principal Mr Kane smiled brightly down towards all the students and teachers.

"This is an exciting time for all," he began speaking. "A time for you to dress up, dance with your friends, and create some amazing memories that will hopefully stay with you for many years to come. But before we go any further, I want to begin today by acknowledging the Traditional Custodians of the land on which we gather today, the Whadjuk, and pay my respects to the Elders: past and present. I extend that respect to the First Nations people—Aboriginal and Torres Strait Islanders."

A respectful silence rang throughout the building.

Mr Kane smiled. "Now, for the remaining time that you are here, the evening will go like this. At seven-thirty you will be served dinner, meaning by seven-twenty everyone needs to be seated in their designated spots and tables. If you do not know where you are seated, please head to the two teachers' tables," he pointed near where Valarie and Ruel were sitting, "and they will guide you to your table. Before *and* after dinner is served you may make your way around the room. The outdoor area is included, but please be careful when nearing the edge."

He looked over to the table where Ruel's old friends, the popular boys, sat. "If me or any teacher finds you mucking around the edge of the outdoor area, such as hanging off the rails, you will be removed from this event. And this goes towards the inside area as well. If we find that you are not being respectful to either the equipment given to us, the staff or the students you will be punished accordingly and you will be removed from the rest of the event."

Mr Kane sighed. "Remember, just because you are not in school uniform does *not* mean this isn't a school event."

"No shit," Valarie heard someone mutter from a table close beside her. She snorted, but quickly covered it with a small cough, smiling innocently at Ruel who looked down at her curiously.

"And any rule breaking of any sort will extend to punishments when back at school. You are representing our school, so we want *everyone* on their best behaviour." He took a moment of silence before continuing. "Phones are not to be used."

Groans and shouts of complaint swarmed the once silent room.

"Students! Students!" Mr Kane shouted through the microphone, drowning out the noise. "This is just like any school event that we've had. Just because you are *not* wearing the uniform does not mean this is not a school event!"

Mr Kane shook his head, rubbing the top of his forehead. "And none of you should be shocked by this—there was an email sent not only to you but your parents as well outlining the behaviours you all will be expected to show tonight."

A voice, Brady Solomen, a boy in Valarie's homeroom, spoke out loud. "Why can't we use our phones?"

Mr Kane looked annoyed. "Because it's school policy."

"But we want to take pictures," Justin Bradson spoke up from beside Brady, his eyebrows creased together angrily. "How are we supposed to do that—save and create memories as you said earlier—if we can't take videos or pictures of it?"

Murmurs began rattling around the tables. Valarie's eyebrow raised, looking at Ruel who only sighed softly and pulled Valarie slightly closer to him.

"There are professional photographers around the room, if you wish for a photo, you can ask them."

"But videos? What about videos?" Brady shouted out.

"Yeah! And not to mention we'll have to *pay* for the photos they take," Caleb Solomen, Brady's twin who was also in Valarie's homeroom, spoke up. "How's that fair?"

The chatter grew louder, the looks became angrier and for a moment Valarie thought Brady would start a fight with the deputy principal.

"Enough!" Mr Kane's voice echoed harshly around the room, making everyone quieten down instantly. "You are nearly adults! You all know the rules, and whether you like them or not you *will* follow them. If you want to complain, go to a bloody therapist or tell your mother, I don't care."

Valarie's eyes widened.

"Now," his voice dropped so he was no longer screaming at the microphone and was now calm. "If I could finish my speech that would be much appreciated." No one complained or commented, making Mr Kane smile slightly.

"As for what you can do before and after dinner, there are photobooths set around the room, as well as a photographer for those who wish to get professional photos taken with their friends or alone. You are not obliged to get your photos taken *except* for one—a photo with your head of house and students. The red house will start first with the yellow ending last."

Valarie groaned.

"Bathrooms are to my right side, and beverages—*non-alcoholic beverages,*" he said to groans, "are on my left. Otherwise, enjoy the night and get involved with some photos and dancing. The best dressed and best couple will be announced towards the end of the night. Thank you."

People began standing up, and chatter started up again, but Mr Kane's voice once more echoed around the room.

"And I forgot one last thing—no one is allowed to leave until the event is over which is eleven-thirty p.m., unless you receive permission."

Ruel laughed softly at Valarie's dramatic groan, his hand coming up to push a piece of her hair behind her ear.

"Come on, gorgeous," he teased as she peered up at him. "Let's get some photos taken."

38. LIKE EVERYONE ELSE

As Valarie expected, the photobooth had a line of students and even some teachers waiting for their turn.

Dinner would be served in just over half an hour and at the rate the line was moving, Valarie honestly didn't know if she'd get the photos done before the food was served.

She let out a dramatic groan, her head leaning against Ruel's upper arm. She suddenly heard him spit something out his mouth, and curiously she looked up at him.

He smiled sheepishly back at her, whispering, "Some of your hair got in my mouth."

"Oh," she said. "Sorry."

He waved it off, wrapping his arm around her shoulder and smiling. "Don't worry about it."

Valarie laughed, comfortably letting her head fall back on his shoulder.

"Is there anyone waiting for photos to be taken of just *three* or fewer people?" An old man, bald-headed and with wrinkles covering his pale face came around from behind where the camera was set up on a tripod. "Anyone wanting professional photos taken?"

Valarie looked over at Ruel who looked back at her, and Valarie quickly got the gist of what he was trying to communicate. Valarie looked at the line in front of her and noticed it was still reasonably long.

"We do!" Ruel called out, raising one arm slightly as with his other one he latched onto Valarie and softly pulled her along towards where the rugged man stood. "We'll get some."

Valarie was shocked to find the line empty. Then again, it wasn't surprising as she knew students would have to pay for it afterwards.

"Ruel," Valarie tugged on his sleeve. "I won't be able to buy the photos, don't bother."

Ruel rolled his eyes, smiling as he pushed Valarie onto the mat next to the sky-blue backscreen. "Who said they're for you?"

She stared at him.

"I'm just kidding gorgeous, I'll buy them for you." He touched his index finger to the tip of Valarie's nose with a small smirk, before turning to look at the camera. Valarie followed swiftly straight after, trying to calm her growing blush before the click of the camera.

"Smile, you two," the photographer smiled toothily. "You, young man, move slightly closer to the lady. Straighten your backs, heads a little higher."

Valarie felt like a doll, being pushed and pulled to perfection, but in the end, she found her body turned sideways to Ruel while her eyes were staring back at the intimidating black lens of the camera.

The camera clicked five times.

Once where they were both smiling at the camera, slightly awkwardly, Valarie thought, as the two struggled to find a good and comfortable position. And it didn't help that her arms were itching to come up to her stomach and cover it but there was no room to do so. Not when Ruel's arm for the second photo wrapped around her waist, her head laying on his chest from the sudden force his arm produced.

The third was taken directly after that, with no chance for Valarie or Ruel to move positions. The fourth was supposed to be the last, with the cameraman suggesting taking a silly photo.

And Ruel decided to stick his finger in Valarie's ear.

With shock written on her face, the camera clicked, and Valarie didn't get a chance to even take a pose. She scoffed, looking up into Ruel's eyes and shoving him playfully—with him only laughing back, grinning cheekily, causing Valarie to not even notice the fifth and final photo.

The cameraman pulled the two aside, flicking through each of their photos and getting their opinions. When they got to the last one, Valarie couldn't help but smile. She decided it might be the best photo she'd ever seen of herself. But what she really fell in love with wasn't herself but rather who she was standing next to.

Ruel was staring at *her*, Ruel was smiling down at *her*, Ruel's arm was wrapped around *her* shoulder. They looked like a couple—and this time Valarie truly believed she wasn't playing tricks on herself.

Not when Ruel whispered from beside her. "We look good."

Once they were done looking at the photos and had approved them the two made their way onto the balcony, deciding they would do the photobooth later in the evening as the line was still busy. The iconic Elizabeth Quay bridge came into Valarie's view.

People—mainly everyone from the Eastern side of Australia, aka the Eastern States—always said how *boring* Perth was and even people within Perth had said so but to Valarie, Perth was beautiful. Yes, it wasn't anything like Sydney with its famous Opera House and Harbour Bridge, nor Melbourne with its shopping and nightlife.

But Perth had the best beaches in the world. Plus, an easy five-hour drive down south and you were in Margaret River where you could find yourself in a lovely small city with beautiful people and scenery. Drive up north and you'd find similar things.

And Optus! Who could forget about Optus Stadium? Plus, the *cactus*. What an iconic piece of sculpture stuck directly outside the train station. (*Even though Sydney has the same sculpture in orange,* Valarie had to laughingly admit to herself.)

The Elizabeth Quay glowed with blue and pink lights that lit up underneath it, shining upwards with the calm river behind it. Valarie leaned her right arm on the ledge, looking out into the distance. Ruel stood beside her.

"What are you looking at, smiley?" Valarie said, grinning, making eye contact with the boy beside her.

He continued smiling. "You, who else would I look at?"

"Anyone," she shrugged nonchalantly. "Literally anyone—I think half the cohort is outside." Valarie was grateful the balcony was big enough that a lot of rowdy teenagers could fit into one area, but space was still available for most to walk around. Luckily, the two found a corner spot where no one was close by.

"Why would I want to look at them when I've got the most gorgeous girl sitting beside me?"

Valarie only scoffed, blushing as she shoved Ruel. "Get real."

"I am real, see," he grabbed her hand, pushing it against his chest. "Feel the *realness*, Valarie?"

"Stop trying to get me to feel you up."

"Don't pretend you don't like it."

She pushed him playfully again. Laughing at his comment to only look away from him. "Stop it."

"Stop what?" He leaned further against the railing, and from the corner of Valarie's blue eyes, she caught a glimpse of him.

"You know," her hand tightened around the metal railing. "Stop *this*."

"What am I doing wrong that makes you want me to stop?"

Valarie's throat bobbed, letting out a heavy sigh as she looked down to the ground, her toes in her heels sticking out from under the glass panels that stopped a few centimetres above the floor, leaving a small gap.

"*This*," she spoke. "You—you're making me feel—I don't know, just stop it."

Ruel smiled slightly. "What am I making you feel Valarie?"

"Things," she spat, eyes looking up once more and finally meeting his eyes. "You—you're acting like I'm everyone else. Like I get the guy in the end."

Ruel's eyebrows furrowed tightly.

"Why are you treating me like—like I am deserving of someone like you? Why are you getting my hopes up?"

"You *are* deserving of love, Valarie," his voice was hoarse, his hands coming up to clutch onto hers, "and I'm not going to stop because I *care* for you Valarie and every time I look at you I get reminded of how *gorgeous* you are. Why can't you see that?"

Valarie's eyes stung. "Because *look* at me Ruel, *really* look at me."

He didn't look anywhere but her eyes. "Why? I already know how you look."

"Don't—" She choked, gulping down the softball lump in her throat. "Don't act like I'm pretty. Don't just pretend because we're friends…"

"Go on a date with me."

Huh?

His eyes bore into Valarie's, determination and a flicker of anger shooting through his pupils.

"Huh?"

"Go on a date with me." He repeated sternly. "Let me show you how gorgeous you are. Let me prove to you how *friendly* I can be."

"Are you fucking with me right now?" Valarie felt like crying— or screaming—maybe a little bit of both.

"Not a chance," Ruel whispered softly, brown and green eyes boring into hers. "So let me take you out."

"When?" Where was an oxygen mask when she needed one?

Ruel looked around for a moment before turning back to her with a small smirk on his lips.

"Now?"

Her eyes popped out. "W-what?"

He nodded. "Let's go."

She couldn't get another word in as his hand wrapped around her arm once more and pulled her towards the two open glass doors and stepped inside, stopping swiftly when they made it to their table to quickly pick up their things.

"How are we going to get out?" Valarie asked in a whisper, looking towards the exit where a teacher stood in front.

"I've got a plan," he whispered back. "But are you okay with this? Before we go any further. I don't want to push you if you don't actually want to."

"You could ask me to swim in a sea of sharks and I'd do it," she said quickly. "Wherever you go expect me to be right behind."

Something inside Valarie twisted when he smiled with a blush on his cheeks.

"I could fucking kiss you right now," he mumbled, and Valarie's eyes widened, his arms moving to sit around her waist and pulling her slightly closer. "But later." He moved his eyes from her lips.

"We're probably going to get into trouble—someone will notice we're gone. But I can get us out of here."

Valarie hesitated for a moment— but just a moment. "Okay. Fuck it, yeah okay."

"Okay."

He smiled.

She smiled back.

"Let's go," his arm moved from her waist and his hand fell back onto her arm, stringing her behind him.

The two swiftly made it to the exit, both slowing down as they neared the teacher who was looking at them in confusion, eyebrows raised.

"Sir!" Ruel put on the most worried and concerned voice he could possibly muster. Valarie tried to hide her shock at the change of emotion. "There are boys in the bathroom, *vaping.*"

The teacher's mouth instantly straightened into a thin line.

"I knew it!" He screamed angrily, steam coming out his ears. "None of the other teachers believed me when I told them our students vape! They all think that stupid smoke detector in the bathrooms scares them off…"

He ran off towards the bathroom, his words getting lost in the crowd.

Valarie snickered under her breath.

"You've probably just snitched on like thirty kids, you do know that right?"

Ruel only shrugged, a cheeky grin curling onto his lips. "Oh well. They'll get over it."

And with the door left unsupervised, Ruel took a step forward, hand falling onto the wood and pushing it open just enough for the two to walk through. But just as Valarie stepped one foot out the exit, a hand fell onto her wrist from behind her and instantly, she flipped around in shock.

"Tessa?"

The girl in question looked between the two and Valarie felt her heart drop out of her chest.

"Tess."

"Stay safe, yeah?" Her voice was a mere whisper.

"Tess."

Valarie was cut off yet again.

"Take good care of her Ruel. Valarie—she's a good friend. A good person."

Ruel hesitated but slowly nodded, giving her the smallest of smiles. Tessa only sighed, her hands gradually letting go of Valarie.

"You'll make a cute couple," she whispered softly to Valarie, but it was clear Ruel overhead her words.

"I'm sorry."

"No, you're not." Both girls gulped. "But it's okay, honestly—I have a girlfriend and I'm totally over him."

"Tess."

"I've always had my suspicion," she laughed softly but there was no malice behind it. "Just—look after yourself, yeah?"

Valarie only nodded. And Tessa walked off, not looking back.

And neither did Valarie.

39. KINGS PARK

Getting to Kings Park playground at seven o'clock on a Thursday night was easier than Valarie expected it to be.

Something changed inside her when Ruel suggested the famous Perth park for their date, and she didn't exactly know what. Maybe it was her inner child happy at the thought of going to a *children's* playground that she'd only ever gone to once in her life, or maybe it was her heart, and how it had beaten faster than usual when Ruel clicked her seatbelt in for her and mumbled in her ear the suggestion.

Whatever it was, Valarie didn't want it to stop.

The drive there took just under ten minutes. Valarie knew she would get into massive trouble when she got back to school next week, but she couldn't find it within her to care. Not when she was here, sitting in the passenger seat of Ruel's car with music blasting from the speakers, a smile on her face and the front windows down.

She felt free.

Free of her trouble, free of the students' eyes and whispers, free of judgemental stares. Free of it all—for now.

She struggled to keep her eyes off Ruel. Honestly, Valarie tried to distract herself from the man beside her, but it was easier said than done. His sleeves were rolled up, a small content grin on his lips as he nodded his head every now and then to the upbeat music.

One hand hung out the window, the other on the steering wheel. His tie and shirt were untucked, his suit slightly wrinkled.

Valarie hadn't seen Ruel this relaxed in months.

Ruel's car rolled into the entrance to the park, finding a car spot easily and parking in between the lines swiftly. Valarie gulped as she looked around the dark area from inside the car.

"Do you think any eshays will be here?"

Ruel snorted. "Nah, if they're going to hang around and cause trouble, they wouldn't be doing it at Kings Park."

Valarie breathed out. "But what happens if there *are* eshays?"

"Then we fucking run," he laughed. "Come on." He slapped her thigh.

Valarie nodded swiftly, her stomach bubbling with excitement as Ruel helped her out of her side of the car, her hand slipping into his own.

"Ah shit," Valarie frowned, looking down at herself.

Ruel's voice was filled with concern. "What's wrong?"

"How the fuck am I supposed to walk around in heels and this big ass dress?" She picked up the end of her dress, fluffing it up and giving an annoyed look to Ruel.

"You can take it off."

"And wear *what?*"

His lips curled into a smirk. "Who said anything about clothes."

Valarie slapped his shoulder. "Stop it."

"It was *just* a suggestion." His smirk didn't falter.

"A shit one at that." She scoffed.

Ruel faked hurt, his hand crawling up onto his heart and squeezing the fabric over it. "How *dare* you, Valarie. I had good intentions and was just trying to be nice."

She didn't comment but only laughed back. "Do you happen to have any spare shoes in your car somewhere?"

Ruel thought for a second. "I might—but they'll probably be my footy shoes. Just be warned, they could stink."

Valarie shrugged. "Couldn't be that bad."

He only gave her a side look, shrugging too before walking behind to the boot of his car, opening it and pulling out a pair of running shoes and socks.

"I have clean socks if you want those as well?"

Valarie grinned. "Yeah, I'll take them too if that's alright."

He only nodded back, walking back towards Valarie just as she began taking off her heels. A groan of relief left her lips as she slipped off the shoes. "Fuck—that feels good."

His lips curled as he tried to hide his grin.

Valarie shook her head in laughter. "Shut up."

"I didn't even say anything," he protested, putting his hands up in the air.

As she slipped on one sock over her foot and switched to the other, she felt the hem of her dress lift and quickly caught sight of Ruel holding up parts of her dress so it didn't get dirty.

"You okay?"

"Yeah," he smiled softly. "Do the shoes fit?"

"A little big but they'll do. Thank you." She stared down at her feet.

"No worries."

The two stared at one another for a moment. It was at that moment she wanted to confess her feelings for him. Maybe grab him by his gorgeous face and kiss it all over.

"Let's go," Valarie said instead, the tips of her fingers edging towards Ruel's hand. "I want to climb the crocodile."

Ruel sniggered. "Of course you do."

Valarie rolled her eyes. "Come on, smarty pants." Her hand slipped into his and this time it was *her* stringing him along behind her.

The two walked through the grass area before hitting the large crocodile statue, Valarie's hand dropping from Ruel's as they stood right in front of it, her fingers clutching onto the hem of her dress as she turned to face Ruel.

"I haven't been here for ages," she confessed. "The last time I was here I would have been around eight for an old friend's birthday party."

"I've only been here once as well," said Ruel. "For a holiday up here when we were still living back in Bunbury. My mums drove me up here for the weekend and one of the first things we did was come here."

"It's a pretty cool place, isn't it," she smiled softly, peering up at the large statue.

Ruel didn't reply and instead began walking towards the large man-made crocodile and began climbing onto the head. Valarie pushed herself up to stand on the statue.

"I could never get to the end as a child," her feet began slowly moving up the head and towards the neck. "The spine towards the end always made me slip off or I'd have to climb with my hands and knees. Never been able to climb it just with my two feet."

Ruel's eyes followed Valarie's slowly moving body.

"I've never been good at things like this—as easy as it looks, climbing *anything* was never my forte."

Her feet made it to the middle of the statue, where the largest part of the crocodile was. From there, it got narrower and narrower.

"But anyways," she shook her head, moving closer and closer to the tail, her right hand wobbling against her side as the other held onto her dress, "things have changed and now I'm a grown woman, with better balance than kid-me, meaning..."

She stopped her sentence, her feet on her side as she slowly and carefully made her way down the start of the tail and all the way to the end—her feet touching the very tip of the tail before she jumped off with a smile.

"I can do *that.*"

Ruel grinned as Valarie made her way towards him, her arms confidently wrapping themselves around his waist as she leaned her head against his chest.

"Where do you want to go next?"

His lips curled into a grin.

They sat on a wooden ledge, a rope ladder below them. Valarie's feet were twisted inside the rope and her hands were in her lap, her dress slightly dirty and muddy (especially the hem) from the climbing and running around she and Ruel had been doing.

For the past half an hour the two decided it would be a good idea to play hide and seek. And Valarie thought it would be a great idea to climb down a slide, stopping in the middle before hitting the ground but not too high up where Ruel would be able to find her.

He, of course, did find her.

And when his voice echoed through the blue slide, saying "I've found you!" Valarie yet again thought it would be a good idea to quickly slide herself down to the bottom, her feet catching on the small wooden planks and sand that was supposed to be the comfortable flooring as she tumbled her way onto the floor, her dress tangling her body inside it.

And when Ruel found Valarie, she looked like a human burrito—covered in dirt, sand and wood, with her green dress completely covering her.

That was when they decided to stop.

Valarie's phone was in Ruel's car, but he'd brought his and from the moment they took a break up on top of the ledge he pulled out his phone and laughed at all the messages regarding his whereabouts.

Most of them coming from his mum.

"I'm totally screwed when I get home." He'd just sent off a message to his mum to let him know where he was and that he was okay. He turned to Valarie. "Do you want to message your mum or dad to let them know where you are?"

Valarie shook her head.

"I don't know my dad's phone number." *And he's probably asleep, drunk, again.* "It's okay."

He didn't comment any further. "Thanks for coming tonight."

She smiled. "Like I said earlier Ruel, I'd do anything you ask." Valarie turned her head down, her eyes looking away from his in hope that would stop the blush that was rising on her cheeks.

"Has this been a good date?"

Valarie's eyes flicked up at the sound of his slightly timid tone.

"The perfect date," she swore a small sigh left his lips. "But it's the only date I've ever gone on. And you've set the standard pretty high so I don't think anyone could top it."

"Hide and seek is the way to win your heart, then, I see?" His voice became cocky as if her answer to his question had not only reassured his mind, but his heart too.

"Exactly," she grinned, nudging his shoulder with hers. "Who wouldn't want to play hide and seek in Kings Park at night in an expensive dress after skipping their school ball with the knowledge their asses were not only going to get beat by their parents but the school too?"

Ruel looked amused. "Sounds like the near-perfect date then."

"Near?" She asked in confusion. "Why near perfect?"

Ruel stilled. But with confidence, he moved himself, so he was facing Valarie, their knees scraping one another.

"Because the night isn't over, and I—I haven't done what I've been wanting to do since the moment I met you."

Valarie swallowed as Ruel's hand gently came up to her cheek, cupping the now warm skin. His thumb rubbed at the softness, flicking off a small bit of sand onto the floor.

Her eyes held his.

"I want to thank you."

Valarie's lips parted slightly as she breathed rapidly.

"For agreeing to come here with me, for—for trusting me with your thoughts and feelings. For opening up to me in ways you may not have even realised. I want you to know *I care*. I care so deeply it…" he sucked in a breath, "it hurts to think about what might be causing you stress, or harm."

He moved in even closer, just a tiny bit more, but it was enough to make Valarie's heart skip a beat.

"You're—you're so fucking gorgeous Valarie and you don't even see it," his head shook side to side with passion, "and it *frustrates me.* Everything about you frustrates me because all I want to do is learn about you, all I want to do is support you, but I can't seem to get a read of what you exactly want from me."

She went to speak but he continued.

"Please, just let me—let me finish."

Valarie acknowledged with a nod.

He let out a jittery breath. "I think you like me, and I hope I'm not reading this the wrong way—*god,* I'd never go out into public again if I was wrong but I just… I would just like some reassurances everything's going to be okay. Does that make sense?"

"Perfect sense," she grabbed his hands, holding them tightly. "Thank you for being so open with me. I—I do feel the same Ruel, don't *ever* doubt that. And I'm sorry I've been so jittery and all over the place with my emotions. I've just been dealing with a few things. But I want to tell you about it."

"You don't have to."

"No, I don't," Valarie whispered, a breeze of wind blowing through her hair, sending shivers down her spine. "But I want to. Because I trust you. And I want to show you I trust you."

Neither wavered their eyes from one another.

"Can I show you how much I care for you?"

She saw him physically gulp.

"Please?" She finished.

Valarie swore she heard him whimper. "If you're going to kiss me, do it already because I don't think I can handle much more…"

She slammed her lips onto his. It was a little harsh, a little uncomfortable for the first few moments, but that was to be expected. Valarie had never kissed anyone before—she had no clue what she was doing.

It seemed as though Ruel didn't care. He desperately grabbed onto the back of her neck, pulling her as close as possible to him until her chest was leaning against his. Their lips never stopping.

It was rushed, needy, urgent as if he'd just taken his first breath of air. Breathing her in like a lifeline. Valarie wasn't going to complain. Not with the way her arms had comfortably made their way around his shoulders, hands rubbing down the back of his shirt, soaking up the feeling of his hot skin against her cold hands.

Who knew a back could feel so… attractive.

Eventually, they had to come up for air, and when they did, they didn't spend anytime rethinking or overthinking what had happened—they just went back to it. This time, more smoothly. There was no awkward moment of 'where do I put my tongue' or 'am I doing this right?'

It was just perfect.

Minutes later, the two finally came to a stop. Valarie, with beet-root-coloured cheeks, wiped off a bit of lipstick that had clung to his lips with her thumb. His hands flattened Valarie's hair from where his hands had previously played around in.

"I want you to know, I don't regret my choice to kiss you. And I'm here, stating out loud, at this kids' playground, that I, Valarie Dale, do like, and always *will like* Ruel Diego."

He pretended to be shocked by her statement. "I don't think I believe you. I might need you to prove it."

"Yeah, and what would you like me to do?"

"Oh, I don't know," his rubbed at his chin, his lips holding a cheeky smirk, "I could think of a few things…"

"If you want me to show you my non-existent tits, you can forget about it."

He laughed. "Just shut up." His lips fell onto hers again.

40. ANGER

It had been four days since Valarie Dale and Ruel Diego decided to string their hearts together and call themselves *boyfriend* and *girlfriend.*

They spent another few hours at the park until it was well into the middle of the night. Valarie had fallen asleep against Ruel's shoulder on their long drive home and when he pulled into her driveway around midnight she spent a few minutes kissing him as a thank you for driving her home.

They hadn't seen each other since. Ruel was grounded by his mum the moment he came home but surprisingly, Valarie didn't receive a single bit of backlash for her runaway moment at the ball.

Her father had actually been leaving her alone, which was a nice change to her week.

Ruel had also been banned from going into his uncle's ice cream shop while Valarie was on shift the moment Mr Diego found out the two were officially dating, confessing he was too scared he'd walk into something he wasn't supposed to see.

But now it was the day before school began for the year, and instead of relaxing on her last day of school holidays, she was sitting in front of Miss Turner, her first name as Valarie only found out the other day being Anastasia. Ana for short.

"When you get angry, what's the first thing you think?"

Valarie pulled on her sleeve. "Er, killing someone?"

"It's not a trick question, Valarie." Miss Turner said. "What first comes into your mind when you get angry? Do you think happy thoughts to try and calm yourself down or do you lose all consciousness?"

Valarie licked her lips. "I…I'm just angry. Nothing really happens—or I don't really think I just *do*. My anger just spews out without letting the sensible side of me calm it down first—before doing or saying something I'll regret later on."

Miss Turner nodded in a hum. "So, you just *snap?*"

"Yes."

"And would you say you see *red?*"

"Yeah."

She hummed again.

"That's completely fine, normal even, but what I want you to try when you start to feel that anger bubbling up inside you is to think. Don't let yourself get angry, don't let yourself get emotional. When you start to feel angry, just start to think of something happy, or a good memory, maybe even a person. Just something that will settle your emotions."

Valarie's mind instantly went to her boyfriend. "I've tried that before, but it didn't work."

"Then walk away. As much as it might be difficult to, just *walk away.*"

Valarie was about to comment, but Ana cut her off.

"From our past lessons, Valarie, and the information you've given me about your home life, I believe you do your best to stay alive. And the actions, or reactions you've had is because you've never had a voice in your own home. Living with someone who disregards your feelings and is well, abusive, isn't always the easiest of things to deal with. And that anger you feel is caused because of the environment you've grown up in but also because you *care.*"

Valarie didn't comment, her eyes glancing down to the floor.

"And Valarie, I want you to know that is a *good thing.*" Valarie's eyebrows furrowed, and she looked slowly back up to meet Miss Turner's gaze.

"Your voice, your loud and opinionated voice is *such* a good thing to have in the real world, Valarie. Because if you keep that anger, that confidence you hold, and just get a bit of control over your temper, you could twist it and use it for the better. You could go off into the world and become an activist or public speaker."

Valarie smiled softly.

"And even if you don't do anything with it, if you can keep your loud voice throughout your future relationships and work, you won't let someone like a boss walk all over you. I reckon you could create a job out of it."

"But the only reason why I have issues with anger and feel angry a lot is because of my father, like you mentioned, so why is that a good thing?" Valarie's voice was tense. "Like yes, it's a good thing I'm not afraid to stand up for myself and stuff, but that's not completely true. I didn't stand up for myself when those girls made that account about me."

"Sometimes you don't need to comment," Miss Turner cut in. "Sometimes the best and most mature thing you can do is just ignore it, not give into the anger that you may feel or allow them to see how upset you are because then you're giving in. Giving them a reaction, which is what they want, at the end of the day."

Valarie's mouth dried up. "Okay then, well what about the anger? Like, I wasn't born with it, I learnt it from my father out of all fucking people and the last thing I want to do is become just like him. I don't want to continue the cycle."

Ana smiled softly. "But you're *not* like him Valarie. You're completely different."

"How?" Valarie scoffed under her breath. "I'm *exactly* like him and I fucking hate it."

"Well for starters you don't drink your life problems away or have a victim blaming ideology. You know right from wrong and can take responsibility and apologise when you do or when you say something hurtful and wrong. You can say out loud, with full confidence, that you need help and have taken the next step to get it." Valarie's lips curled. "And you're already better than him. Because you're *not* him. You're mature for your age and independent—and yes, you may be too mature and independent purely because of the environment you were forced into. But there isn't a lot wrong with that. It has its good and bad sides." Miss Turner said tenderly, her eyes boring into Valarie's teary blue ones. "You're not him Valarie, don't ever think you are."

"You're going to make me cry." The two both laughed gently, a hiccup leaving Valarie's lips. "That's—that's sweet. Thank you."

Miss Turner just smiled. "I want to chat with you about a few things you can do to control your anger, but firstly, tell me everything that happened at your ball."

Valarie's ears turned pink.

Only two people knew she and Ruel were dating, and they were her therapist and Ruel's uncle. Maybe she shouldn't have told Miss Turner *everything,* but the excitement Valarie felt when someone asked about her and Ruel with nothing but pure curiosity about their relationship, made Valarie spill the beans.

After her ramble, Ana had three things to say. One, that she was happy that Valarie was happy, and two that she was proud of her for opening herself up and allowing herself to trust Ruel with not only her heart but her body too. But lastly, and it was something that replayed in Valarie's mind on her bus ride home—"Do not let your world revolve around him."

Valarie scoffed under her breath at her comment.

Her life consisted of three things before she met Ruel: food, sleep and an angry father. She lived for nothing—usually waking up to silence, the abuse from last night's dinner still lingering in the air, and then school, just to come home and repeat it all again.

Life was shit. And the only emotions Valarie felt consisted of anger and despair, as she found herself struggling to keep afloat every time she walked through the hallways at school.

And then Ruel Diego came into her life. Without a warning he walked right into her heart and planted himself there for good. All the pain, all the anger just faded when she was with him.

And now they were dating. She had a boyfriend.

Valarie *fucking* Dale, fat depressed girl who always talked shit about high school relationships and had a toxic upbringing was dating a *man*.

So, of course she loved him, of course she clung to him like she was on life support. *That's what love is, isn't it?*

Because without him, she had nothing. She was *nothing*.

Her front door creaked open as Valarie swiftly made her way inside, a drop of sweat falling off her forehead from the summer heat. Two voices whispered harshly against the loud sound of the aircon. Valarie's ears perked up, her eyebrows knitting together as she dropped her shoes off to the side, walking towards the kitchen.

"... it's been nearly four months and now you're asking for things."

"... just some help, you said you would if I ever asked for it and well, now I am."

Valarie peered towards the brown living room couch, her eyes nearly bulging out of her sockets when Cindy Dale came into her view.

When the mother and daughter made eye contact Cindy's voice instantly dropped. She pushed herself up so she was standing facing Valarie.

"Mum?" Valarie hesitated.

"Valarie," her mother sighed, moving around the coffee table in the middle of the room. Though, the small smile Valarie saw on her mother's face disappeared in a near instant and out came a look of anger. "Why the *hell* did I get a call from the school the other day saying you went *missing* from the school ball?"

Valarie's eyes widened as she glanced towards her father, who seemed to be equally as shocked as her. Once the initial shock had subsided her face expressed outrage, her fingers curled into fists.

"It's been a week since the ball, a little late to the party aren't ya?'" Valarie tried to laugh it off, tried to ignore the bubbling emotion of *anger* inside her.

"*Don't* try and joke Valarie. This isn't a laughing matter. Do you understand how much trouble you're going to get into once you're back at school? They have already begun talking about the punishments with me!"

Valarie rolled her eyes. "It's not the biggest deal on the planet Earth, mother."

"Where even did you *go*? Did you go off to do—do *drugs?*"

Valarie gaped, her eyes widening. "You know I don't fuck with that shit."

"Well, lately I don't know much about you at all!"

Silence rang through the house. Valarie's fingers twisted against the couch. She ran her tongue over her teeth, letting out a small scoff just as her father moved so he was standing beside his wife.

"And who's fault's that, huh?" she spat, eyes boring into her mother's. "When was the last time I saw you, talked to you? You just fucked off to wherever you went without a word and now you wanna come in here and start talking about *me*? About *not knowing me*?"

Cindy shook her head heatedly. "You *know* why I left, why I had to go. It wasn't my choice."

"Yeah, because you cheated on Dad. I'm not surprised he kicked you out." Her voice grew louder, the ringing in her ears growing noisier, and for a split second, a glimmer of relief hit her when she caught the eyes of her *sober* father. "What did you expect, Mum?"

"That's none of your business young lady," Cindy cried, anger laced in her tone. "That's between me and your father."

"Well, when you leave your seventeen year old daughter in the hands of an abusive guardian, it tends to affect other people."

She ignored her father's wince against her words.

"Do you even fucking care?" Valarie took a step closer to the couch. "Do you? Because while you were gone, I was stuck with *him*. Cleaning up the mess *you* left me. You act like you care, but you knew exactly what would happen after you left."

"I didn't have a choice!"

"You could have messaged me!" Valarie screamed savagely. "You—you just fucking took off, no explanation, no sympathy, no apologies. But here I am, nearly three months later and the first thing you want from me is an *apology*?"

"You don't know how hard it was for me."

"I don't fucking care, Mum," her voice rang around the room. "Do whatever the fuck you want—leave me, make excuses for why you couldn't have messaged me, checked in on me, *called me*. Blame everyone else but yourself for the fucking mess you made."

"I didn't abuse you," her voice was harsh, hoarse with fury. "I didn't do those things to you—your father did. Don't start getting angry at me because of the way he treated us *both*."

Neither woman cared that he was in the room, neither even made eye contact with him.

"But you were the one who married him, you're the one who stayed."

"I was a victim!" Cindy cried, tears streaming down her face.

"I was a victim too!" Valarie's body launched forward against the couch as she sobbed, her eyes struggling to see through the constant tears that had been furiously running down her cheeks for the past minute. "I—I did *everything* to protect you, I stood up for you, took the mental hits for you and what do you do? Can't even fucking remember my birthday. You know, for the longest time I believed you were perfect, this—this amazing woman who loved me. But in reality, you don't fucking care about anyone but yourself."

Cindy took a step back as if Valarie's words had physically hit her. "I did everything I could to protect you."

"Oh really?" Valarie laughed manically.

Think happy things. Walk away. Don't make it worse.

"Then why did you leave? Why didn't you protect me?"

"I've done a lot of things to protect you Valarie, you just don't know about them."

"Sure." Valarie nodded her head, taking a step back, "Sure you fucking did…"

Matthew took a step forward suddenly, a hand slowly lifting as if he was trying to hold back his wife and daughter. "Let's all just calm down."

"Fuck you!" Valarie laughed boisterously. "Fuck *both* of you actually. Don't you fucking tell me to calm down Matthew and *you* Cindy, don't bother trying to act like you care about me or my life. Don't come storming in here and act as if you've been a caring mother, as if you've been here to witness what's been happening in this house the past months."

"Valarie," Matthew spoke quietly. "You know I'm sorry, I apologised and I'm trying to be better."

"Apologises don't take away the bruises on my neck, Dad," she spat, voice filled with nothing but resentment. "Or the pain you've caused. I don't want your apologies. I want you to fuck off and I want you to take Cindy with you."

"You know I can't do that..."

"Then don't fucking talk to me," she spoke through her teeth.

In and out, in and out.

"Don't speak to me, don't look at me, don't fucking care about me. I don't need *either* of you." *Ruel. Ruel. Ruel.* "My life would be so much fucking better if you didn't exist in it."

Cindy and Matthew both gasped.

"I hope you both rot in hell."

Walk away. If you cannot control your anger and cannot find a way to calm yourself down. Walk away.

Walk away, Valarie.

Her mouth was dry like she'd just eaten a mouthful of sand. Snot was bubbling against her nostrils, her cheeks so red you'd think she'd been standing in the summer sun for the past fifty minutes without sunscreen. The inside of Valarie's palms stung from her sharp nails digging into them from how tight she had been clenching her fists for the last minute.

Silence rung throughout the house but the ringing in Valarie's ears and her heavy breathing was a lot louder.

Walk. Away.

With one more glance between the two shocked and tearful adults, Valarie Dale walked to her room, her heart filled with nothing but anger.

She needed Ruel.

She picked up the phone laying in her pocket and called his number. It rang through once, then twice, and by the third time she began to freak out.

Is he over me? Has he left me? Forgotten I exist? Where is he? Is he with someone else?

The fifth ring passed, and Valarie nearly dropped her phone on the ground from how shaky her hands were, but he finally picked up.

"Hey gorgeous, how are you?"

His voice sounded raspy, like he'd just woken up.

A breath of relief escaped Valarie's lips, her hands tightening around her phone like her life depended on it, holding the speaker up to her ear as closely as she possibly could.

"Nothing," she whispered shakily. "I just need to talk to you."

"Need me?" He teased, and from Valarie's end of the phone she could hear the rustling of movement, the ruffle of bedsheets. "You okay?"

"Need you."

"Hmm," Ruel hummed, his voice smiley. "What do you need?"

"Can I come over?"

"Ah shit, I can't sorry. My mum's grounded me from the car at the moment due to well, y'know, skipping the ball and stuff."

"Oh. Okay."

"But I can stay up and chat, I just need to be quiet." He quickly cut in.

Valarie's lips twitched. "I'd like that."

41. PDA

As Valarie Dale got ready for school, it hit her that this would be the last first day of school for her. There wouldn't be another summer break where Valarie would be counting down the days until school was back on, preparing herself for the inevitable list of assignments and exams and drama she'd have to deal with. There would be no more school checklists for Officeworks or buying of new water bottles as last year's grew mould when it was left at the bottom of her school bag all summer break.

It was a harsh reminder, as Valarie slipped on her trousers and socks, that today was her *last* first day of school. And when the school bell rang for the last time at the start of October, she'd never hear it again.

It was kind of scary in a way—but exciting.

What would she do? Valarie had, of course, thought about all the things she'd love to be when she was older, but whether she'd go to university or not was another question. University was expensive and just more time of her being in a school environment, which was the last thing she wanted.

But first, she needed to figure out what she wanted to do.

One of the first things she could remember being serious about was film directing. It was the only reason why she took the Media class in Year 10. Her teacher back in Year 7 mentioned the idea to her after Valarie confessed she often made short films at home on her iPad.

But then she turned fifteen and hadn't touched her iPad since she was thirteen. And she was grown enough to realise it was very unlikely that a little Perth girl like her would make it to the big Hollywood world.

Plus, she had no desire to go to the USA.

Then came History. When she was first introduced to the class back in Year 10 and learnt all about the Vietnam War, all she wanted to do was learn more.

But then she realised she needed to pass the class to go further with it. Also, there weren't many jobs when it came to History. It was either you teach it, or… don't.

So now she was stuck. As she sat in front of her mirror, applying some mascara, Valarie realised that she was finishing school this year. And she only had about eight months until she was done. Forever.

And just under four months until she turned eighteen.

And in five minutes, Ruel Diego would be arriving to pick her up for school.

Valarie usually wouldn't put anything on her lips or any extra things on her face but today—today Valarie had put on blush, a little bit of contour and an extra blotch of concealer on her face. Just enough where it looked natural but made her face somehow look *better.*

She even went as far as waking up earlier than she normally would, ironing her school clothes which she'd *never* done before and using a roller under her chin and jawline in the hope it would become more defined within an hour.

Her hair was the biggest issue though. Usually, Valarie would just leave it in its wavy way, shoving it up in a bun or something that took nothing longer than ten seconds. But today, she'd put it into a tight ponytail, with her hair at the top frizzing crazily and Valarie nearly burst into tears at the fact her hair wasn't staying down or straight.

She finally managed to get it to calm down.

A honk came from outside her house, and instantly a smile grew on her lips. Valarie rushed outside, grateful neither her mother or father were anywhere to be seen, with her backpack filled with her laptop and a pen on her shoulder, closing the door behind her as her eyes met Ruel Diego's who stood beside his car, a grin on his lips.

She jumped at him, her hands wrapping around his shoulder as her head landed on his chest. He laughed softly, amused and pleased with Valarie's reaction, and didn't waste time wrapping his arms around her waist.

"Hey, gorgeous girl."

"Morning pretty boy."

She leaned up and pressed her lips against his, smiling into the sweet kiss when he swiftly kissed back, his hands tightening around her waist as he pulled her closer.

"You only saw me a few days ago," he chuckled softly when they pulled away. "Missed me that much, huh?"

His teasing tone brought a blush to her cheeks. "Too long ago."

Ruel sniggered, his lips falling onto her forehead and leaving it there for a moment or so. Valarie closed her eyes at the contact.

"Let's go to school, yeah," Valarie groaned and Ruel only smiled in return, his finger touching the top of her nose cheekily. "Oh come on, it won't be that bad."

"And due to your unauthorised departure from such an event, you will both be receiving an after-school detention every day for the next week and gum duty for a month." Valarie and Ruel blinked at the two teachers in front of them. "This is unacceptable behaviour from the two of you! Do you understand how serious this is? Walking out of one of the school's most formal events? We spent a lot of money for you to be able to attend and *this* is how you repay us?"

A hand came onto the older woman's shoulder, from the teacher beside her who looked at the two with a slightly sympathetic look.

"How about," Ruel's head of house, the blue colour, gave a tight smile towards the two teens who sat beside each other in the room. "Let's all take a breather. And just understand, that we come with good intentions. Mrs Baker here was just worried."

Valarie's head of house looked displeased at his kindness but didn't utter another word.

"At the end of the day, Ruel and Valarie, you both know exactly what you did. And you knew it was wrong and shouldn't be surprised at the reaction from not just myself but Mrs Baker. You both should be grateful there isn't suspensions or worst included in these punishments, but luckily because of your clean records this is your first and last warning. Are there any questions?"

"I have work after school most days," Valarie cut in, smiling sheepishly. "Is there any way I could change my punishment for something else?"

Mrs Baker talked up swiftly, "Absolutely not! You should have given that a thought before you went running off like a lunatic."

"Mrs Baker!" Mr Obster gasped in exasperation. "Will you please keep quiet."

The older women just gulped.

"Valarie, there is a possibility that we could change the time of your detentions, but we wouldn't be able to change the punishment as a whole. Would you be able to come earlier to school? Possibly around seven?"

Valarie winced at the time but nodded her head anyway. She couldn't afford to miss work.

"Yeah—that could work."

Ruel's head was turned towards Valarie, a small frown on his lips. "I could talk to my uncle. He wouldn't have an issue with you missing some time."

"It's fine," she shook her head, eyes meeting his. "Honestly."

Ruel shook his head sharply. "But you'd have to get up at like six, five even? That's way too early, especially if you're working until late in the evening, every day. I know you've been struggling to sleep recently."

"Ruel," Valarie smiled, her voice tinted with admiration as she moved her hand to his knee, squeezing it softly. "Thank you for your concern, but I'll be okay."

Ruel's lips squeezed together as he swiftly turned his head to face the two teachers. "It was my fault. I… I practically forced Valarie to come with me, not leaving her a choice. She's completely innocent in the matter."

"As much as I admire your care for you *friend*," Mr Obster spoke, "the two of you were involved and no matter how much you may have 'forced'," he put up two air quotes with his fingers, "Miss Dale here to join you, she still committed the same act as you did which was leaving the school ball without a parent's consent or without explaining to a teacher your reasons why you needed to leave."

Valarie's hand squeezed harder around his knee.

"Now, we all know that you didn't leave because of an emergency or a life-threatening situation, you left because you *wanted to*. And the truth of the matter is that we, the school and staff, have an obligation to all our students which is when put them under our care—we *care* for them." He spoke softly, yet his tone was strong and stern making the inside of Valarie's gut twist with discomfort and guilt. She felt like she was getting into trouble from a caring father. "We have a duty of care when you are put under our supervision and the student's parents put their trust in us. Now imagine if something were to happen to you both, and the backlash not only this school and staff would receive but other parents too. We understand you are teenagers, and at times you enjoy breaking the rules and find them annoying or unneeded, but in the real world, you will face rules that you might not like. And you're going to have to follow them."

The teacher only sighed, fixing up the edge of his glasses before finishing his speech.

"So just keep that in mind next time you think of breaking any rules. Is it really worth it? Breaking a rule just to annoy some teachers and get your parents worried, and in the end, you end up with punishments for your actions."

Valarie's eyes met Ruel's for a moment.

"So, now that's been established. Starting from tomorrow and ending next week on Wednesday, you Valarie will need to be at Mrs Baker's office at seven a.m. sharp for your detention. Ruel, you will need to be at my office when you get out of your last class for the day."

"Actually, sir," Ruel cut in. "Do you think I could join Valarie in the morning detentions? I think it would be better for me too."

The older man curled his lips, looking between the two before nodding his head and sighing. "Sure thing. Just remember, you're arriving at school at seven in the morning."

"I know."

Mr Obster smiled slightly. "Okay then. Great. So, I'll see you both here, at lunch to start your gum duty. Everyone clear on what is expected from them?"

Valarie and Ruel both nodded simultaneously.

"Okay. You both can go off to homeroom now," he smiled, standing up. Valarie and Ruel followed along with his movement. "I'll see you at lunch."

"Bye."

"Thanks."

The two quickly made their way out of the room, heads down as their shoulders brushed beside each other. They walked out the door, picked up their bags that were sitting on the ground and walked down the hallway.

"This sucks." Valarie groaned, her head falling on Ruel's arm.

"But I'd do it again if it meant I got to kiss you."

Valarie smiled softly, her eyes looking up at him as he wrapped his arm around her waist. "I would kiss you right now, but I hate PDA."

"Same."

The two smiled, laughing together as she leaned her head on his chest and hugged him.

"Eww!"

Screams and teasing childish tones came from a group of boys near the end of the hallway, some even whistling at Valarie and Ruel's closeness. Valarie rolled her eyes, moving herself to come beside Ruel instead of in front and faced the Year 8.

No wonder why the voices sounded so high.

"... K–I–S–S–I–N–G ..."

Valarie just threw her middle finger at them.

"Hey!" Ruel playfully slapped Valarie's shoulder. "They're just kids, leave them alone."

"Shitheads more like it," she muttered.

Ruel laughed out loud.

42. UNBELIEVABLE

Valarie was a little late to her homeroom. There was no one to blame but her own selfish needs—she had struggled to walk away from Ruel.

But the last thing Valarie needed was to add time onto the punishments she had already been given, so she swiftly made her way to class.

Once she made it inside, she noticed eyes trailing after her but didn't bother to comment or give attention to the obvious stares. Valarie smiled when Miss Candlewood looked over at her and held out a piece of paper.

"Morning Valarie, here's your timetable for the year." Valarie instantly looked down at the sheet, eyes moving up and down as she took in her subjects. "Glad to see you're still in my class for Biology."

Valarie grinned.

Her subjects consisted of Business General, Human Bio ATAR, Drama General, Math General, English General and Economics General. Valarie was reasonably pleased with her courses and the teachers she had for most of them. It was basically the exact same timetable she had last year just without all the ATAR and History classes.

"I'll see you later then, Miss," Valarie said, looking at the teacher before walking off towards where Harmony, Addison and the rest sat. Brody and Justin were arm wrestling while Layla and Jenny were facing one another, their full attention on each other as they whispered intently. Harmony and Addison were giggling together, about *whatever* they were talking about.

Valarie gulped at the sight.

She brushed down the end of her ponytail, sighing when her finger got caught in her hair before quickly pulling it out. With a boost of confidence, she made her way towards the group of students, some of whom she had called her best friends just a short time ago, and put a smile on her lips as she sat down, ignoring most eyes turning to her.

Valarie lifted her head to meet the eyes of the group before speaking. "Good morning."

Valarie could have sat anywhere else. She could have even asked to go to the toilet and spend the rest of her time there, but she didn't.

She would try her best to be friendly. Because that is what Ruel would want.

"Morning," Addison chirped, seemingly unaware of the awkward silence that hung in the air ever since Valarie decided to enter their space. Or maybe she was aware of it but didn't find it within her to care. Maybe she was doing exactly what Valarie was doing and acting like everything was fine. Be the better person…

Valarie internally laughed at the point. *Addison, being the better person? Yikes.*

"Hi."

"Valarie," Harmony's shy voice came from the other side of Addison, her chair scraping against the carpet to move her seat more on an angle so she could see Valarie completely. "How are you?"

"I'm fine, thanks for asking." Harmony looked down. "What were we talking about?"

She knew she was being annoying. No one likes it when someone uninvited walks into your conversation, but Valarie really couldn't care less. Because yes, she would be the better person—she'd do her best to stay calm and mature. But if she caught Harmony or any of the girls slipping up *on anything,* she wasn't afraid to call them out on it. And on everything else too.

But calmly, of course…

"Er," Harmony began but Addison cut her off.

"Just about Natasha's back-to-school party coming up this Friday after school."

Valarie nodded her head slowly, leaning back on her chair as she brushed down her school shirt. "Cool. I assume you're going?"

Harmony went to speak, but Addison cut her off again.

"Of course," she grinned. "But I don't know if you're invited. Farm animals usually aren't allowed inside."

Okay, fuck being mature.

"Nice to see you're hanging out with your own kind Addison," Valarie sneered. "Cunts and snakes seem to mix well together."

"Fucking pig…"

"Hey, let's just calm down everyone," Layla Whitlock nervously laughed, running a hand down her hair as she looked between the two girls. "No need to be rude or disrespectful."

"Shut up, Layla," Addison's nose twitched. "This has nothing to do with you."

"Well, I think it does," Layla crossed her arms around her chest. "When it involves my friends."

"Friends," Valarie scoffed under her breath, turning to face Layla, whose eyes widened. "What is this *friend* thing you're going on about?"

Layla frowned. "Valarie…"

"Save it." Valarie spat, standing up. "All of you." Her eyes skimmed over the four of them, Jenny included who hadn't muttered a word before moving around her chair, brushing past the teacher where she quickly muttered *bathroom* before walking out completely, bringing her bag along too.

She never should have gone and sat there. What was she thinking, being able to stay calm and mature, when even *looking* at them made her angry. She internally pinched herself, slamming the bathroom door open when she finally arrived and quickly moved herself to stand in front of an empty sink, turning the tap on as she cooled herself down by running the water over her hands and lower arms.

The bathroom door creaked open moments later. Valarie peered up in the mirror to meet the eyes of an awkward Layla. Valarie scoffed again and swiftly turned the tap off, turning around and walking towards the door when Layla quickly stood in front of it.

"What's wrong?"

"What *isn't* wrong?" Valarie spat. "That's the question you should be asking. Now why are you here?"

"I came to check up on you," she spoke softly, stepping away from the door slightly. "Are you okay?"

"Are you?"

"Stop changing the question."

"Well stop fucking bothering me like you care!"

"I do care."

"Don't seem to be doing a very good job at it."

"What's wrong?" Valarie crossed her arms over her chest. Layla let out an irritated puff of air. "Stop being a bloody baby and tell me what's wrong!"

"No one cares!" Valarie cried. "No one fucking cares about me."

Layla took a step forward, her eyes widening in shock. "Valarie," Layla said sympathetically. "I care. I really do."

"As if," she scoffed, wiping away at her red cheeks. "You didn't bother inviting me to the ball, you didn't even come up and ask me how I was. No one messaged me during the summer break or bothered to check up on me. I literally sat in my bedroom rotting away like a dead corpse and none of my so-called *friends* cared. *Especially* after what happened at Harmony's party..."

Layla took a second to respond. "I'm sorry that happened to you. I... I know how shitty you probably feel, especially coming back to school, but I didn't know about it until recently." Valarie's eyebrows shot up. "No—seriously I'm not lying. Me and Jenny left early, probably not long after I saw you take off—by the way, I need to know what happened between you and Ruel that night."

Valarie's lips twitched.

"So, I didn't know what happened, and it wasn't until Ruel got in contact with me that I found out what happened." She gulped. "He was pretty upset, angry to be honest, but I didn't know, truly."

Her head shook from side to side, and she tilted her chin downwards. "And I don't have an excuse as to why I didn't try to contact you, check in on you. So, I'm sorry. I got all caught up at the ball and over the summer break with James... I didn't even think... I didn't think about you."

"I was so lonely." Valarie said. "I... I was dealing with a lot of shit over the Christmas break, and no one cared. I needed a friend and no one but Ruel gave a shit."

"I'm sorry."

"Are you?"

Layla took a second to respond. "Yes, I am."

"Okay."

"I know it doesn't sound believable."

"No, it does. But I just..." Valarie took a breath in. "I need to get my shit together. Because frankly, I don't know what to believe anymore."

And then she walked out.

43. GUM DUTY

Valarie went straight to her first class for the day.

After a long hour of listening to the teacher talk about what was on the year's agenda, she made her way to her Math class and instantly took in a breath of fresh air when her eyes caught onto Ruel's, sitting on a two-seater table at the back of the class. Valarie quickly took the empty spot beside him, ignoring Harmony and Addison who were also in the same class.

"I'm so happy you're here," she mumbled to Ruel as she kissed his cheek when she knew no one was looking before opening up her math book. "I think I'd lose it if you weren't."

Ruel grinned as he leaned back in his seat, rubbing his hands down the front of his shorts. "Miss me that much, gorgeous?"

Valarie's cheeks turned pink. "Yes. And I'm not afraid to admit it."

Ruel smiled, kissing her cheek just like she'd done to him moments ago before leaning back and putting his hand on her knee under the table. "Well, I can admit I missed you too."

"We sound like high school couples."

"That's because we *are* a high school couple."

Valarie rolled her eyes. "Yeah, but like, we sound like those annoying high schoolers who make it *known* they're dating to the whole world."

"What's wrong with that?"

"I used to hate on them. Fucking despised them, and now I'm one of them."

Ruel shrugged, rolling his head to the side to crack his neck. "Oh well, who fucking cares. And anyway, I don't think we're that bad. We barely show PDA and for anyone who might be looking we could just be really close friends."

Valarie just smiled as their teacher began speaking. The two stayed quiet for a few minutes, letting the teacher talk about what was expected of them and all the stupid shit they repeat at the first class of every year.

"Wait—why are you in this class if you're really good at math?" Valarie muttered randomly during the middle of class.

"I don't want to do the exams," his shoulders lifted as he leaned forward and put his elbows on the desk, his head slightly turned towards Valarie but not enough for it to be obvious he was talking and looking at her. "Last year most of my subjects were ATAR and since I dropped out of school halfway through, it was really difficult for me to catch up on all my work and pass the exams—so this year I'm just taking it easy."

Valarie just smiled softly. "Fair. And sorry for changing the subject, but I've got something to tell you ... about what happened this morning..." Her eyes caught sight of Harmony and Addison smiling together, giggling at whatever they found funny. She just sighed and shook her head, turning back to face Ruel.

Valarie told him about everything that happened during homeroom, the chat with Layla in the girl's bathroom and the bitter taste that was left in her mouth afterwards. How Addison had been so rude to her, and Harmony's quietness.

Twenty minutes had gone past, and the teacher had finally stopped talking. A piece of paper was being handed out to all the students. Valarie and Ruel didn't even bother looking at the paper.

"So, what are you going to do about Layla and Jenny? I mean, I'm not sure about Jenny, but Layla, well, I know you were close with her."

Valarie scratched at her head. "Yeah, I know. Well actually, that's the problem, I don't know. My feelings are all so fucked up and I'm all in my head. I don't want to blame Layla or anything because, at the end of the day, she doesn't have an obligation to check in on me and y'know, invite me out and shit but it just—I need her to understand how hurt I am."

Ruel's hand clutched onto her thigh, squeezing in comfort.

"You're allowed to be hurt. She treated you like shit Valarie, don't get it twisted."

"But it's more complex than 'she's wrong I'm right.' I just don't know," Valarie shrugged. "But I won't go too much into it. Because Layla apologised—and at this moment she's the only person who's reaching out to me."

"What about Harmony?"

The two looked over to Harmony and Addison, before looking back to one another.

"She chose her friends. And she chose *her.*" Her eyes caught onto Addison once more.

Ruel frowned. "I never liked Addison. Especially after Harmony's party."

"Well, I did," Valarie puffed out some air. "And I regret it every day, liking her, trusting her. But it doesn't matter anymore. I'm just going to ignore her—and Harmony. No matter how much it hurts, I'm just going to leave the whole situation alone. We have one more year. Literally, like six months until we leave school and then I'll be out, away from everyone."

Ruel smiled.

"And anyways, no one seems to be talking about the account about me anymore, so that's one less thing I need to worry about."

Ruel frowned slightly, his head leaning on the palm of his hand as he looked Valarie in the eye. "Just because no one is talking about it doesn't mean it won't hurt. And I can see it—every time you talk or think about it you get this small crease on your forehead and your shoulders slump as if all the words people said about you are running through your mind."

Valarie's shoulders slumped.

"But they're not correct, you know that, right?" Valarie gulped, looking down at her lap. Ruel's hand returned to her thigh. "You know that, right?"

"Well, it's kind of true…" she said, and Ruel's lips curled tightly. "I mean, like obviously I'm not an animal or anything but I am… *big.*"

"That doesn't matter," Ruel shook his head instantly, his voice stern. "I couldn't fucking care if you're the skinniest person alive or biggest. Nothing about that matters. Valarie, I like you for *you.*"

"But it matters," Valarie shrugged nonchalantly. "To me anyways. You know I… I've struggled with my weight for years. And never been able to do anything about it because everything I've tried always failed. Ruel, you cannot say the first thing you didn't notice about me was the size of my stomach."

"I didn't." He said immediately, "Honestly. Look at me, Valarie."

And she did, hesitantly, but she did. "The first thing I noticed about you was the colour of your eyes. And then the freckles on your face, and then the shape of your lips. Then, when you got closer, I could see the curls in your hair and *then* your body. But I didn't care—not one bit." His voice was stern. "Valarie, think back to the first time we met, in that science room. I know you noticed me, and I know you were looking at me. So, think back and see if you saw me *once* look at you in disgust or however you may fear I could have looked at you."

Valarie just stared at him, silence lingering between the two for some time as Ruel's lips slowly curled into a smile. The longer she stayed silent, the more Ruel smiled.

"I ... I can't."

"Exactly," Ruel nodded, beaming. "You know why? Because every second that passed with my eyes on you, the prettier you got. And to this day, every time I look at you my heart skips a beat from how gorgeous you are."

"You're going to make me cry in class."

"Well don't," his thumb rubbed under her cheek for a split moment before pulling away. "I'm proud of you, for today, this morning. That you were able to stand up for yourself and also *trust* Layla to open up to her slightly. You did the right thing, Valarie. And they don't deserve you. Remember that."

He was proud.

Proud.

When recess came around, Valarie decided to sit with Layla and Jennifer. Jennifer took the time to apologise. It was similar to Layla's apology earlier that day. With the confidence from the two being sincere in their apologies and the comforting smile from Ruel, Valarie opened up to both Layla and Jennifer about their relationship.

Once recess was over, Valarie made her way to Business class, hand in hand with Ruel and Layla beside them, while Jenny went off to her Accounting ATAR class. Oliver was in that class too and Valarie rolled her eyes when he muttered *pig* when she walked past him.

Next was Economics, which she spent alone as none of her friends were in it either. The moment the bell rang to indicate the lunch break had started, she quickly rushed to the office, picking out some rubber gloves and taking a scraper from where Mr Obster had shown her it was located.

Ruel arrived about two minutes later, a frown on his lips as he picked up some gloves but not before kissing her on the cheek when he knew no one was looking. A groan left his lips when a teacher walked into the room and informed the two that they would be spending their time inside the science building, picking out gum from the lockers.

With their eyes down, and embarrassment ticking away in Valarie's brain, the two walked through the halls to get to their location, brushing past familiar and non-familiar faces until they finally made it inside. She was grateful that no one was allowed to sit inside it during lunch so they could pick at gum in peace.

"Well, this is romantic," Ruel sniggered from beside Valarie, putting down his empty box designed for gum pieces to be put into. "Don't you think?"

"Yeah, *super* romantic," Valarie grinned slyly, turning to face Ruel as she held up her spatula with a large piece of green gum sitting on top. She waved it in front of his face, and he swatted his hands at her as he took a step back. "Doesn't this turn you on?"

He licked his lips, smiling when she began laughing. "Totally— you picking up gum is making me want to do unholy things to you."

She shoved his shoulders playfully. "Don't be gross."

"It's the truth, nothing gross about it."

Valarie just continued to giggle, bending down slightly as she continued picking at another piece of gum.

"How many are we supposed to get before we can go to lunch?"

"I think it's more of a time limit," Valarie shrugged, moving to another open locker. "So technically we could sit here and make out instead of picking up gum. But if we go back with an empty box, I reckon we'll get into huge shit."

"How about we just drop out?" Ruel dropped his things, putting an elbow on a locker floor and facing Valarie who was still bent over picking at a piece of gum. "Y'know, be the next Bonnie and Clyde and run away together."

Valarie paused her movement but did not lift her head or move her body. "They killed like fifteen people or some shit?"

"I could name fifteen people I want to murder."

Valarie just chuckled, shaking her head as she leaned up, turning her body to face him. "I'd rather not go to prison for the rest of my life, thanks."

Ruel just shrugged, crossing a foot over the other. "Jail couldn't be worse than this place, surely."

"I think it would be," Valarie laughed in slight shock from his comment. "Dressed up in fucking orange all the time and sleeping in the same room as paedos and shit—no thanks."

"You'd probably look hot in a jumpsuit," Ruel grinned.

Valarie rolled her eyes but struggled to hide her smile. "Maybe we could roll play it one day."

"Just—go pick some gum," Valarie cut him off, glaring at him while he just laughed. "Make yourself useful, before you get us into trouble."

Ruel just grinned.

Valarie struggled to calm her erratic heart.

44. HARMONY DAVIS

The rest of the week went by fine.

Valarie spent her time as far away as she could from Harmony and Addison, but that wasn't too difficult as Layla and Jennifer spent their time with her which provided a nice and good distraction from the ever-lasting problem of the fact that her once best friends had now decided Natasha and her friends were the perfect people to be hanging with.

Ruel also helped—a lot. He changed his detention times to be alongside her every early morning, picked her up for school and dropped her home, along with gum duty. And though the detention and gum duty sucked, Valarie was grateful she was doing it with him and as time went on, she generally didn't mind doing gum duty or having detention as it gave her a free pass to be alone with him. She even at times got excited for it.

Over the week Valarie felt the happiest she'd been in a while. It surprised her that out of all the places and times in the world she'd felt the happiest, it would be at school—but chatting with Layla and Jennifer during recess and class times with Ruel usually beside her was just *nice*. It was perfect.

Friday came around, and her last class was English. She made her way out of the classroom, picking up her bag from outside and stuffing her pen and old laptop within the large pocket before she made her way towards the carpark. It was an unwritten rule, that most Year 12s parked in a certain sport.

She leaned her back against his car door once she reached his car, eyes pondering and gazing at the stairs where Ruel Diego would always come down, to only swiftly look away when she saw Natasha, Oliver, Harmony and Addison walking down the steps.

And suddenly the road became really interesting and intriguing.

She could hear their loud laughs, and it was like an alarm waking you up from your fantasy. They were loud, louder than most and it seemed they didn't care either.

Valarie peered up, holding her head low and trying her best to seem like she was still looking at the ground instead of the four people. She looked at them all, but they seemed to linger on Harmony Davis more than anyone. Valarie watched Harmony's twenty-five year old boyfriend Connor push himself out of his car and pull Harmony into a daring kiss. Once they pulled apart, Harmony pulled Natasha into a side hug, a grin on her bright red lips. Valarie's throat seemed to tighten, and she felt her stomach twist and turn at the sight.

It isn't your life. It isn't your problem. Don't worry about it.

Valarie breathed out, forcing her eyes to move away from the group before she threw up, to only make eye contact with Ruel Diego, his lip curled in a grin. As he got closer to Valarie, he began frowning.

"You okay?" His voice murmured, the back of his hand coming up to gently touch her forehead once he stood in front of her. "You don't look too well."

Valarie gulped. She let out a shaky breath as her eyes flickered to Harmony for just a second before looking back at her boyfriend.

"Yeah. Fine."

Ruel sighed, turning to look behind him as he quickly caught sight of exactly what Valarie was looking at. He sighed once more, his hands coming up to wrap around her shoulders and softly pulled her into his chest. Valarie didn't hesitate to make herself comfortable within his arms and let her shoulders slump against him.

"Don't worry about them, Valarie," he muttered in her ear.

"I don't care about them. I care about *Harmony.*"

Ruel moved his head, so he was looking down at the girl in his arms. "What about Harmony?"

"Her new boyfriend. It's—it's wrong." Valarie gulped. "Like—I know she's an adult and all, but it's just weird."

Ruel didn't say anything back but instead moved Valarie to the side so he could open the car door, slowly nudging Valarie inside, with her complying instantly. Ruel quickly rushed around the other side, pulling himself into the driver's side and starting up the car.

"Let's go talk somewhere a little more private."

Valarie smiled at his comment, but she still shook her head. "I can't, I have work."

"Not anymore."

She huffed as he pulled out of the parking spot. "I can't, Alan needs me."

"He'll be fine," he promised, making Valarie tug on her sleeve. *"Trust me,* that man has been alone in that shop for the past fifteen years. He'll be perfectly fine."

"Okay… but if I get into trouble, I'm blaming you."

"You do that."

Valarie just leaned her head back against the car seat.

And close to fifteen minutes later, after Valarie had messaged Ruel's uncle she was unable to come into work that day, his car was parked on top of a small up-hill sand dune, the boot of the car facing the ocean. Valarie looked around from where she stood outside just beside the car, and there was no one in sight.

"Where did you find this place?"

"I used to go dirt biking with my mum whenever we took trips up here. And I found this spot." He shrugged as he laid out a blanket in the large boot space, where he had pushed down the back seats. "Hop in."

Valarie smiled softly, pushing herself into the car from behind and sitting on the edge, her feet dangling off the edge. Ruel quickly took the empty spot beside her.

"Now talk—about your thoughts and feelings."

"We'd be here until Christmas if I said everything."

"Then I guess we'll be spending Christmas together."

His little cheeky grin made Valarie's heart flutter and she quickly moved her eyes away from him and towards the open sea before she leaned in and kissed the daylights out of him.

"It's Harmony. I can't stop thinking about her."

"Do I have some competition?"

Valarie snorted rather unattractively, but she couldn't find it within herself to care. "Funny. Real funny, Ruel."

"I know, it's my best personality trait."

"That and being an annoying dickhead."

Ruel smirked. "You love me."

"Possibly."

The two fell into silence for a moment before Ruel spoke up again. "Sorry, I'll stop fucking around now, continue."

Valarie licked her lips. "Well basically—you know I've known Harmony for ages, right?" He nodded his head. "And so, since I've known her for ages, I've also been there through *everything*. As in every breakup. And she's had a few."

Ruel stayed silent as Valarie puffed out a bit of air, manoeuvring herself so she was turned slightly towards Ruel.

"Now—listen, I might sound like a bitch when I say this, but it's just how I feel and how I interpret everything okay? So please, don't judge, just let me explain."

Ruel just nodded, giving a comforting smile while Valarie took another deep breath.

"She's an attention seeker. A big fucking attention seeker who does and will do anything for a man's attention. And I know it's mean to say but it's just the truth. Harmony is a beautiful girl with a heart of gold but as the years have gone on, she's become... *more desperate.* Every year, sometimes multiple times in a year she'll have a new boyfriend. It's like she can't live without one. At the start, in Year 7, I didn't think much of it because she was a pretty girl, you know, and so of course she was going to get people's attention, but as the years went on it just kind of got out of hand."

She let out a breath of air as she wrapped her arms around herself.

"Every time she had a boyfriend, she's always chosen them over me. And she never listened to me either. She's a good friend, or—or *was,* but she cared for me, I know she did. But every boyfriend she's had hasn't been nice, or good for her. I tried my best to support her and did my best by just being a good friend but as the years went on her, boyfriends got worse." Her head tilted down slightly. "And the longer they stayed the worse she became, and it's been like this for her whole high school life. She'd get a boyfriend, say she loved him and he was the one, while he was either secretly cheating on her or treating her like shit. And me being me, I tried to warn her, *every single time* she had a boyfriend I would always say *'I don't trust them'* or *'They're not good for you'* but she never fucking listened and would just tell me I was wrong."

Valarie gulped.

"And of course, in the end when the guy finally broke up with her because she'd *never* break up with them, she'd come running back to me after leaving me in the dust for however long they were dating, with tears in her eyes and a broken heart. And me being me, I would always take her back, just for the cycle to repeat again and again."

"That's toxic," Ruel mumbled.

"I know. But you see, Harmony was my first friend. I know it sounds kind of weird but back in primary school I had *no one.* All the students *hated* my guts. The bullying got pretty bad, and no one cared. So, when I moved schools for high school and Harmony came up to me, back when she had braces and always had a smile on her face, and introduced herself to me, it—it meant a lot."

Ruel smiled sympathetically.

"I wasn't seen as a human for most of my childhood. I was seen more as a piece of fat or something to tease. So, when Harmony came up to me, on the first day of Year 7 and promised me she'd be my best friend for life, I was finally seen as a human being. Ever since then, I've struggled to move away from her, even though I know she's difficult and toxic and probably not your perfect definition of a friend, but she was *my* best friend. She was the first person to treat me with kindness and it's something I'll never forget."

She wiped under her eyes, rubbing away the tears that were beginning to show.

"I love her Ruel, as much as she can be a pain in my ass, I love her, and I *understand her.* I get why she shows off her body trying to gain attention whether it be good or bad, I understand why she feels the need to always be in a relationship or fall in love every time a boy shows her the tiniest bit of attention. I get it because I *understand her.* I know her, I've witnessed her highs and lows, and I could tell you what she's thinking just by looking at her. She's my best friend. My best friend who at times treated me like shit and always chose me last, but she was still my friend."

Ruel rubbed his hand over her thigh in comfort.

"But it's just—as the years went by it got worse. And worse, to the point that she was taking people back who had cheated on her, and she *knew* about it. She'd let her boyfriend talk shit about me right in front of my face. And anytime I asked her to do something her first response would always be *'Can my boyfriend join?'"*

She let out a puff of air.

"I stayed because not only did I care about her, but because I thought—I thought as she got older, she'd change. She'd become more mature and realise that how she was treating me wasn't okay and that the relationships she was getting into weren't healthy. But she never did. It only got worse, especially when Addison started getting close to her at the end of Year 10. Addison, before Year 11, didn't often involve herself with Harmony or us. She was usually with the popular girls. But recently, she's been getting close with Harmony and let me tell you, she hasn't helped one bit. I actually think she made Harmony worse."

"I could be wrong. But ever since Addison kind of joined the group and started hanging with us Harmony has become… more obsessed. She's started talking about boys even *more* and now— now she's dating this twenty-five year old or something and Harmony's never gone for someone that old."

Valarie huffed. "I don't know Ruel. I'm just worried about her because she keeps putting herself into these relationships and though I don't know much about *this* relationship it seems no matter what she does she always finds herself in a toxic one. And I'm just scared that one day she gets into a *really* toxic relationship."

"Like—like domestic violence?" He was hesitant to ask, but when Valarie nodded her head reluctantly, he let out a sigh.

"Fuck. That's heavy."

"I know!" Valarie explained. "But how could I not think that? After everything I've seen her ex-boyfriends say and do, it's the path she seems to be going down and I'm *really* worried about her. But now she won't even talk to me, and every time I've seen her Addison is near and I just get so angry too, every time I look at her, I think back to what she's done and how she's treated me. I just—I don't know what to do."

"If she does get into a situation where she is in a toxic environment like that, it isn't your fault. I want you to know that."

"But if I knew how she was, maybe I could stop it, inform her."

"Yes," Ruel cut in. "But has that worked in the past? Have you told her how you feel about the relationships she's been in? Valarie, if anything happens to her, you're not at fault."

"I want to help. I want to protect her, and I want to be there for her but she just—she won't listen and I'm so tired of her treating me like shit." She shook her head, "I could be wrong, and maybe I am, maybe I'm overreacting and seeing this shit all wrong but I just—I don't know anymore."

"You cannot help someone who doesn't want to be saved."

Valarie breathed out a shaky breath. "Fuck. This was deep. Sorry for just dropping this on you."

Ruel smiled softly. "I'm glad you told me. It seems you've kept this to yourself for ages."

"I have," she nodded shyly. "But I just—I feel like a shit person for not doing more, but I just don't know what to do either, you know?"

"I get it."

Valarie leaned her head against the side of the car, pulling her knees to her chest. "Let's change the subject, shall we? Like, should we go to this party tonight?"

Ruel raised his eyebrows, giving her a *'really?'* look. Valarie just laughed slightly in return.

"Yeah, good answer."

"I'd rather jump off this hill into the ocean and drown than go to that party."

"A bit dramatic."

"Am I wrong though?"

"Not really."

The two sniggered, and when Ruel wrapped his arm around her shoulders and pulled her into his side, kissing the top of her forehead, she felt the weight lift off her shoulders, especially when he muttered, "I'm proud of you Valarie. For opening up to me and trusting me enough with how you've been feeling recently."

Valarie struggled to hide her blush, but inside her heart and mind, she was also proud—proud of herself for opening up to Ruel, to allow him to know her thought process and feelings on a situation she'd been handling alone for the past six years.

45. WHAT HAPPENED TO YOU?

The moon was shining against the ocean. *Beautiful,* Valarie thought, with her head twisted sideways as she laid on Ruel Diego's clothed chest. It wasn't the most comfortable position for the two of them, with his back bent and leant against his car boot, legs spread outwards and the end of his ankles hanging off the edge. While the girl of his dreams lay against his chest.

It had been a few hours since school finished, and Valarie knew her father was probably curious as to where she was. *If he's even noticed I'm gone, that is.* But unless the world came to an end, Valarie wasn't leaving. She didn't want to.

"What's going on up in that pretty head of yours, hmm?"

His fingers ran softly through her hair, tapping his index finger against her forehead. Her eyes tore away from the sea in front, staring up at the boy who was already looking at her.

"Nothing really."

He hummed again. But secretly, he wished to ask something else.

What happened to you?

Ruel was aware of his girlfriend's troubles. Maybe not all, maybe not even some—but he knew something was going on. And though the past few weeks had been perfect, better than perfect he'd argue—there was always the underlying thought of *what happened?*

Like a pair of sunglasses, Ruel had put shades over his eyes and ignored the many pondering questions he had for her. And the anger he once felt for her over Christmas, as for a moment he thought *he'd* done something wrong, had disappeared the moment he saw her again.

What did you go through during the summer break?

Why are your eyes dimmer than usual?

Why do you always cover up your body, and why was the ball the first time I saw anything below your neckline.

What are you feeling?

Why'd you disappear for months?

He was scared. Truthfully, he was fucking frightened to ask. And not because of her reaction, but because of the answers she might give. But he needed to know. He needed to know more about her.

"Would it be okay if I ask a question?"

"Depends on the question." She let out an airy laugh. But all Ruel did was gulp.

"What happened... over summer break." He felt her tense up within his arms, and subconsciously, he tightened his hold around her, scared that she'd run away. Again. "Why did you just... *disappear.*"

They sat in silence for a while. Realistically it was only a few seconds, but for him it felt like an eternity, as his mind was running at a million miles an hour.

Fuck... I fucked up. I shouldn't have asked. I should have left it.

"I... I was just struggling mentally over the break."

Valarie's therapist would be so proud.

"Do you mind explaining more?" When he didn't get a response, his hands began rubbing up and down the side of her arms, and softly he whispered out into the night. "You don't have to if you don't want to. It's just, I want to help."

Valarie shrugged as if trying to show she didn't care about his question. But she knew she was lying, and it seemed Ruel did too. But he didn't push it, nor her, and for that reason, she sat up, curling her arms around her legs and pushed herself to the side of the car, trying to ignore the small patch of skin that had been revealed from where his shirt had rolled up his body.

She gulped.

"I just was really lonely and yes, I know you tried to call and get in touch with me but—I don't know how to explain it. It's just, y'know when you want to do something but you're not in the mood, like your body is so exhausted and you cannot find it within yourself to do it?"

He hummed softly, his eyes staying on hers while his fingers gently traced up and down her thigh for comfort.

She sighed, pushing her hair back against her ear. "That was me. The whole break. I was depressed. That's the easiest way to explain it. I just fell into this deep hole where I had no clue how to get out. I didn't eat, I just slept all day. There were times I didn't leave the house for days because I just didn't want to.

"To be honest Ruel, the summer break is kind of blurry for me, like I remember parts of it, but I couldn't tell you what I did. It's like it just blanked from my mind and now—now I'm here." Valarie smiled softly. "With you, and I've never felt happier. *You saved me,* and now I can leave everything else in the past."

He got lost in her eyes, drunk off her affection—but she never answered the question, and the millions more Ruel wish to asked.

What really happened to you?

46. YOU'RE CRAZY!

Valarie Dale didn't know what to think.

When she opened her heart up to Ruel Diego on Friday night, in the back of his car with his hands on her body as he listened to every word she spoke—she was frightened. Mainly at his reaction, at what he'd think of her or judge her for. But it ended on a high note, because she was confident that he truly did care.

He understood and it was really all she ever wanted.

As scary as it was, his caring reaction nearly made her spill *everything*. And she meant *everything*. From the bullying in primary school, to the abuse she'd faced at home—she wanted to let him in on every little detail of her life.

And it fucking terrified her.

But she knew, by the time the sun had set, that it would have to wait another day.

That night, just as she was about to go to bed, a message popped up from her Instagram page. Valarie had only recently jumped back onto the social media app, now knowing after being at school for the past four days that everyone had seemingly moved on from everything that had happened last year to something different.

Comfortably, Valarie opened the notification only to find a direct message from Natasha Campbell that made her heart stop for a moment. It was a picture of her and Ruel at the school ball, with the word "pig" written over her face.

It made Valarie backtrack for a moment, and her palms began to sweat, but she didn't hesitate to write a response.

"Say it to my face, bitch."

It made her a little smug when Natasha didn't respond for a moment, leaving her on 'read' for a few minutes until another message was sent. This time, it was a written paragraph.

"He'll never love you. You know that right?"

Valarie gulped.

"You don't deserve him, and never will. Watch out Valarie Dale, because when the day comes where you realise Ruel is faking it, I'll be right there filming it."

The words shouldn't have stung. But they did, and Valarie hated herself for it.

Her thoughts went haywire. Her insecurities suddenly gained a mind of their own, filling her head with thoughts.

Does he really like you though?

Is this a joke someone's put him up too?

Am I pretty enough? Good enough?

Valarie wasn't sure what to do anymore. Wasn't sure what or who to believe. But after Friday night, she couldn't deny the fact she had major feelings for Ruel. And she really hoped he wasn't faking his.

He was three minutes late.

It was a miracle Valarie hadn't lost her head by the time four minutes went past—Ruel always arrived on time, in fact usually, he was early. So why now? After bailing on taking her to and from work on Saturday, without a proper explanation and no further communication, he was now late to pick her up for school.

Have I done something wrong?

She looked down at her outfit, wondering if maybe the issue was how she had dressed, before realising he didn't even know what she was wearing today, so how could it be that. So, then her mind went to *her.*

Have I said something?

The last time she saw him, it was Friday evening, and now it was Monday. She chatted with him for about three minutes on Saturday but that was it.

Ten minutes later, he finally rolled into her driveway, and instantly she took a seat beside him.

"Hey gorgeous." He quickly swooped down to plant a quick kiss on her cheek, rolling onto the road to begin their journey to school a moment later.

"Hey," she said quietly, running her hands over her stomach anxiously. "How are you?"

"Great, yeah," said Ruel.

The silence that fell over the two of them caused Valarie's mind to go haywire.

She wanted to ask what was wrong. What she'd done, and how she could fix it. But before she could ask, the music from the radio got louder.

"I love this song!" Ruel said suddenly, smiling as he nodded along to the music.

Valarie just smiled timidly back, pretending to enjoy it too.

"You alright? You've been quiet all day?"

It was lunchtime. Valarie's eyes hadn't wavered from where her food lay out in front of her. Layla Whitlock had asked the question, one Valarie knew she'd been wanting to ask all day but hadn't.

She'd been unusually quiet, and she knew it. When the two rocked up to school Ruel didn't notice any off behaviour, and it wasn't until she didn't hug him back like she usually would that he began to ask questions.

But she tensed at his curiosity, and that confidence from a few days ago about wanting to spill every thought and memory to him, disappeared in an instant.

She put walls up around herself and hadn't really talked for the rest of the day.

"Hmm." She hummed in response to Layla's question. And Ruel—*oh, Ruel*—the whole time he hadn't pushed her, hadn't cornered her to open up, he had just been beside her.

He'd just understood she needed time.

She didn't deserve him.

A shaky breath left her lips. Gulping she suddenly stood up, saying, "I'll be back," before walking off to the women's bathroom.

She needed a moment to herself. She needed to get her thoughts together because it wasn't fair. It wasn't fair that the stupid fucking words Natasha had written to her on Saturday were still affecting her.

It wasn't fair that she was becoming insecure in her relationship with Ruel all because he didn't talk to her over the weekend.

Valarie needed to get her shit together. Quickly.

The bathroom was packed, of course. Valarie wasn't too surprised—it was very rare for not a single person to be inside. Mainly because it guaranteed privacy from teachers.

Valarie didn't bother muttering apologies when she knocked into a few girls who had taken over the majority of the walkway.

She was too busy in her own head to even be able to create a sentence. Quickly, she made her way to the end of the hall, where another set of mirrors and sinks lay—but she stopped in her tracks when she was met with the sight of Natasha and Addison, shoulder to shoulder laughing at something on their phones.

Giggles erupted from the two blondes, but all it did was cause a bubble of rage to settle within Valarie's stomach.

Rage at the fact Natasha could say such mean words to her online and didn't care about the aftermath. Rage that she *trusted* Addison and thought they were friends just to find she'd been getting close to Natasha the whole time.

But most of all, she was enraged at herself.

Doing her best to follow the anger management steps her therapist had been running through with her, she went to turn around and ignore the two girls, but she stilled in her path when Natasha shouted the word '*pig*'.

Valarie clenched her fist, shaking her head for a moment before continuing.

"Yeah, that's right. Walk away cunt." Valarie could hear Addison laugh from beside Natasha. "You don't deserve him!"

That made Valarie snap around to face Natasha, who grinned devilishly.

"Come on Valarie, you can't think Ruel will ever love you back? It's ridiculous watching you think that."

"Piss off, Natasha," Valarie muttered. "Seriously, I don't need your shit today."

"I'm just trying to help," Natasha shrugged, shoulders knocking into Addison as a small giggle slipped between her lips. "Someone's gotta be truthful."

"Well, I appreciate your concern but it's highly un-needed. As in not needed at all."

Just as Valarie went to walk away Natasha spoke up once more. "Valarie," she took a few steps towards her. "I know you're really struggling right now, but know I am really trying to help."

"Struggling to walk, the fat cunt." Addison muttered under her breath causing the pout Natasha was wearing to turn into a smile as she laughed at Addison's comment.

Valarie just rolled her eyes, ignoring them both and beginning to walk away once more. But just as she went to step around the corner, a loud *slap* sound came from down the hall.

Valarie swiftly looked behind her and saw that Addison had *slapped* Natasha right on her cheek. The force was so strong the skin was already turning red.

"Oh my God!" Valarie stopped herself short as she quickly made her way over to the two girls. "Addison, what the fuck?"

"Why did you slap her, Valarie?" Addison suddenly cried out, her face all squeezed together as if she was crying.

But she wasn't.

"Why would you do that?" A crowd began forming around the three, whispers and gasps coming from all directions.

"I—*what*?"

"You're crazy, Valarie! Fucking crazy! Someone get this girl *away* from me." Addison pulled Natasha into her chest, comforting her as she backed away from Valarie.

Moments later, a teacher, Miss Brown, had appeared beside Valarie, taking one good look at her and the situation before grabbing at Valarie's arm. "Come on, I'm taking you to your head of house."

"Wait—but..."

Miss Brown didn't let her speak, only shoving her through the crowd and outside. Valarie noticed though, as she was physically removed from the situation, that students had begun consulting with the two girls, as well as a teacher who had followed suit, all checking in on them both.

"Miss you don't understand..."

"Oh, I understand *perfectly.*" Miss Brown sneered, knocking on Mrs Baker's door. "And I'll make sure they do too."

The moment both were allowed in, the teacher, without even letting Valarie get a single word out had begun speaking.

"Sorry to disturb you on your lunch break, but there has been an incident in the women's bathrooms. Valarie has physically assaulted another girl."

At the explanation, Mrs Baker's dropped her sandwich onto her desk. Instantly, she stood up and ordered Valarie to take a seat.

"Who was it?"

"Natasha Campbell." The teacher replied coolly. "A lovely girl she is. And her friend Addison witnessed it all."

Valarie gaped.

"Well then," Mrs Baker nodded. "Thank you for bringing this to my attention and bringing Valarie here. If you could please make sure Natasha makes her way to first aid and send Addison to my office. It would be highly appreciated."

The teacher nodded before walking off, closing the door behind her.

As innocent as Valarie knew she was, she had a *real* bad feeling as she sat across from her head of house. Her palms were sweaty and she wouldn't be surprised if sweat was dripping down her face too. Her eyes were wide with shock and her lips were dry.

"Mrs Baker, I..."

"Valarie," Mrs Baker cut in. "What in the god's name are you doing? First, you have your little runaway moment during the school ball and now *this*? I've never had any issues with you in the past. What is happening?"

"This is all a big misunderstanding. I didn't physically assault anyone! Addison was the one…" And as if she was answering her name being called, Addison suddenly walked into the office. She crossed her arms over her chest as she stood in the corner of the room.

"Addison," her head of house acknowledged. "Please take a seat."

Addison shook her head. "I'd rather not sit next to her… if that's okay?"

Oh, she really does know how to act, doesn't she?

Valarie rolled her eyes, and unfortunately for her Mrs Baker caught sight of it.

"I understand. Addison if you could explain to me what happened, from the beginning."

Addison nodded her head, putting on a frightened face before starting. "Well, me and Natasha were innocently minding our business in the bathroom when Valarie came up to us and started going on this massive rage rant about how mean we were being to her and saying *awful,* just *awful* things."

Mrs Baker began writing her words down.

"And then, Natasha being Natasha, kind as always, defended me—stuck up for me you know, and then suddenly," she sniffled, "suddenly Valarie just slapped her. *Oh,* it was *horrible."*

Addison sniffled once more. "It should have been me you know, I—Natasha wasn't doing anything wrong," she sighed. "And well, afterwards, luckily Valarie was pulled away from us because I was frightened she'd harm me or do something even worse."

Mrs Baker dipped her head. "I'm sorry this has happened to you Addison. I appreciate your honesty and wiliness to open up to me. I understand you might be frightened, but know we take these matters *very* seriously and there will be consequences."

Valarie finally picked her jaw off the floor and managed to get some words out of her mouth. "That's bullshit."

"Young lady," Mrs Baker snapped, causing Valarie to nearly whimper. "Enough." She turned back to Addison. "If you don't mind dear, could you please fill out an incident report in the other room while I chat further with Valarie?"

Addison nodded, sniffling once more before grabbing the items handed to her by Mrs Baker and walking off, leaving Valarie and her head of house alone.

And it finally hit Valarie. As she stared back at Mrs Baker, whose eyes were narrowed in on her, that no matter what she said or did, they wouldn't believe her.

No one would.

47. BELIEVE ME

It had been three days since Valarie Dale got expelled.

That same lunch she 'assaulted' Natasha, Mrs Baker had explained the consequences of physically assaulting another student, and that she was left with no choice but to expel her.

It was actually an easy process, surprisingly enough. They got all the written and physical evidence they needed, which wasn't hard as Addison had written a very *detailed* incident report and they had seen the very obvious bruise on Natasha's cheek. Mrs Baker quickly pulled the deputy of students aside, they sat in their office for about five minutes and then Valarie was informed she was no longer a student.

Her mother was called, but unsurprisingly, she didn't pick up, and then her father.

Valarie was more scared about seeing her father than getting expelled.

By the time everything had wrapped up, Valarie was off and didn't even get to say goodbye. Because she didn't have a locker, purely because she didn't need one, there was nothing to pick up. Just like that, she had finished high school.

The whole car ride home her father didn't say said a word, shockingly enough, and much to Valarie's pleasure. But she knew he'd question her, and the time came the moment they were behind closed doors.

She did her best to explain the situation and felt grateful she was able to get more than five words out, but she knew he didn't believe her. Even though he didn't outright say it.

It was then he said he was going to organise a meeting with himself, her and Miss Turner in the next couple of days to discuss options moving forward.

As if Miss Turner was her mother or something.

Which left Valarie to deal with... everything else.

"So that's what happened." Valarie finished, her eyes trained on Ruel Diego's face, waiting to watch the discomfort and confusion he originally came in with disappear. She knew he would be curious, and after work on Thursday he got the chance to see her.

He'd driven her home and parked his car in her driveway before asking questions.

He was quiet for a few moments, and it did nothing to help Valarie's worry.

"So, what do you think?" she managed to say.

"Er," Ruel rubbed his hand over the back of his neck. "Listen, Valarie, I..." He shook his head. "Addison and Natasha have been saying some er—interesting things at school. Everyone believes you did it you know. The bruise is right there on Natasha's face and everyone knows how close Addison is to her. You were also the only one there and frankly..."

She cut him off in horror. "You don't believe me?"

"No!" he said, running a hand through his hair. "No, I'm just trying to say that... if you did it, I understand. And I wouldn't judge you for it. You don't have to lie to me."

"But I *didn't* do it." Valarie said coolly. "I didn't. I *swear it.*"

"And I believe you," his hand fell on her thigh. "But I'm just saying, I would understand if you did. And I understand it's a lot to take in. Valarie you've been *expelled.*"

"And I didn't do it, so why are you acting like I did? I'm telling you the truth."

A split moment, that's all it took—she would have missed it if she blinked but she didn't. She saw.

She saw his hesitation.

"Just say it Ruel," she said while her heart broke in two. "Just say you don't believe me and move on. Don't lie to me. Not to me."

He sighed. "I do believe you. I was just saying... I don't know what I was saying, okay. But let's just move on, forget about it."

But I can't.

"Okay," her head nodded. "Okay, sure." Valarie opened the car door and made her way to her front door. She stood still for a second after hearing the words "I'll message you!" shouted from her boyfriend's mouth. But she didn't look back.

And maybe if she had looked back, he would have messaged her like he said he would.

"How are you today, Valarie?"

Valarie flicked her eyes to her father, who sat right beside Miss Turner.

"Er, fine."

She hummed in response. "I'm glad to hear that. I haven't had the chance to discuss with you in private everything that's been happening, and I promise that will come, but it was actually your father's idea for me to bring you in today."

Of course it fucking was.

"We both understand it's been a difficult and tough time for you the past few months. And especially this week. After discussing further with your father we've come up with a plan that we believe will be the best course of action for your future."

Believe. What a fucking word.

Valarie nodded slowly.

Miss Turner continued. "Well, your father has gotten in contact with your grandparents over in Melbourne. And they were very kind to offer you a place to stay if needed. And it got us thinking. How would you like to stay with them for a little while?"

Her jaw slacked open. "Er, I don't—I don't know."

"That's okay, I understand it would be a big change, and something you'd need time to consider."

"If—if I said yes, how long would I stay."

"However long you like," Matthew answered.

However long I like. She leaned back in her chair, and thought about the effect of this change. She realised there wasn't really a negative.

It would get her away from her father, it would get her away from school and the people inside it. It was a new chapter in her life.

"I believe this is the best course of action for you Valarie," Matthew spoke up. "I—I know it's been tough on you, and I'll be honest here, I cannot handle working on our relationship while I'm dealing with handling myself."

But what about Ruel?

Her eyes began watering at the thought. "I—I don't know... there's a lot to consider."

But there wasn't.

Because realistically, she knew there was nothing for her here. No family, no friends, no school—nothing.

But Ruel...

He didn't even believe you.

"When do I need to make the decision?"

"Well... about that," Matthew said awkwardly. "I kind of already bought you a plane ticket for tonight."

"Oh."

"I thought you'd say yes straight away, I'm sorry I assumed."

"Well, it looks like you've chosen for me."

"No," he shook his head, "that's not what I was wanting to..."

"I'll fuck off," Valarie shrugged, doing her best to keep her face emotionless. "I'll move, yeah—I'll piss off to Melbourne just like you want."

"It's not what I want."

Valarie looked him dead in the eye.

"Well, it's what I want."

Ana narrowed her eyes. "Valarie, I don't think you've thought about this enough... You can miss planes, there is always the chance to leave another day."

"I don't need to think about it anymore," she said, as firmly and nonchalantly as possible. "I've made my choice. I'll move to Melbourne. And I'll leave tonight."

49. BYE

The car was quiet.

The sound of her suitcase, packed without care, ruffled in the back seat of her father's car. The road was quiet too, which wasn't surprising as it was closing in on midnight.

Her heart felt heavy, weighed down by her thoughts.

Is this the right choice?

Valarie Dale stared out the car window, waiting for the text message. The confusion, the anger, the hate.

Because Ruel Diego would *hate* her.

But he wouldn't understand.

He would read the letter she left on his door with a furrow across his brow and tears running down his face. He'd have so many questions it would make his head explode. He'd hold the hand-written letter to his chest as his knees crumbled to the floor.

Valarie liked to think, anyways, that he'd care enough to cry about her sudden departure. That it would hurt so much it felt like his heart was ripping in two.

But would he even notice?

A tear slipped down her cheek.

This is the right thing to do. She had to remind herself, convince herself. Because if her own therapist thought she was lying, who would believe her over in Melbourne?

She hadn't visited the city since she was twelve years old. Just before she started high school. The only contact she had with her grandparents was via letters, which they sent twice a year—one at Christmas, and one on her birthday.

Would they even remember her?

It was then Valarie realised they might not believe her either. *Crazy girl, she's always had her anger problems.*

What would the neighbours say? Would they warn their kids not to get too close to the fat girl?

She's trouble, I'll tell you.

But then Valarie reflected that moving to Melbourne surely could not be worse than what she was dealing with right now. Whether she was the talk of the town, or they didn't care at all, Valarie Dale believed she'd done the right thing.

She was leaving.

Pulling into Terminal 1, she realised she had no desire to get out of the car. She was always looking for a way out, a way to escape her father, but scarily, she was content where she was.

They were parked in the drop-off area for two minutes before Valarie spoke up. "Bye, I guess." Valarie went to open her car door, but it was locked. "Let me out."

"Don't stress Valarie," Matthew finally spoke. "I'm not trying to keep you in, I just want to talk."

"You've had half an hour to do that."

"Well—very true, but I still want to talk."

"It's what you're doing at the moment."

"I want to say I'm sorry." He ignored her snarky response. "For everything, and I want you to know you'll always have a place to call home. If you ever need it in the future. I'm just one phone call away."

"Cool, can you let me out now?"

"I believe you," he said. "I know you didn't hit that girl. That's not like you."

"You don't know shit about me Matthew, so don't try and act like you do."

"You're right, I don't. And it's no one's fault but mine." He spoke sincerely. "And I'd love to get to know you, when you're ready."

Valarie didn't respond, once more trying for the door, and this time it opened. Swiftly, she pulled her luggage out the backseat and laid it on the side of the road.

Her eyes connected with her father's.

"Call me when you make it to Melbourne. Or anytime."

Nodding, Valarie waved him off, but he didn't move. They stayed staring at one another, until he finally sighed and started up his car.

"I love you, Valarie," he said through the open window.

She didn't say it back. And from the looks of it, he didn't expect her to either.

And there she stood, alone at ten thirty at night, with nothing but memories to fill the empty gaps in her suitcase, and her future in the hands of *fucking Melbourne*.

Valarie Dale watched her father speed off, along with her phone, which she knew was turned off, dead and stuck under the passenger seat of his car.

And there it was.

The silence.

A small content smile grew on her lips.

THE END

ABOUT THE AUTHOR

C.A. Blake is a young author who lives in Perth, Western Australia. You can usually find her listening to music, cleaning her house, or reading. She loves to travel and wishes to experience the world.

If she's not reading, she's writing and with her best friend Lulu (her cat) right beside her—there's nowhere else she'd rather be. (Well, except maybe on a plane.)